MORGUE ON WHEELS

To hell with death! Camellion sprinted to the right and began to trigger the SMG, which he had switched to full automatic—*PHYTTTTTT!* The two troopers in the rear seat of the jeep tried to get out while the two men in front stood and leveled AKR submachine guns at the Death Merchant. A dozen full-metal-jacket 5.45 × 39 mm projectiles burned air close to Camellion. Close was not good enough. The Death Merchant's tidal wave of .45 THV slugs washed all over the jeep and drowned the four Russians in a flood of copper death. The termination had taken only twelve seconds. A ton of TNT could not have made the pig farmers more dead.

The DEATH MERCHANT series

QUANTITY SALES

Most Dell Books are available at special quantity discounts when purchased in bulk by corporations, organizations, and special-interest groups. Custom imprinting or excerpting can also be done to fit special needs. For details write: Dell Publishing Co., Inc., 1 Dag Hammarskjold Plaza, New York, NY 10017, Attn.: Special Sales Dept., or phone: (212) 605-3319.

INDIVIDUAL SALES

Are there any Dell Books you want but cannot find in your local stores? If so, you can order them directly from us. You can get any Dell book in print. Simply include the book's title, author, and ISBN number, if you have it, along with a check or money order (no cash can be accepted) for the full retail price plus 75¢ per copy to cover shipping and handling. Mail to: Dell Readers Service, Dept. FM, P.O. Box 1000, Pine Brook, NJ 07058.

(Death Merchant #67)

ESCAPE FROM GULAG TARIA

Joseph Rosenberger

A DELL BOOK

Published by
Dell Publishing Co., Inc.
1 Dag Hammarskjold Plaza
New York, New York 10017

*This book is dedicated to
J.J.A.*

Dell ® TM 681510, Dell Publishing Co., Inc.

ISBN: 0-440-12375-5

Printed in the United States of America

December 1986

10 9 8 7 6 5 4 3 2 1

DD

It has happened to them according to the true
    proverb,
The dog turns back to his own vomit,
and the sow is washed only to wallow in the
    mire.

—2 Peter 2:22

Technical advice for all
Death Merchant books is
supplied by
Colonel George E. Ellis
of
Le Mercenaire

Special Psychiatric Hospitals in the Soviet Union, reserved for dissidents who have an "absence of social adaptation," instill discipline and "cure dangerous antisocial behavior" by neuroleptic drugs, forced labor, beatings, and other tortures.

There are the Soviet concentration camps. The official Soviet designation for such living hells is *ispravite'notrudovaya koloniya* in singular form, meaning corrective labor colony or ITK. In these camps, prisoners are worked literally to death, their deaths hastened by a starvation diet.

Considering the Soviet talent for hypocrisy, it should come as no surprise that above the gate of each ITK is the motto: "Honest Labor: The road home." Nazi concentration camps had a similar slogan: *Arbeit macht frei!* —"Work shall set you free."

The only difference between Nazi Germany and the Soviet Union is that Soviet totalitarianism has endured and is still a cancer on the world community.

Richard J. Camellion
Votaw, Texas

Chapter One

Ten miles east of Yakutsk, Zoya turned the Volga M-124 left onto the highway that led north to the village of Taria. Her hands were steady on the wheel of the Soviet automobile, which resembled a 1973 Plymouth, and her manner didn't betray the nervousness that had to be twisting her insides into Gordian knots.

It wasn't every day—or even every ten years!—that Zoya Beliyev became the central figure in a plot to free a Soviet scientist from a special psychiatric hospital, a psycho prison. In her wildest imaginings, she had never considered the possibility that the day would come when she and two "comrades" would march into a KGB administered psycho prison and present official orders from KGB headquarters in Moscow that instructed the hospital administrator and the chief psychiatrist to turn Georgi Ulomov over to three escorts, who would take him to Moscow where he would be charged with treason and bound over for trial before a five-judge tribunal.

If Zoya Beliyev appeared relaxed, Richard Camellion looked as calm as a clam in a coma. Dressed in a dark-brown suit, his face with the features of a man in his middle forties, the Death Merchant didn't reveal any of the worry that had been gnawing at him ever since he had come ashore. In another month, if not sooner, the "season when water freezes," as the Russians were prone to say, would begin. Winter in Siberia was always very cruel. The temperature would remain fifty degrees below zero for weeks on end. Engines would freeze, tires split, and the façades of buildings would peel like old waterpaper. The black-bodied, white-sheened clouds would come, and the merciless *purga* would blow and bury the land in blizzards. Under such terrible conditions, it would be impossible to travel the three hundred miles to the east coast, to the Sea of Okhotsk and rendezvous with the *George Washington*.

Alexey Perchany, a stocky man with wide shoulders and a narrow, nondescript face, said from the rear seat, *"Tovarishch* Scott, my first concern is how we will escape if something goes wrong. How will we reach the car and get through the gates?"

"We have the advantage of surprise, and we have enough explosive to blow the gates," the Death Merchant said, unperturbed. "And quit calling me 'Comrade.' Damn it! For the past three weeks I've been asking you to call me either Scott or Arnold. That is my name." He gave the woman a quick glance. "Zoya, you're sure that the shortwave set is in Vartanyan's office?"

"I am certain," she replied in Russian, her low voice tinged with only slight nervousness. "Lidia Tamis and two other women cleaned his office only three days ago. The radio was there. The telephone exchange system is in the general office in front of Administrator Vartanyan's office."

"In our favor is the sheer improbability of the plan," Perchany offered. "Vartanyan and Dr. Libinsky would never imagine that three individuals would come to the hospital and pose as KGB agents as part of a plot to free a mental patient. It has never been done. It is also standard procedure for Moscow to send special escorts when the *vlasti*—the powers that be— want a particularly important prisoner moved."

"What's your second concern?" Camellion asked.

"I think it is foolish of us to inspect the wards." Perchany paused to light a strong Fet Frumos cigarette, a common brand in the Soviet Union. "We know that Ulomov is at Taria. Why don't we present our orders, take Ulomov into custody, and be done with it?"

"I agree with him, Arnold Scott" Zoya said firmly. "Why should we take the extra risk?"

The two had a right to be concerned. Their lives, too, were at stake. Camellion was patient. "We don't necessarily have to inspect the wards. What I should have told you is that I don't want to have to ask for Georgi Ulomov until I'm positive that Vartanyan is not suspicious. I don't even intend to mention Ulomov's name until I'm sure."

"He will see Ulomov's name on the order of transfer," Zoya said quickly. "Why not mention him? If we do not get him out

this afternoon, we never will. We will not have a second opportunity."

That's what you think, sister! "First, we'll have to produce
our identification, everything except our *kharakteristiki.* Then
Vartanyan will offer us tea or something stronger and ask us
how our trip from *Moskva* was, and were the militia in Yakutsk
polite enough when they loaned us this car. I'll have more than
enough time to evaluate his words and know whether he sus-
pects us. My uneasiness lies in another direction."

"It is the lack of confirmation of the order that worries you,"
Perchany said bluntly. "Is that not so?"

To lie would have been foolish and counterproductive. "It
is," Camellion admitted promptly. "My own people have as-
sured me that the KGB administrator of a mental hospital–
prison never phones *Moskva* to confirm a prisoner transfer, even
one who is prominent socially or scientifically. You in the
Charodeika Otdel have given me the same guarantee. Yet I
don't like it. Such a lack of check procedure is poor security to
me."

"To you—*da!*" Perchany said earnestly. "But not to the
KGB. After all, why should the KGB worry about such mat-
ters? Who has ever opposed them in this closed society? Who
would dare pose as KGB officers? Where could they get the
forged identification?" He gave a short and bitter laugh. "This
is not the United States with its cowboys and Indians."

"The *malenky chelovek*—the little man—is helpless in our
society," cut in Zoya, a pleasant, oval-faced brunette with large,
expressive eyes. "People are driven into one of two camps by
the authorities: open dissenters, to be prosecuted and turned
into 'nonpersons' and social outcasts, or collaborators with the
legal repression."

"There is much cynicism among our people," Perchany said.
"The honest man makes the silent ones feel guilty because they
haven't spoken out. They cannot understand how he had the
courage to do what they could not bring themselves to do, so
they feel impelled to agree with the State and speak out against
him to protect their own consciences. I tell you, *Homo
sovieticus* is a special breed of moral coward."

"There is still some hope." Zoya spoke rapidly. "More and
more ordinary people are *samizdat* and forming into tiny

groups with trusted friends to fight the State in nonviolent ways. It is a good sign."

The Death Merchant remained silent, the word *sumizdat* tumbling around in his mind. Courtland Grojean had said the same thing: that more and more Russians were going underground.

The briefing, six weeks ago, had not filled Camellion with any gee-golly-gosh enthusiasm. The mission itself was so dangerous that Grojean had surprised Camellion by saying that while the CIA had triple-checked every detail and taken every precaution: "I wouldn't give you a fifty-fifty chance of pulling it off. If you turn down going over there, I wouldn't blame you."

All the Death Merchant had to do was go into the Soviet Union and grab Georgi Vladimir Pytor Ulomov—from right under the noses of the KGB! A particle physicist, Ulomov was in the KGB psycho prison.

Camellion had gotten down to practicalities. "Why is Ulomov all that important to the Agency? If you want a big shot for propaganda purposes, why not try for Andrei Sakharov, the 'father' of the Soviet H-bomb?"

"It's not prop, Camellion." Grojean had then explained that Ulomov was more than a physicist; he was also a brilliant climatologist who was an authority on microclimatology and atmospherology. Furthermore, he was an authority on the experiments of Nikola Tesla, the Hungarian-born genius who had immigrated to the United States and had made amazing discoveries in radio transmission, wireless communication, and alternating-current transmission. When Tesla died in 1943, he had been conducting weather modification experiments in Colorado: "And some were partially successful."

A big, bright light had begun going off in the Death Merchant's mind. So that was the magic ingredient! *Weather modification!* The nation that could fully control the weather could control the world.

"That's right, Death Merchant. For that reason, we—"

"Don't use that stupid title!" Camellion's strange blue eyes had blazed in anger.

"Sorry. Anyhow—"

Anyhow, Dr. Ulomov, who possessed four Ph.D.'s, had been

working on a weather modification program that had not failed, although there had been dire results for the Soviet Union.

"Remember the bitterly cold winters of 1976 and 1977?" Grojean had asked. "Ulomov and other scientists managed to establish terrestrial electric resonance and were able to create relatively stable ELF magnetic fields. They then used the extremely low frequency magnetic fields to divert the jet stream flow in the northern hemisphere. But something went wrong and some of the fields backfired. In 1977 Moscow and parts of the USSR had the coldest winter recorded in modern times."

Dr. Ulomov and his staff continued the weather modification experiments. His troubles with the Soviet state began in 1983, when he began to speak out against the immorality of tampering with other people's weather. He was immediately warned to shut up, that he was "slandering" the Soviet state. However, Ulomov's conscience finally overcame common sense, despite the numerous warnings from the KGB, which since September of 1983 had been monitoring his mail and his telephone. The straw that shattered the KGB's patience was Ulomov's daring but foolish attempt to organize a committee of Soviet scientists, who, as a group, would demand that the government stop all weather-control experiments.

On March 10, 1984, Ulomov was arrested and charged with "anti-Soviet agitation and the spreading of lies for the purpose of undermining and weakening the Soviet regime." An ordinary citizen would have been tried and sentenced to twenty-five years in a corrective labor colony. Ulomov was too prominent in scientific circles. Surely he had to be insane to disseminate such slanderous fabrications about the glorious Soviet Union! Obviously, the poor man needed treatment. Why, he was as crazy as a person who believed in God!

Accordingly, Ulomov was taken to Moscow's Serbsky Institute of Forensic Psychiatry and was quickly judged "mentally incompetent" and "suffering from dangerous paranoid delusions." But not to worry. The sympathetic State would do its best to "cure" him.

The CIA's chief of the covert section had offered the question: "I suppose you're wondering why we waited until now to smuggle Ulomov out of Russia?"

The thought had tiptoed across the Death Merchant's mind.

The CIA had not been able to help earlier because the scientist had not been accessible; he had been too far from any of the Soviet Union's vast borders. Ulomov had been in four different special psychiatric hospitals—two in Moscow, one in Leningrad, and one in the Ukraine. Finally he had been moved to Special Psychiatric Hospital UZh-15/5 ITK-14. Collectively, in the vernacular, the hospital and the associated prison camp were called Tarialag (*lag* being the short form of *lager,* prison).

A short distance from the village of Taria, Tarialag was in southeastern Siberia. Yakutsk, a large city not far from Taria, was only three hundred miles from the Sea of Okhotsk, that vast body of water north of Japan. As far as Camellion was concerned, Grojean might as well have asked him to go to another planet!

"It wasn't until recently that we had any kind of an operational network in the Soviet Union," Grojean had said very seriously, "and it took us eleven years to develop it. A tiny part of the network is in Yakutsk."

The Death Merchant's expression had changed to one of pure skepticism. While anything is possible, many things are highly improbable, or at least extremely difficult. Recruiting spies in the USSR fell into the almost-impossible category. Foreigners were watched too closely by the KGB. Americans in particular were kept under constant surveillance, be they embassy personnel (or members of the U.S. Consulate in Leningrad), tourists, or businessmen.

Those Soviet spies who were recruited were almost always "walk-ins"—KGB or GRU agents, who, stationed in foreign countries, made surreptitious contact with American officials. Often these eventual double agents had been cultivated by American journalists working for the CIA.

"We call our Soviet web the *Charodeika Otdel,*" Grojean had said. "In Russian, *Charodeika* means—" Catching his mistake, Grojean had smiled. "How silly of me! Of course you know what the word means!"

"Any particular reason for calling the web the Sorceress network?"

"None. We grabbed the name out of thin air." Grojean had then given Camellion a long, sly look. "There are eleven Soviet citizens in the Yakutsk network, all Russians, born and bred."

Camellion had never thought that the members were American Indians. But just hearing the Fox say it made him furious, and he knew why Grojean had said it. Camellion despised any political system that consisted of only the leaders and the led, the privileged and the pariahs. He especially hated the Soviet system that would turn the entire human race into brainwashed robots, into sheep with only automatic reflexes, into "record players" who could sing only the "praises" of world communism.

The Death Merchant was contemptuous of the Soviet people. Not only were they moral cowards, they were all liars and hypocrites who placed personal comfort—such as it was in pigland —above ethical integrity. Forever a pragmatist, Camellion realized, although reluctantly, that much of his prejudice was based strictly on emotion and had no foundation in fact. In a sense, the Soviet people were to be pitied. There was their external toughness that came across in public as passive fatalism, total indifference, and pushy discourtesy. Soviet agencies, such as Intertourist, whose employees worked with foreigners, even told their people to smile more than usual because Westerners expected it.

It was all a sham. Since their public life was the world's biggest living lie, the Soviets wore a mask. In public they were critical, careful, cagey, and even rude. In private they felt very inferior to the rest of the world, to foreigners of whom they were always suspicious.

The Death Merchant had glared at Grojean. "And naturally you're going to tell me that those pig farmers in the network are to be trusted! You expect me to go over there and put my life in their hands! I would have to! No other way would be possible."

Grojean had looked at the ceiling and admitted that there was always the possibility that one of the eleven could be an informer, or even a career officer of the KGB or the GRU. He had added very quickly, "But if any of them aren't playing it square with us, I'd know it. We have highly placed contacts in not only Special Service Two of the KGB's First Chief Directorate, but also in the Ninth Direction of the Fifth Chief Directorate. You know what SS-Two is—counterintelligence. And the Ninth Direction of the Fifth Chief Directorate handles dissidence and administers the special psychiatric hospitals and the ITKs. It's through our agent in place in the Ninth Direction that we've learned so much about the hospitals and the labor camps. That's how we also know that Ulomov is in good health, despite all the triftazin, aminazin, and other drugs they've pumped into him."

The Death Merchant hadn't remained alive by taking anything at face value. Even God could make mistakes—and had. Didn't he create the human race? Grojean wasn't God. He wasn't even a tenth-grade angel. Yet he was willing to trust damned pig farmers in the KGB! Uh-uh. How much was he willing to trust the trash?

"I'd say ninety-nine percent," Grojean had snapped, slightly angry at Camellion's negative attitude. "We've paid both moles plenty of hard cash. All of it's stashed in a Swiss bank. We'll not give them the numbers of the accounts until after we've brought them to the States and debriefed them. You know damned good and well that the KGB doesn't believe all the crap about Marxism. They *know* the good life is in the West, and they want a piece of it!"

Turkey turds! What about the Russians who would actually be helping Camellion? Hopefully they had an IQ higher than an onion!

Zoya Trisnanova Beliyev, a member in good standing of the Communist Party, was the leader of the four-cell web in Yakutsk. Thirty-four years old, she was divorced, lived with her grandmother in a three-room house, and was a sociologist who taught four days a week at the Pichorvesk Institute in Yakutsk. She was also one of the "New Siberians," that group of volunteers who began to arrive in the late fifties to replace the millions of slave laborers released after the death of Stalin.

Alexey Lazar Percheny was a veteran truck driver who worked for the Soviet *Zchor'l Pokazukha*, the state-operated trucking system. His job for the past seven years was to drive a big Vanda tractor and two trailers from Yakutsk to the port city of Okhotsk and haul back freight for the state-run *Kommissiony* stores.

The other nine members of the Sorceress network in Yakutsk held a variety of jobs. One was a clerk; several were minor functionaries. Sergei Tsipin was a member of the militia. The youngest member was twenty-six, the eldest seventy-one. All the men had served their six years in the Red Army. Maxim Chenko, the seventy-one-year-old, had received the Stalin Medal during World War II. A master sniper, he had killed eighty-nine Germans. Now a pensioner, he served the network by delivering messages.

After Grojean had given the Death Merchant a few more hours of details, he had regarded Camellion with businesslike eyes. "Camellion, either you are going to accept the assignment or you're not. What's it going to be?"

The *George Washington,* one of the new class of Alpha nuclear submarines, had taken the Death Merchant to the Sea of Okhotsk. At 0330 hours the Death Merchant and five SEAL commandos, all six in scuba suits with a closed-breathing system, reached a lonely stretch of beach and dragged two black plastic drums onto the wet sand. In each container was a wooden box about the size of a footlocker. In the two boxes were arms and ammunition, a complete makeup and cosmetic laboratory, an AN/URC-101 SATCOM tactical transmitter with dish-to-satellite attachment, ten pounds of pentolite, and RC detonators. Finally, there were numerous meticulously forged identification books and documents. Some of them identified Camellion as an ordinary citizen, a worker in various jobs; others as an officer in the KGB, including a major in the Ninth Direction of the Fifth Chief Directorate. There were also a dozen domestic or internal passports—the *kharakteristiki,* absolutely vital to every Soviet citizen because it contains not only information about birth, parentage, and national ethnic group but such other data as education, army service, social record, and so on.

In each passport was a *propiksa,* the residential permit. In the Soviet Union, one has to have state permission to live anywhere.

There were also a dozen institutional work passes in blue *poryidok* workbooks. The *poryidok* was a history of one's total work record. Finally, there were the various permits to prove that one had been authorized to do whatever he might be doing. This was the all-important *spravka.*

In the darkness and in the cool of the late summer's early morning, the Death Merchant and the five SEALs had gotten down in the sand and put on night-vision goggles that could detect blinking signals from a flasher that operated on "invisible" infrared.

It had been only fourteen minutes before Roy Blessy, one of the SEALs, detected IR flashes to the southwest—1-2-3-4-5 flashes. Pause. Then another five red eyeblinks—a fifth of a mile away. The two Russian contacts had arrived and were waiting.

The Death Merchant had immediately returned the signals with his own IR flasher.

"Scott, it could be a trap," Lieutenant Robert Hoxmier had warned. "How do you want to play out the string?"

"Leave the boxes where they are, and you and your men get out of here," Camellion had told him. "If it is a trap, there wouldn't be anything you could do to help me." He handed the IR signal flasher to Hoxmier. "Swim back to the sub and wish me luck."

Hoxmier had shaken his head in wonderment. "The chances you intelligence boys take! You're all nuts!"

"We have to be. A sane person wouldn't do what we do."

Camellion had then moved out and, listening to the waves behind him breaking on the shore, headed toward the area where he and the others had seen the signals flashed. If it were a trap, the KGB had possibly gone to a lot of trouble for nothing. Camellion would simply bite into the capsule attached to one of his left molars. The capsule contained enough potassium cyanide to kill a dozen men—if he got a chance to use it. The KGB was a lot of things. Stupid it was not. If a trap were in the works, the KGB could dart him with an extremely powerful "sleeper" that could put him out in seconds—before he could terminate himself. The CIA had prepared for such an eventuality. There were four artificial but very realistic looking "moles" on Camellion's powerful body. Each "mole" contained 6 milligrams of T-14yB, the deadliest neurotoxin in Uncle Sam's chemical warfare arsenal. The moles were really a case of tremendous overkill. T-14yB, code-named "Tilly," was six times more virulent than the poison from the puffer fish, whose toxin was 150,000 times more venomous than curare. If evenly distributed, twenty-four milligrams of Tilly could wipe out Moscow. Camellion was walking death!

There was no trap by the *Zapravleniye,* the KGB border

guards. Alexey Perchany, who had flashed the signals, and Lavrenti Kirov, his relief driver, had been waiting, nervous and afraid. An hour and thirty-seven minutes later Camellion and his equipment were hidden in a special make-do compartment in the first trailer behind the Vanda diesel, a hollow space among crates of refrigerators toward the front of the boxcar on wheels. Crawling over the tops of the crates and shoving the equipment boxes in front of him as he did so had not been an easy task.

With crates to the left and the right of him, and in front of and behind him, the only danger Camellion faced was the tractor and its two trailers turning over. He'd be crushed like a grape in a bag of gravel.

Sixteen hours later the Death Merchant was in Yakutsk, safely hidden in the tiny room beneath the potato cellar.

Gazing pensively out the car window, Camellion thought of the vastness of the land. Siberia stretched from the Ural Mountains to the east four thousand miles to the Bering Sea, the total area almost one and a half times the area of all fifty United States.

He watched the countryside roll by. Everything was still green, but faint yellows and browns were beginning to tinge the leaves of the birch and oak trees, and the land looked sad, as if summer had become a monotonous burden. Here and there was an *izba,* a peasant cottage, with its gaily carved window frames, the gray clapboards weather-worn from lack of paint. The peasants cooked with fires fueled by wood, and the chimneys of the *izbas* extruded smoke that stretched horizontally across the windless sky.

"We'll be going through Taria very soon," announced Zoya Beliyev.

The main part of Taria—population 209—contained only the green-fronted (freshly painted) *Kommissiony* store, a physicians' building, a State records office for grain and produce, vegetable stalls, a small restaurant, and the bright-blue building of the two-man militia.

There were four *babushkas* and three *dedushkas* resting on benches on the wooden porch of the *Kommissiony* store, the four grandmothers, with their broad, flat faces worn as smooth as the wood of a well-used washboard, as sturdy as the men. In their cheap, dark dresses, they sat like the three grandfathers, their legs spread apart, their hands clasped around their bellies. The faces of all seven were Mother Russia, the picture of a sturdy benediction or of a merciless memory.

In only a few minutes Taria was behind the Volga, and Zoya was driving on the open road. Tarialag was only four miles away.

Alexey Perchany broke the silence. "The labor camps are a disgrace," he said in almost a snarl. "The special mental hospitals are even more of a disgrace. But the worst abomination of all is that people pretend that neither exist. Our people are as bad as the Germans. In World War II, the camps of death were all around the German people. They went to bed and got up with the stink of burning flesh in their noses, and they ignored it. The human slaughterhouses were not there, they told themselves."

"Our people are afraid. We cannot blame them," Zoya said, her voice almost harsh. The Death Merchant sensed that she was speaking more for his benefit than for Perchany's. "That is why Soviets lie so much. Deceit is a compensation for weakness, for a feeling of inferiority before foreigners. As a nation, we can't deal with others equally. We feel they are more powerful than we are, and so we compensate by deceiving them."

"Garbage!" snorted Perchany. "That's a lot of psychological and sociological manure. It's still a shame on our national honor that people remain quiet about injustice. It's like inviting guests to share the main meal on the day of Father Christmas and having a pile of cow manure in the center of the table and pretending it's not there."

The Death Merchant smiled at the comparison. The Soviet Union made him feel uncomfortable in any number of small ways. Mother Russia lacked even those little things that Americans took for granted—billboards, roadside fast-food establishments, and so on. And one was always aware of the fear. Even though quiet and under the surface of daily living, it was a terror that extended to even the authorities. This was especially true of those in the Party leadership, or the *apparatchiki,* the people who had jobs in the Party *apparat.* So great was this fear that even photocopy machines were kept under lock and key and could only be used by special permission, lest the documents reproduced be used for "illegal" purposes.

There was another incongruity, this one purely psychological. Camellion did not like Russians, and Zoya and Alexey and the other members of the small network were as Russian as borscht and vodka. The Death Merchant also hated traitors. While lower than the bottom side of a pancake, KGB and GRU officers were at least fighting for the land in which they had been born. Technically Zoya and the others were traitors. *Who's kidding whom?* Battling conflicting emotions, the Death Merchant realized there was a vast difference between traitors who sold secrets for personal gain, for money, and people who, loving their nation, were fighting its gangster oppressors. Grudgingly, Camellion found himself admiring Zoya and Perchany and the others—*Even if they are pig farmers.*

There were no signs pointing the way to Tarialag and its special psychiatric hospital. There was only the turnoff, a wide brick road that led straight to the hospital and the camp.

"Soon." Zoya did not sound happy. "It will be only three kilometers after we cross the Kolga River. It is only a short distance ahead."

Only two miles. The Death Merchant reached down, picked up the Soviet-made briefcase, opened it, and looked inside one compartment to make sure that everything was in order. There were ten ounces of pentolite made up into four packages, with a remote-control detonator attached to each numbered packet. Next to the explosives was the central detonating station with its numbered throw-switches. In another compartment was a 9 mm Vitmorkin machine pistol. The only reason it was in the briefcase was because of the length of its barrel. Besides, KGB agents carried 9 mm Makarov auto-pistols. So did Camellion and Alexey Perchany, in shoulder holsters. So did Zoya Beliyev, in her handbag.

There was another grim reality: It was possible that, if a knot got tied in the string, he might have to put a bullet into Zoya or Perchany, or one of them might have to terminate him. If one of them was wounded, he or she could not be left behind to be questioned by the KGB. The KGB could make anyone tell everything. Any person, even the Death Merchant, had that threshold when pain became intolerable, and if the KGB made

Zoya, or Perchany, or Camellion talk, the Sorceress network would go down the drain, at least in Yakutsk.

Some "river," the Kolga! Camellion thought. The Kolga was only a thirty-foot wide, shallow creek, with a simple truss bridge over it.

Finally, there was the hospital. There wasn't any sign to indicate what lay behind the faded yellow walls, whose large double gates were solid and metal-covered. They, too, were a faded yellow. There was only one large sign on one of the walls: NYET! NEFOTOGRAFIROVAT!—NO PHOTOGRAPHS!

A quarter of a mile north of the hospital were the gates of the corrective labor colony, 841 acres of work, misery, and starvation.

Zoya Beliyev stopped the car in front of the gates and honked the horn.

Welcome to hell!

Chapter Two

The two guards in the watchtower motioned to the guard below to open the gates. The three were not the least bit suspicious about what was going on. It was normal enough for some official of the KGB in Yakutsk to visit the hospital or the labor colony. Even when *nachalstvo*—big shots—from *Moskva* came on business, they used a militia vehicle from the central station in Yakutsk.

The gates swung inward. Zoya drove the Volga inside the compound and parked in front of the two-story administration building. Five other vehicles were already there: three olive-drab jeeps and two passenger cars, a Zhiguli and a Zaporozhets.

"Those jeeps could outrun us," Perchany said gloomily.

"They could, but they won't," Camellion replied.

There wasn't a lot to be seen, and what they could see didn't fill them with happiness. The administration building was the same faded mustard yellow as all the other structures. To the rear of Administration was the two-story ward that, shaped like a Greek cross, housed 150 "mental patients." To its right was a square building that was the living quarters of all the personnel but the attendants. The attendants were *bytoviks,* nonpolitical prisoners who had committed some minor civil offense and were serving short sentences. They were not *lagerniks* from the corrective work colony, but common criminals from the jails in Yakutsk, more often than not sadistic brutes who beat the mental patients and subjected them to other physical painful abuse—with the permission of the administration. The *bytoviks* lived in the hospital with their charges.

Smaller buildings were for storage and maintenance. In one corner was the powerhouse with its gasoline generator. The terrible blizzards of Siberia often brought down the power lines coming from the Cibek electric generating station west of Yakutsk, and the petrol-powered generator was a precautionary measure.

"Don't lock the doors," warned the Death Merchant just before he and Zoya and Perchany got out of the car. "It would appear suspicious to anyone who might be watching."

With Zoya and Perchany on either side of him, Camellion strode into the general office of the administration building and sized up the layout. There were five metal desks, a row of old-fashioned, five-drawer wooden filing cabinets, the inevitable photographs of Karl Marx and Nikolai Lenin on a rear wall, and five bored faces behind the desks, faces that lighted up with curiosity as the Death Merchant walked up to the first desk, reached into an inner pocket of his coat, pulled out a red leather KGB ID case, flipped it open, and thrust it under the nose of Vasily Bukivitch, the chief clerk.

"I am Major Valantin Veskaya," Camellion barked with all the authority of God giving a directive to Moses on the mountain. "I'm attached to the *Upravleiny Delami* in *Moskva.* I and my assistants are here to see Comrade Vartanyan. Our time is limited."

Bukivitch's eyes widened slightly and instantly he was on his best fawning behavior. The *Upravleiny Delami!* The Administration of Affairs was the main department of the Communist Party's ruling Central Committee, the Politburo. *Chort vozmi—* damn! Why did the big shots always have to show up without warning?

Bukivitch, calming himself, stared at the pale-blue card in the leather folder. There was Major Veskaya's photograph and the words *Komitet Gosudarstvennoy Bezopasnosti*—Committee for State Security, the KGB. In the upper section of the leather folder was the emblem of the KGB, the yellow shield and the vertical white sword. In the center of the sword was the five-pointed blood-red star, a black hammer and sickle in its center.

"Yes, sir. Right away," said Bukivitch. "One moment, please." He pressed the button on an interoffice communicator and leaned close to the box. "Comrade Vartanyan, Major Veskaya and his two assistants from Moscow are here to see you, sir. They are from the Administration of Affairs, sir."

"Send them in," the voice from the box said.

With the kind of smile reserved for high officials, Bukivitch got to his feet. "This way, please, Comrade Major Valantin Veskaya."

Looking neither to the left or right, Camellion and his two assistants followed Bukivitch to a door on the far side of the room. As they walked, the Death Merchant noticed that the telephone exchange was in the northwest corner of the room and was being operated by a pretty young woman in a remarkably stylish dress. *She has to be warming the bed of some high official!*

Bukivitch tapped lightly on the door, then opened it and motioned for Camellion and Co. to enter. After they were inside the office, he pulled the door shut, and Camellion, Zoya, and Perchany found themselves looking at Feliks Vartanyan, who was putting on his suit coat, and another, younger man.

Of medium height, raw-boned, with wide blue eyes, a thin mouth, and in his mid-forties, Feliks Vartanyan looked like the sensuous man he was, a man for whom the greatest pleasures in life were eating and drinking.

The other man, sitting in a chair close to the door, was ten years Vartanyan's junior. Fleshy, and looking as though he were smelling a disagreeable odor, he had a peculiar slant to his eyes, indicating he was either Mordovian or a Chuvash. Like Vartanyan, he was dressed in a typical Russian suit of poor material and poor cut.

"I'm Feliks Vartanyan, the administrator." His face curious, Vartanyan stepped forward and shook hands with Camellion, who introduced himself and his two "assistants," Captain Arkady Sukhodrov and Lieutenant Raisa Kartopki.

After introducing slant eyes as Tibor Igchenko and mentioning that he was the assistant administrator, Vartanyan motioned toward chairs in front of his desk. "Sit down, Comrades, please. I trust your journey from Moscow was pleasant?"

"Is this your first visit to this area of Siberia, Comrade Major Veskaya?" Igchenko asked pleasantly. "I suppose you flew?"

"Would you care for some refreshments?" Vartanyan sat down behind his desk. "Tea? Or vodka? Or perhaps some local Kroshev wine? It's very good if you like your wine sweet."

"Nyet stimko chorvt, Comrade. Unfortunately we must hurry and get back to Yakutsk," said Camellion, who saw that the

shortwave transceiver, a UHF Zhko H-68 SIV, was on a table against the west wall.

Vartanyan nodded sympathetically. "I understand. The Administration of Affairs is always very busy managing the affairs of our great and glorious nation."

"Especially in these trying times, when living in the same world with the warmongering Americans has become so difficult," Igchenko added quickly, trying to score brownie points, for who knew what the three from Moscow were really up to and what they might report to the KGB center?

For the same reason, because Feliks Vartanyan was very cautious, he stuck faithfully to protocol.

"Comrade Major Veskaya, I must see your identification, and the identification of Captain Sukhodrov and Lieutenant Kartopki."

"To be sure," agreed the Death Merchant. "I would have had to report your lack of security to the home office if you had not requested that we identify ourselves."

Camellion pulled out his ID case, got up, and handed the case to Vartanyan. Zoya Beliyev and Alexey Perchany followed suit. Vartanyan checked each individual identification, then returned the cases to their owners, who then resumed their seats.

"Major Veskaya, what is the nature of your business here?" Vartanyan folded his hands on the desk.

"We have come to take one of your patients to Moscow," Camellion said. "He is to be charged with treason and tried."

"I see. And you have the release forms and the authorization from the Fifth Chief Directorate?"

"Of course, Comrade Vartanyan." Camellion picked up the briefcase and opened it.

"What else do you have, Comrade Major Veskaya?"

A note of warning sounded in the Death Merchant's brain. What else? What else could there be? *How should I answer the pig farmer?* Before he could frame a reply, Feliks Vartanyan asked again, "Comrade Major, what else do you have for me?"

Thinking that success was never permanent any more than failure was forever, Camellion gave the only answer he could. "And I said I have all the necessary papers."

"Yes, you did." Vartanyan nodded at Tibor Igchenko, who promptly pulled a Stechkin machine pistol from under his coat and snapped, *"Ruki verx*—hands up! All three of you—*ruki verx.* Get to your feet!"

Wondering where he had slipped up, the Death Merchant raised his hands and stood. The same big question mark in their own minds, Zoya Beliyev and Alexey Perchany also got up and moved their arms toward the ceiling.

"I don't know who the three of you are, but we are going to find out damn soon," Vartanyan said, urgency in his voice. He stood and put his hands flat on the desk. "First we'll have a look in that briefcase. Hand it to me, Tibor."

Igchenko took several steps toward Camellion and motioned with the 9 mm Stechkin in his right hand. "Step back," he ordered. "Don't even think of trying anything. I'd just as soon kill you as not."

Camellion saw that Igchenko wasn't nervous and that his finger was steady on the trigger. But he had still made a fatal mistake in confronting a man like the Death Merchant: He had come within striking distance.

Camellion's left leg came up in a karate high kick with such incredible speed that neither Igchenko nor Vartanyan saw the tip of his foot crash into the underside of Igchenko's right hand. Igchenko's arm flew upward, his hand releasing the pistol, which shot over his head and landed on the floor ten feet behind him, hitting the rug with a dull thud. A well-made weapon, the Stechkin did not discharge from the force of its striking the floor.

So quickly had Camellion disarmed Igchenko that by the time the astonished man and Vartanyan fully realized what was happening, they found themselves staring into the muzzle of the Death Merchant's 9 mm Makarov, which he had jerked from his shoulder holster with a lightning motion.

"We're members of the Ubangi Committee for the Rights and Freedoms of World Eskimoism," he said softly to the open-mouthed Vartanyan and to Igchenko, who was holding his right hand and wondering if any bones were broken.

By then Perchany had drawn his Makarov, and Zoya had taken hers from her handbag.

"The guards in the watchtower will have assault rifles," she reminded Camellion nervously. "What do we do about them?"

"Open your coat, Vartanyan," ordered Camellion.

Vartanyan did so. He wasn't armed.

"If they as much as sneeze, kill them," Camellion said to Zoya and Perchany. He picked up the briefcase, placed it on the desk, opened it, and took out the Vitmorkin machine pistol and a Russian noise suppressor.

"Listen to me," he said to Vartanyan and Igchenko. "In a moment we're going into the front office." He finished screwing the silencer onto the end of the barrel. "Then, Comrade Vartanyan, you will telephone the two guards in the tower and tell them and the man at the gate to come inside. Tell them it's a special briefing. Tell them anything, but get them inside, or you're dead. Both of you, move over to the east wall and face it."

"Listen, whoever you are. You can't get away—" Vartanyan began.

"Move, or I'll blow your head off right now!"

As soon as Vartanyan and Igchenko, their hands above their heads, were facing the wall, Camellion opened the briefcase, took out a 2.5-ounce packet of pentolite, turned on the detonator, and placed the little brown packet in front of the shortwave transceiver on the table.

The briefcase in his left hand, Camellion moved over to the two hospital officials, the Vitmorkin and its silencer held loosely in his right hand.

"Lower your hands. We're going into the front office. Do as you're told, or I'll kill everyone. Lieutenant Kartopki, open the door and keep well ahead of our two friends."

Nodding, Zoya shoved the Makarov pistol into her handbag, hurried to the front of the office, opened the door, and stepped out smiling at the four men and one woman who glanced in her direction. Right behind her came Vartanyan and Igchenko, with Alexey Perchany and the Death Merchant right behind them, neither attempting to hide his weapon.

The five office workers stared in disbelief when they saw the Vitmorkin and the Makarov. Then Zoya pulled her Makarov from her handbag. Was it a purge? Had the three newcomers come to arrest Comrades Vartanyan and Igchenko?

"On your feet! Hands flat on your heads," ordered the Death Merchant. "March to the east side and line up—*davai bistri*— hurry up! Igchenko, go with them—move or die!"

As Igchenko and the office staff moved to the east side of the large room, Camellion thrust the muzzle of the silencer under Vartanyan's big nose. "Phone those three guards, Comrade. If they aren't walking through the door a few minutes from now, you'll be in hell in a hundred and twenty-five seconds. Get on that phone, spinach face."

A look of fear frozen on his face, Vartanyan picked up a phone from the nearest desk and told the two guards to come into the administration building: "And bring the guard at the gates with you."

The Death Merchant realized that he was taking a risk that Vartanyan had actually phoned the guards. He was gambling that Vartanyan wasn't crazy brave or so fanatical that he would be willing to give his life in exchange for a half victory.

"Comrade Major, the three guards are coming," Perchany said in less than half a minute, a note of relief in his voice. "And they're bringing their assault rifles with them." He stood in front of the office, to one side of a window.

Camellion, who had shoved Vartanyan over with the other Russians, nodded and sat down on the edge of Bukivitch's desk. In his right hand was the Vitmorkin machine pistol, in his left hand a 9 mm Makarov autoloader. *Grojean! You goofed it! You gave me a tangled string full of knots!*

The three unsuspecting guards opened the door and came into the office, not realizing this was their last day on earth. They had time only to see six men and one woman standing by the east wall, and another woman and two other men with weapons in their hands. Camellion opened fire with the Vitmorkin machine pistol. *Phyyyt-phyyyt-phyyyt!* The silencer whispered its short, quiet tune and the three guards went down, their AKS-74 assault rifles making a loud clatter as they hit the floor. The corpse of the last goon was still settling on the floor when Camellion swung the Vitmorkin to his left and expertly began squeezing the trigger.

A Vitmorkin machine pistol (an improvement on the Stechkin MP) holds twenty 9 by 19 mm cartridges, staggered in a wide magazine. After the Death Merchant completed the necessary terminations, there were only nine cartridges in the clip and one in the firing chamber. The floor also had new additions: seven cold cuts by the east wall.

"Good! They were all KGB," Zoya Beliyev said in a satisfied voice. "They deserved to die twice over."

"They still couldn't defend themselves!" Camellion spit out the words savagely. "Still, the fewer people around to give a description of us, the safer we'll be tomorrow and in the days that follow, if we don't get our heads blown off today." He turned to a grim-faced Alexey Perchany. "Watch the main door."

Camellion opened the briefcase and took out another packet of pentolite. He turned on the detonator, ran over to the telephone exchange, and placed the explosive on the table, against the switchboard. Then he hurried back to the front of the general office.

"Zoya, once we're outside, start the car and drive it through the gates," he said, handing Perchany one of the AKS-74s. "Alexey, open the gates." Camellion took the control station of the remote-control detonators from the briefcase and dropped it into a coat pocket. He closed the briefcase and handed it to Zoya. "Get hold of yourself, Zoya," he said ruthlessly to the woman, who, despite her earlier words, was now looking shaken. "This is all-out war. Death is never important. It's only life that counts. Let's go." He moved toward the door.

Outside there was only the sky, the emptiness, and the hint of approaching winter. Carrying an AKS, Perchany ran to the double gates. Zoya got inside the Volga and turned the key in the ignition. The Death Merchant, ready with an AKS, moved forty feet from the administration building and began watching its front corners as well as the fronts of two other buildings sixty feet to the east. Though he had no way of knowing, it was time for the changing of the guards.

Zoya had backed up the Volga and was turning the wheel to head the vehicle toward the now open gates when three guards, each carrying an AKS AR, came out of a building to the east. A cut above the average Red Army Ivan, KGB guards are well trained. They didn't know what was happening, but when they saw Camellion—a strange civilian—with an assault rifle, they realized that they were not confronting normal routine. Zoya's spinning the rear wheels of the Volga and another civilian standing by the open gates convinced them that something very serious was happening.

The three pig farmers stopped and brought up their AKS assault rifles, one of them yelling, *"Ruki verx! Ruki verx!"*

"Hands up" were the last words the Russian would ever speak. The Death Merchant's 7.62 by 39 mm projectiles chopped out his stomach, cut his spine in two, and turned him into a gory mass of ripped rags. The second man went down minus his head and most of his neck, both of which had been exploded by Camellion's slugs. Dimitri Pushlin, the third man, did succeed in getting off a short burst in Camellion's direction —for all the good it did him. Seeing Pushlin swing the muzzle toward him, the Death Merchant jumped to one side and in the next few moments stitched the guard from navel to neck, the grand slam of steel knocking him backward. As his corpse dropped to the ground, he resembled a broken bladder of blood. Pushlin's own chain of projectiles heated air two feet from Camellion, although four had come dangerously close to the rear of the Volga.

The Death Merchant turned and sprinted toward the open gates. Zoya had taken the car through the gates and was now waiting, engine running. Perchany waited by the corner of the outer left wall, his assault rifle trained on the compound.

The moment Camellion was through the gates, he took the remote-control box from his pocket and turned it on. Since he hadn't bothered to check the number of the packet he had placed by the telephone exchange, he threw all the toggle switches, his reward two *BERRRRBLAMMS* so close together they sounded as one. The shortwave and the phone exchange were now memories.

"Let's get out of here," he said to Perchany. *We're fourteen miles from safety! It might as well be four hundred!*

Zoya Beliyev's nervousness at coming face to face with sudden and violent death did not interfere with her driving. A Volga could reach 90 mph (except the souped-up Volgas used by the KGB), and she sped away, once reaching 73 mph.

"What went wrong, Arnold Scott?" asked Perchany who, in the rear seat, was staring out the window. "How could Vartanyan have known we were not genuine *Kah Gay Beh* officials from *Moskva?*"

"I don't know," Camellion said in a hard voice. He pulled the magazine from the AKS to see how many cartridges were left. "Twice he asked me what else I had for him. I suspect there's a code word that's used when special political prisoners are transferred from a special psychiatric hospital."

"Jeeps!" The word exploded from Perchany's mouth. "Four of them! I think. I can't be sure at this distance. A bit more than a kilometer behind us."

The Death Merchant's expression of cold distaste did not change.

"How far to the Kolga River, Zoya?" He opened the briefcase.

"Less than half a kilometer." Her voice trembled. "I'll s-speed up."

"They are coming up fast," Perchany said. "Those damned jeeps can reach a hundred kilometers an hour."

Camellion took the last two packets of pentolite from the briefcase, the last five ounces of the powerful military explosive he had with him. He noted that the packages were numbered six and eight.

"Zoya, after that next curve just up ahead, we'll be on a straight stretch to the river," he said. "Then give it all you've got. We have to reach the bridge, or we're dead."

She only nodded, her eyes glinting with fear and excitement. She had increased speed, and Camellion warned her, "Watch the curve. You'll have to go under forty to make it."

He could detect a faint musky odor emanating from her—the stink of perspiration. It wasn't that Zoya was not clean. There were times when the cleanest of Russians had body odor, unless they bathed three times a day. In all of the vast prison that was the Soviet Union, you couldn't buy any kind of deodorant or antiperspirant. You either washed constantly or smelled constantly. Even the toilet paper manufactured by the State had the "softness" of newsprint.

"Scott, you are going to use explosives on the bridge?" asked Perchany, the scowl on his face deepening as he watched the jeeps, which were getting closer.

"I can put a big enough hole in the bridge to stop pursuit," Camellion said, his body swaying to the right from the momentum of Zoya's taking the car around the curve. "My concern is that the guards back at the hospital or the camp might have a field radio and use it to contact the police either in Taria or Yakutsk."

"There isn't anything we can do about it," said Perchany with growing vehemence, "except shoot it out with the bastards."

"We can do plenty about it," Camellion said blandly. "We can grab another car. We should meet half a dozen or so between here and Taria after we're on the main highway. Since we're in a militia car, with a hammer and sickle all over the front doors, we won't have any trouble stopping a vehicle. All we have to do is turn on the siren."

"And you will kill the driver and whoever is with him," said Zoya with calculated restraint.

Camellion gave her a cool look of subtle condemnation. "That's right. We're not playing a game. We can't afford morality without setting ourselves and the rest of Sorceress up as naked targets. Is that what you would have us do? I think not!"

"Arnold Scott is right, Zoya," Perchany said emphatically. "We cannot concern ourselves with innocent bystanders. Freedom can never be won with weakness. We must be as ruthless as Lenin and his Bolsheviks were."

"I know," Zoya said hesitantly. "It's only that. . . ." Her voice trailed off.

"There aren't any 'thats' or 'ifs,' " Camellion retorted. "There's only success and failure, life and death. Watch your driving. There's the bridge ahead. Give us all the speed you can get out of this pile of junk now, but slow down to almost a stop as soon as you reach the bridge."

The four jeeps of KGB guards were only a sixth of a mile away by the time Zoya reached the bridge over the Kolga River. She slowed the car to five miles an hour, and Camellion opened the door, got out, and ran around to the rear of the Volga. He placed the two small packages of explosives on the wooden flooring of the thirty-foot-wide span, each one ten feet from the outer sides of the bridge. Then he ran back into the car and took the remote-control station from his coat pocket. Camellion waited until they had driven for half a minute before pushing up toggle switches six and eight.

BLAMMMMM-BLAMMMMMMMM! The entire bridge shook and, where the two packets had exploded, there were only two gaping holes whose edges were twisted metal braces and jagged, splintered flooring. There was a creaking sound and a low groaning. The bridge near the explosions sagged a few inches.

The first jeep of the guards pulled up to the bridge and stopped, the driver and the other five men cursing. By then the Volga was a speck in the distance.

Zoya had left the side road that led to Tarialag and had just turned onto the main highway. Now they were only a mile from the village of Taria.

In the distance were the hazy outlines of the village's outer buildings, shimmering against the backdrop of the blue of the low sky and the bright, brittle sunshine of the late afternoon. For some odd reason, the panorama ahead reminded Camellion of the outskirts of Los Angeles.

Sunset was only a few hours away, a sunset that would have been strange to Americans. There wouldn't be any bright reds or orange or yellow. Because the region was so far north, there would be only a whitish glow.

"Ah . . . do you see what I see, Zoya?" A smile twisted itself on one side of Camellion's mouth.

Coming from the opposite direction, on the other side of the road, was a white Zhiguli.

"We can take that car over without any problem," Perchany said.

"We have to. That Zhiguli is more than our salvation," Camellion replied. "It's our transportation to Yakutsk." He reached out and turned on the siren. "Zoya, cut in front of him."

Chapter Three

Tobacco smoke drifted lazily to the ceiling in the office of the dead Feliks Vartanyan, much to the discomfort of Lieutenant Colonel Boris Rudneva. The KGB specialist in terrorism and counterinsurgency was an officer in Special Service II of the First Chief Directorate and, with Major Anton Cheklitt, his aide, had flown from Moscow to Yakutsk to investigate the massacre at Special Psychiatric Hospital UZh-15/5.

Half sitting on the front edge of Vartanyan's desk, bracing himself with his left foot on the floor while he swung his lower right leg back and forth, Rudneva studied Captain Gennady Kipeka, the head of the KGB guards at the hospital.

"Comrade Kipeka, tell us again where you were when you first realized there was trouble," Rudneva said gently.

Kipeka, a big man with the wide, dull face of a peasant, shifted uneasily in his chair. Ever since the thirteen had been gunned down, he had worried constantly that the blame would be dropped on his shoulders.

"Colonel Rudneva, it was three-thirty in the afternoon when I heard the first shots," Kipeka replied in a straightforward manner. "I am positive of the time because I looked at my watch. At the time, I and Lieutenant Tusbikov were inspecting the snow breaks around the generator house. At maximum, winter is less than two months away, and here in Siberia we have snowstorms that are much worse than in Moscow."

"What did you do after you heard the shots?" asked Rudneva, his voice still soft. All the while he kept his gray-green eyes riveted on the uncomfortable Kipeka, who was dressed in a brown uniform with red shoulder bars. Every button was in place, his boots so polished one could have used them as mirrors.

"I attempted to phone Comrade Vasily Bukivitch, the officer on duty in the hospital's front office. When he didn't answer the phone, I tried to contact my office in the main guard station. I could not get a reply. It became clear to me that Comrade Trina Makrivev was not at the switchboard in the front office. Then Comrade Tusbikov and I heard the firing of AKS assault rifles. We gathered nine men and hurried to the front area. On the way, we heard the explosions.

"When we reached the front of the area, we found our murdered comrades. We rushed into the administration building and found it was full of smoke from the explosions. The switchboard had been completely destroyed. The shortwave had also been blown to bits, and part of the office wall. It was only yesterday that the rubbish was removed completely. I instructed my men not to touch anything until after you, Comrade Colonel, had seen the destruction."

"And of course you found the bodies in the front office," Major Cheklitt said, getting up from the desk and standing straight.

"*Da*, where they had fallen. I knew the terrorists must have escaped in a vehicle, and we gave chase in jeeps. We would have caught up with them, but just as we were closing in, the murderers exploded a section of the bridge over the river and prevented us from continuing the pursuit. We had no choice but to return to Tarialag."

Major Cheklitt crushed out his cigarette in an ashtray on the desk.

"There is no doubt in your mind that the vehicle of the terrorists was a militia car, a Volga?"

Kipeka nodded emphatically. "I am positive, Comrade Major."

Colonel Rudneva asked, "Why didn't you and your men use one of the field radios to contact the militia in Taria or the *Kah Gay Beh* station in Yakutsk? The Taria militia and, our own people in Yakutsk have told us that it was almost an hour and a half before they were informed of the massacre. I should like to hear your explanation, Comrade Captain Kipeka."

Kipeka did not hesitate. "Comrade Colonel, as I have already told you and Comrade Major Cheklitt, our field radios were removed four months ago as a precautionary measure against a patient using them, a patient who might try to escape."

"And what idiot ordered that nonsensical measure?" Cheklitt demanded angrily.

"The directive came from *Moskva*, from the Ninth Direction of the Fifth Chief Directorate. A month later an officer from Yakutsk picked up the field radios, fourteen to be exact."

Cheklitt glanced at a calm-faced Rudneva, his heavy black brows forming a deep V of a frown of disgust. Those dumb bastards in the Fifth Directorate were always making asses of themselves with ridiculous security measures.

Colonel Rudneva's eyes were steady on Kipeka.

"How did you get word to the outside?"

"I first made certain that fires could not result from the explosions and placed the hospital under full alert. Then I sent several of my men to tell Comrade Major Gusbichev, the commander of the corrective labor camp, what had taken place. I next sent three men to Taria. They walked all the way to the highway. There they flagged down a motorist, who took them into Taria where they phoned the *Kah Gay Beh* in Yakutsk and reported what had happened. There isn't anything else I can tell you, Comrade Colonel."

"Very well. *Spasibo*—thank you," said Rudneva. He turned, reached down, and shut off the tape recorder on the desk. "You may go about your duties, Comrade."

He glanced at where the shortwave and the table had been. There was a two-foot hole in the wall, and although the debris had been cleaned up, there were still bits of metal and wooden splinters on the floor.

Captain Kipeka got up from the chair, saluted smartly, and left the office. Rudneva sat down behind the desk and smiled slightly. He had accurately analyzed Kipeka as being one of life's dullards, a follower who had found a home in the uniformed *Kah Gay Beh*. Fine. He would always go by the book and do exactly as ordered. *Da*, like Americans, he was naive about the world and prone to simplicities.

Rudneva turned his attention to the chief psychiatrist of SPH UZh-15/5, the fat-faced Dr. Stephen Libinsky, who was sitting in a chair in front of the desk. Of ruddy complexion and fifty pounds overweight, Dr. Libinsky would have made an ideal Father Christmas at children's parties.

Libinsky didn't wait for the questions. "I can't add anything of value to what Captain Kipeka has already told you," he said in his loud bass voice as Rudneva switched on the tape recorder. "At the time of the incident under investigation, I was with a most recalcitrant patient and doing my best to reverse his dangerous paranoid thinking. We had treated this poor fellow with haloperidol, and he was suffering from extrapyramidal derangement caused by the drug, such as headache, dryness of the mouth, double vision, intense physical restlessness, and a constant desire to change body positions.

"The only remedy in such cases is to place the patient in compulsory immobility. I told the orderlies first to subject the patient to wetpack treatment. This is a form of immobilization in which the patient is tightly wrapped in wet sheeting. This patient certainly needed intensified treatment. He had been convicted of practicing yoga. As you know, yoga is a very dangerous form of mysticism which can lead to independent thought and behavior detrimental to the State.

"As I was saying, the sheeting tightens as it dries, this causing intense pain, which acts as reinforcement to help reshape thinking in regard to our glorious Motherland. If this method—"

"Dr. Libinsky, we are not interested in a recitation of your various treatments of psychotic patients," Rudneva said dryly. "We only want to know if you have information about the murders."

Libinsky's heavy-lidded eyes looked first at Rudneva, then at Cheklitt. He found the dark-haired Cheklitt very attractive—and so young to be a major! He could not have been older than thirty.

In his forties, Rudneva could have been a young cadet officer in the Soviet Army. He was tall and muscular, his face, with its angular features, straightforward. Libinsky envied his flat stomach and narrow hips. Why, his waist couldn't have been more than eighty-three centimeters! Libinsky also sensed that the intelligence and antiterrorist specialist was a strong-willed, strong-minded individual who could expertly keep flunkies in control and skillfully adapt to adverse conditions. Above all, he would be a dangerous enemy.

"I know nothing about the terrible crime," Dr. Libinsky said casually. "The first I and my staff knew about the act of terrorism was when three of Captain Kipeka's men came to the general ward and informed us that the entire complex was under a state of full alert. They explained why. I was horrified at such brutality. I did examine the bodies of our murdered comrades and confirmed that they were dead. There wasn't anything else I could do. However, since Comrades Vartanyan and Igchenko were dead, I did appoint myself temporary administrator." He paused slightly. *"Gospodin*—gentlemen. I am busy and have much work to do. If there isn't anything else?"

"Spasibo, Dr. Libinsky," Rudneva said in a proper official tone. "Continue your duties."

"Do svidaniya," Libinsky said cordially. His double chins bouncing, he got to his feet and started to waddle toward the door, Rudneva and Cheklitt following him with a strong gaze that reflected their dislike of the pervert.

A well-educated man, Rudneva despised psychiatrists in general and Soviet psychiatry in particular, although he never voiced his opinions, not even to his wife. Survivors spoke their true thoughts to no one, trusted no one. Soviet psychiatry was exceptionally backward, mainly because theory and methods of treatment had to conform to official ideology and materialistic dogma. This meant that the problem of responsibility and irresponsibility could achieve its full scientific resolution only on the basis of Marxist-Leninist philosophy. The entire system was a lot of crap. The chairman, the Council of Ministers, the Politburo—they were all full of shit. The *Kah Gay Beh* was full of shit. The government and the social structure were a sham, a monstrous joke spinning around what was and what was supposed to be—every bit of it, theory and practice, make-believe. There were always the blind, millions of brainwashed idiots who believed the system actually worked, who were convinced that the Soviet Union was the greatest nation on earth. The fools even believed all the propaganda crap about the "warmongering" United States. Such imbeciles, true victims of their own vapidity, exhibited the twisted logic of weaklings who had tricked themselves into believing in a Supreme Being. Many of the old ones were like that. Even during the years of terror, during the era of Stalin, when millions were being carted off to the slave-labor camps, the peasants were stoically muttering that the brutality was the "will of God." Why, they even admired Stalin, calling him *krepki khozyain*—strong master!

At the opposite end of the psychological spectrum were the idealistic morons whose stupidity of conscience forced them to speak out openly against "injustice." They were the dissidents who were either sent to corrective labor colonies or ended up in a special psychiatric hospital. God help the fools who found themselves in SPH UZh-15/5. Dr. Stephen Libinsky was not only a sadist; he was a homosexual who liked his victims young.

The First Chief Directorate had a file on Libinsky two inches thick. In reality, the Home Office didn't give a damn what the overweight cocksucker did, as long as he did it *in* a special psychiatric hospital and *to* a patient. The more he subjected patients to physical abuse and emotional devastation, sexual or otherwise, the better the powers in *Moskva* liked it.

Only once did the *Kah Gay Beh* have to step in and order Libinsky to stop using a method of treatment he insisted would shock a patient into having "proper thoughts about the State." General Pytor Lom-Karaganda, the director of the Fifth Directorate, didn't mind the drugs and the brutality inflicted on patients by orderlies. He didn't mind the insulin-shock therapy that threw patients into hypoglycemic shock and, after repeated treatments, gave them heart and kidney ailments and severe diabetes. But there were limits. Using a small hose to force high-pressure air into a patient's bowels via his rectum—"to change his thinking"—was too much. It had to stop. The treatment killed too many patients. Dr. Libinsky was warned that the system demanded that patients be cured, not killed by having their intestines exploded by air. Cured meant that a patient admitted that his thinking had been wrong, that he had slandered the State, and that he was certain that the Soviet Union was indeed a true paradise on earth. Some even left SPHs even believing their own lies. That was the irony of the system. A person could enter a SPH sane and leave emotionally and mentally warped.

Colonel Boris Rudneva gave a little snicker after Libinsky closed the office door behind him. "Too bad, Anton. You missed a prime opportunity to have your horn blown, if not bitten off!"

A man who blushed even when told a blue joke in male company only, Cheklitt reddened, then laughed good-naturedly. He realized that Rudneva, knowing his tendency to blush easily, was only kidding. Anton Cheklitt liked his boss and had been his aide for three years. He especially admired Rudneva's methods and efficiency. He had certainly made true believers of those Allah-howling savages in Afghanistan and had done much to prevent peasants from helping the murderous *mujahidin* who were slaughtering brave Soviet soldiers protecting their homeland.

Rudneva's method had been simple and effective. He had told the peasants and farmers that if they helped the "freedom fighters" in any way, their small children would die. To emphasize that he meant exactly what he said, he and his *Opergruppa* specialists went from village to village and chose three children at random, two boys and a girl, all under the age of seven. The children had been taken 150 yards aloft in a helicopter and thrown out. Rudneva had then announced to the horrified villagers and the grief-stricken parents that the next time, all the children of the village would be executed. Indeed, Boris Rudneva did his job very well.

Before Major Cheklitt could reply wittily to Rudneva's joking, the door opened and two old women walked in. One carried a broom and a dustpan, the other a handful of rags and a carpet sweeper that must have been old when Stalin was a baby.

Both women wore rundown boots and thick stockings of coarse homespun. Old, faded kerchiefs were tied peasant-fashion under their chins. Their dresses were shapeless brown sacks, tightened only by their wide hips and pendulous breasts. Rudneva and Cheklitt didn't need to be told they were cleaning women. What bothered Colonel Rudneva, who was always security conscious, was how they could walk in, apparently any time they felt like it.

"Who are you women?" He got to his feet, an angry expression on his face. "Who told you to come into this office?"

The old women stopped and stared fearfully at Rudneva and Cheklitt, their manner as servile as a dog about to be whipped.

"I am Maria Maximovna Zedoseeva, *Khozyain,*" one woman said timidly.

"My name is Lidia Pavlovavitch Tamis, *Khozyain,*" the other woman said fearfully. "*Grazhdanka* Zedoseeva and me live in Taria. We have come to finish cleaning this office and the larger room in front." She put down the carpet sweeper. "We ask your forgiveness for disturbing both of you *khozyaini.*"

Rudneva wanted to laugh. The poor fools! But he said in a deliberately angry voice, "Stop calling us 'masters.' Officials are not the masters of citizens. Our nation is a democracy. Before you start work, tell me: Were either of you in the general area when the terrorists committed their terrible crime?"

Maria Maximovna Zedoseeva gasped and put her hand over her mouth.

"Oh, no, comrades!" Lidia Tamis's voice trembled. "Citizen Zedoseeva and me were not here. We came to work the next day, and Comrade Captain Kipeka instructed us to return home and come back the following day. The next day—that was yesterday—we did not complete the cleaning. That is why we are here today."

"And you walk in without knocking?"

"*Da,* Comrade. We always have," Lidia Tamis answered. "Is it improper to do so?"

"It is. From now on, knock and ask permission to enter," Rudneva told her. "Now continue with your duties."

He moved from behind the desk and looked at Major Cheklitt, who had gotten to his feet.

"There isn't any more we can do here. We'll return to Yakutsk."

"We're not going to question Comrade Gusbichev?" Cheklitt lighted another long Red Mist cigarette and carefully blew smoke away from Boris Rudneva, who neither smoked nor drank alcoholic beverages.

"He knows as little about what happened as these two cleaning women. Come, let's get to the helicopter."

They didn't continue the conversation as they left the administration building, walked across the yard, and hurried through the gates now manned by four guards. The three-seater ZOK-2 chopper was parked in the area in front of the gates. Two of the guards were watching the craft; they stepped back, saluted, then turned and walked back into the yard as Rudneva and Cheklitt got into the bird and secured the seat belts over their laps. However, Rudneva didn't start the engine immediately. Instead he said thoughtfully, "Anton, I fear we are faced with the impossible. I am sure of one fact: Whoever the terrorists were, they were experts. They planned well and came well prepared with explosive devices that were either detonated by timers or else by remote control."

Concerned about the note of worry he detected in Rudneva's low voice, Cheklitt, an avid reader of British detective fiction, said, "Sherlock Holmes said in one of his cases that if there aren't any answers after everything has been checked out, one must then turn to the impossible, even if the impossible is improbable."

Rudneva said contemplatively, "An autopsy proved that the people inside the office were killed with a nine-millimeter weapon. No strange fingerprints were found inside either office." He turned and looked straight at Cheklitt. "I ask you, how is it possible for two or more persons to go inside the administration building, all the way to the last office, and not leave a single fingerprint? We know they did not wear gloves. The temperature that day was almost seventy degrees."

"We're not without information," Cheklitt said. "We do know that the terrorists had expertly forged credentials identifying them as members of the *Kah Gay Beh*'s Fifth Chief Directorate. We —"

"*Nyet!* We know nothing about the actual terrorists who came to the hospital," Rudneva corrected his aide. "What we actually know is that two men, posing as *Kah Gay Beh* officers, had identification so perfectly forged that it fooled the Yakutsk militia into lending them an automobile. Your—"

"One called himself Major Valantin Veskaya. He was the tall red-haired man. The shorter man was supposed to be a Captain Arkady Sukhodrov."

"Your hypothesis, however, is valid, Anton," Rudneva said gravely. "I believe the two who acquired the Volga were members of the group who came to the hospital. Captain Kipeka said that when he and some of his men chased the Volga, they did not get close enough to see how many people were in the car. There couldn't have been more than five of them. The most important questions to be answered are who and why." He gave a short laugh. "I think we could use the services of Sherlock Holmes and—wasn't his assistant named 'Wattles?' "

"Watson," said Cheklitt, smiling. His mood changed instantly. He frowned and flicked the stub of his cigarette through the window. "None of it is logical. There aren't any terrorists in all of the Soviet Union. Our nation is not Europe or South America with their lax laws and inefficient police. Where did they come from? Why did they go to the hospital? Colonel, could the motive have been revenge, either against Vartanyan or Dr. Libinsky?"

"Revenge was not the motive," Rudneva said firmly. "Revenge does not explain how the perpetrators obtained such expertly forged credentials and the explosives. Revenge does not explain the precision and high quality with which the operation was carried out."

A troubled expression dropped over Cheklitt's face. "But, Colonel, there has to be a reason. I can't believe that all of it was an act of pure terrorism—killing simply for shock effect! Such an act wouldn't prove anything and would accomplish nothing."

"It proves that we have come to the impossible that, supposedly improbable, has become very possible," Rudneva said grudgingly. "I believe the kills were not the true goal of the terrorists. The murders were only a coverup after the terrorists realized they had failed in their prime objective."

"Their prime objective?" repeated Cheklitt, his mind trying to catch up to whatever his chief's conclusion might be.

"Their goal was to free one of the mental patients. They probably told Vartanyan and Igchenko they had been sent by the home office to pick up the patient and take him to *Moskva.* They also had the papers of release and transfer to prove it."

Seeing the disbelief spreading over his assistant's face, Rudneva smiled. His tone was fatherly. "I know, Anton. You find that incredible. Be honest with me."

"Yes, and no," Cheklitt admitted. "Yes, because no one has ever tried to break out a mental patient. No, because there always has to be a first time. If you are correct, Colonel, all we need is the who."

"I think you know the answer," Rudneva said evenly. "But you do not like to admit that an enemy intelligence service has penetrated this far into our nation. There can be no other answer."

Stunned, Major Cheklitt leaned back on the leather seat, groping for appropriate words. He had no doubt that Colonel

Rudneva was right. Special paper and inks were used in *Kah Gay Beh* identification documents. It would indeed take the technology of a foreign intelligence service to come even close to producing expert forgeries.

"Da, foreign agents are the only logical answer," Cheklitt said at length, becoming excited. "But how could they have gotten in? Why, they would need *propiksi,* workbooks, and of course passports and *spravki,* and since we do not have the free —" He stopped short and a fearful, embarrassed look flashed over his face.

"Were you going to say 'freedom'?" Rudneva chided him.

Cheklitt regained his composure. "I was going to say that since our country does not have the foolish permissiveness of many of the nations in the West, enemy agents in our land would have to have a very secure safe station. That means some of our own people—Soviet nationals—have to be helping them —Russian traitors in every true sense!"

"Exactly—and those traitors will be in Yakutsk," Rudneva said very seriously. "Taria, Bikopek, and other villages are too small. Strangers would be noticed immediately. But not in a city with a population of almost four hundred thousand."

"What action will you recommend to the front office?"

"There can be only one course of action. More agents have to be brought into this area and a quiet search begun. It's probably the American CIA, and I don't think its *otdel* here in Siberia can be very large, maybe ten or twenty people at the most. I mean native Russians. I doubt if the CIA sent in more than two foreign field specialists. They—"

"The Americans?" Cheklitt tilted back his head slightly in surprise. "The Central Intelligence Agency?"

"Who else but the *Amerikanski* have the capabilities? Not the British or the French or the West Germans. All this time we were looking for the impossible—for terrorists among our own people. But it wasn't terrorists who came to the hospital. It was American agents, helped by Soviet traitors!"

Cheklitt considered a moment. "In that case, we have very serious trouble. The Home Office will never admit that enemy agents have established an intelligence network in our country, especially in Siberia. General Dalstroy will demand more than theory."

"It's not difficult to see how the American agents came to Siberia," Colonel Rudneva went on. "The coast of the Sea of Okhotsk is only four hundred eighty-two kilometers away."

"If *Moskva* accepts your theory, Dalstroy and his Chief Border Guard Directorate will catch hell from the Central Committee," Cheklitt said gloomily. "General Dalstroy has always insisted that his boys are so good that even a foreign bird couldn't slip over our borders."

"Vadim Dalstroy has always been full of shit," Rudneva said quietly. "Any asshole knows that our borders—except in the European sector—can't be adequately guarded. They're too vast, too twisted, too rugged."

He started the ASh-84V eighteen-cylinder radial engine of the ZOK-2 helicopter, adding in a louder voice as the three-bladed rotor began to revolve faster, "We'll get back to Yakutsk and have our pilot fly us to *Moskva* tonight."

He checked the gas producer tachometer and other instruments, then worked the cyclic and throttle. The gray-green chopper shot upward into the dreary sky.

Major Anton Cheklitt continued to be puzzled in more ways than one. How could Rudneva always guess so accurately—anyhow, nine times out of ten? A strange man, Rudneva. Unlike many other officers of the Soviet Union's secret intelligence service, Rudneva never ran around on his wife. He was odd in other ways. He always traveled with a dozen old-fashioned alarm clocks, their ticking helping to put him to sleep.

Cheklitt hated his life as a member of the *Kah Gay Beh*. Compared to the average *grazhdanka,* he had a privileged life. Yet, in a sense, he was in even more of a vulnerable position than the average citizen. All he had to do was make one tiny mistake. So be it. One had to accept his situation in life and lean with the wind. Keep your mouth shut and survive. It was like Colonel Rudneva was fond of saying: The world was ruled by men who believed in ideas, not people. . . .

Chapter Four

Mrs. Joseph Camellion's only son, Richard, was not a happy man. Six days and six nights had become memories. The first effort to grab Dr. Georgi Ulomov had failed; he was stuck in a tiny room beneath a cellar, and the KGB was quietly tearing apart Yakutsk in an effort to find the "terrorists" who had invaded the special psychiatric hospital attached to Tarialag. Camellion's only pleasant surprise was that Zoya Beliyev and the rest of the Sorceress network had not let panic set in. If anything, the Yakutsk members had become more determined than ever—at least Zoya, Perchany, and Kirill Tarkovsky and Sergei Tsipin, the two Russians who had come this night to the small house of Zoya's grandmother on Donskoi Prospekt, in the northern section of Yakutsk.

Tsipin suddenly got up from the daybed, which also served as the living-room couch, and went over to one of the room's three windows.

"Sergei, you checked all the shades when you first arrived," Zoya said with a frown of consternation.

"I know I did. I want to be sure for my own peace of mind," Tsipin said determinedly. "I can't stand the thought that someone outside might be able to look in."

Having bent down and reassured himself that the end of the shade was several inches past the sill, he returned to his chair and sat down.

Only twenty-five years old, Tsipin was of medium height and slightly on the fleshy side. He was a good-looking young man—straight nose, square jaw, wide-spaced brown eyes, and a head of thick, slightly curly chestnut hair. For three years he had been a member of the Yakutsk militia and stationed at Post 17. In the Soviet Union, the militia served as the "local" police in each city, town, and village.

"As I was saying." Zoya, in a faded blue bathrobe, turned to

Tarkovsky. "After we commandeered the car from the man on the highway, we abandoned the militia vehicle and drove the Zhiguli straight through Taria. I then drove to the city. We didn't have a bit of trouble. We abandoned the Zhiguli on Keskivko Street, not far from the auditorium. The three of us then went our separate ways."

Tarkovsky's thin face became puzzled. "Separate ways? But *Tovarishch* Scott is staying here with you, Zoya Beliyev!"

"That is true," she admitted. "But he could not come here to my grandmother's house until late at night. This block is filled mostly with the elderly, and they retire early. Of course, if anyone did see him entering, they would only think he was a visitor, perhaps my lover. No great harm would be done in either case, but it pays to be cautious."

Tarkovsky and Tsipin looked at the Death Merchant in admiration.

"You walked around alone in Yakutsk?" exclaimed Tarkovsky, who was a square-shouldered man, with close-cropped blond hair and mustache to match, his jaw muscles, conspicuous at the corners of his mouth, suggesting he was in the military. He wasn't. He was in construction and was the foreman of "high walkers," those iron workers who bolt the steel girder skeletons of buildings together. He had one of those old-young faces and his age could have been from thirty-five to fifty.

"I walked a lot," said Camellion, who was sitting on the floor, his back against the front of the small couch on which Zoya was sitting. His gray shirt and brown pants and shoes were all of Soviet manufacture. "I stopped in restaurants and lingered over tea or vodka. But the very first thing I did was go into a washroom and remove my red hairpiece and mustache and fake mole on my left cheek. I also tore up all the papers identifying me as Major Valantin Veskaya and flushed them down the toilet. I became citizen Aleksandr Gvishiani, a driver on your local *elektrichki,* one of your local commuter trains, and I had all the papers to prove it—as long as I wasn't hauled into some police station."

"I did the same thing after the three of us left the Zhiguli and its owner," Zoya said. "I went—"

"You took the owner of the car with you?" Sergei Tsipin's eyebrows went up. "Didn't you kill him?"

"We didn't have to," Zoya said. "He was so drunk when we stopped him, he could hardly drive. He was a physician and had a bottle of vodka on the seat beside him. We made him get into the backseat with the third member of our group and forced him to finish the bottle. When we left him, he was passed out."

"Then you also were in disguise, Zoya," said Tsipin.

"I went into the ladies room of the hotel on Priponskiev and took off my dark wig and removed from my mouth the two clips that widened my cheeks. I stuffed all of it into my handbag. I also destroyed my identification as an agent of the *Kah Gay Beh.*" She gave a quick little laugh, then leaned down and looked at the Death Merchant. "Do you know what, Scott? I forgot all about the gloves until I got home."

"Gloves?" Tarkovsky said in surprise. "How could you be wearing gloves in this weather?"

"Scott, you tell him," urged Zoya.

Camellion explained that he and Zoya and "the third person with us" had worn special Latex rubber gloves, so transparent that the fingernails and veins showed through. The special gloves worked especially well for women because they didn't have hair on the back of their hands. With men's gloves, hair had to be attached, a single hair at a time for realistic effect.

Sergei Tsipin grinned, showing tobacco-stained teeth. "Our superiors in the militia are still wondering why there weren't any strange fingerprints in the two offices. We have heard that the *Kah Gay Beh* can't understand it either."

Kirill Tarkovsky finished lighting his pipe and looked from Zoya to the Death Merchant. "Do you have any idea why the administrator and his assistant at the hospital became suspicious?"

Zoya leaned down again and looked at Camellion, her eyes asking if she should confide in Tarkovsky. It was a matter of security. The Sorceress *otdel* in Yakutsk was arranged in two-man cells, with only Zoya knowing the identity of all ten members. For this reason, Tarkovsky and Tsipin, the two members of Cell 3, did not know that Alexey Perchany was the third member of the trio who had gone to SPH UZh-15/5.

Camellion replied in an even tone, "We've since learned that a new regulation was put into effect only five days before we went to the hospital. It seems that now when the *Kah Gay Beh* sends agents to any hospital to transfer a mental patient, there is a special code word that indicates the identity of the patient to be transferred. The password is given at the time the officers identify themselves. I didn't give the code word. Vartanyan and Igchenko knew the three of us were fakes."

Camellion could tell that Tarkovsky was on the verge of asking how he had learned so quickly about the new regulation. Actually, whether Tarkovsky and Tsipin knew about the AN/URC-101 transmitter wasn't that important. If the KGB closed in, they'd have so much on him that the radio wouldn't matter.

After he had returned to the house and found Zoya anxiously waiting for him, he had calmly eaten a supper of black bread, cabbage, and *tvorog*—sweetened homemade cottage cheese. With Zoya at his heels, he had then gone down to the room beneath the cellar, brought up the shortwave transmitter and its hand-held dish antenna, and had mounted the dish to the top of one of the poles supporting the clothesline in the rear yard. With Zoya scared stiff that some stray soul might spot the dish in the dark night, Camellion had turned on the AN/URC and sent two words to be bounced off one of NSA's SPINTCOM satellites orbiting the Soviet Union—*Blue Cow,* the phrase that meant the first attempt to free Dr. Ulomov had failed and that more input of data was needed.

There was a problem with operating the AN/URC-101 in Siberia. Because of space limitations, Camellion had not been able to bring any black boxes with him. Since the AN/URC-101 did have a built-in scrambler and could frequency-hop over 35,000 UHF channels in the 225-399.995 MHz AM and FM range at the rate of 6,500-C per second, Soviet listening posts could pick up only what sounded like meaningless static. But even static could be tracked by mobile units with sophisticated equipment, if the static was from a fixed location and if the sender was stupid enough to remain on the air very long.

Shortly before dawn, the Death Merchant got his reply via the CIA's powerful shortwave station in Otaru, in northern Japan. It was then that Camellion had learned about the new KGB regulation. Grojean's office explained that they had just learned about the recent order the morning of the previous day. The Agency's mole in the Ninth Direction of the Fifth Chief

Directorate had not been able to send a message by shortwave any earlier. It was just one of those things—sorry.

Zoya recrossed her legs, and in doing so her right leg slipped from underneath her bathrobe. Camellion could see her leg, to his left, from the corner of his eye. It was unshaved. That was another thing that turned him off Russians: Soviet women did not shave their legs or underneath their arms. But then, in social customs the Soviet Union was 150 years behind the rest of the world's modern nations.

The Soviets made toilet paper, paper cups, and ice-cream cups from the same grade paper. Coffee or hot tea would drip through the bottom of a paper cup in about twenty seconds. Prolonged use of Soviet toilet paper could be so injurious to one's health that all the Preparation-H in the world wouldn't help.

Public restrooms were scarce. There weren't any public drinking fountains. A citizen would put a few kopecks into a vending machine and water would drip into an ordinary glass. The next person would drink from the same glass.

Nothing worked in the Soviet Union, not even logic. While he had waited for dark and killed time by walking around in Yakutsk, Camellion had seen a sign over a bar in one of the hotels: OPEN 24 HOURS. CLOSED FROM TEN IN THE MORNING UNTIL FOUR IN THE AFTERNOON. In all of Yakutsk, there were only six service stations for all the cars. In Camellion's opinion, a nation that didn't even distribute telephone books to its citizens was a long way from world domination. Another annoyance was the Russian habit addressing each other by their full names. However, this was strictly a social custom that dated back hundreds of years. All nations had their own peculiar customs and habits.

"Sergei Tsipin, you've told us that the militia is assisting the *Kah Gay Beh* in its 'search' of Yakutsk," Camellion said, speaking rapidly. "I should like to know how the secret police can be looking for people it can't identify, even among the Russian people."

Tsipin thought a few moments. "All I can tell you is that the militia is supplying vehicles for groups of special *Kah Gay Beh* officers who choose several blocks at random. The militia cordons off the blocks and the special officers go in and question all the people within the area. We in the militia have discussed this procedure among ourselves. We don't know what the *Kah Gay Beh* expects to find. And there isn't any word filtering down from the top either. The militia is not helping with the actual investigation."

"Do you know how many special *Kah Gay Beh* officers came from *Moskva?*" Zoya asked, sounding worried.

"*Tovarishch* Scott, what did you mean when you said 'even among the Russian people'?" Tarkovsky interrupted, his tone and his face somber.

"By now the *Kah Gay Beh* has concluded that the invasion of the hospital was not carried out solely by Soviet nationals," asserted the Death Merchant. "*Moskva* has to have arrived at that conclusion from logical deduction. It knows that expertly forged *Kah Gay Beh* credentials had to have been used. Even if there were local terrorists, where could they obtain such identification? How could they forge it? Where would they get the special paper and inks?"

"What's your conclusion?" asked Tsipin.

"The *Kah Gay Beh* is working on the premise that the Soviet Union has been penetrated by foreign agents and that it was they, helped by Soviet citizens, who engineered the bust-in at the hospital. What the *Kah Gay Beh* doesn't know is why. They don't know anything about the three of us mentioning the prisoner transfer. The people who could have told them are no longer in this world."

"A hundred or so *Kah Gay Beh* officers came from *Moskva,* I've heard," Tsipin said nervously, his right foot brushing against the side of his wooden-cased chess set. "That's what we heard. We do know that the officer in charge is Lieutenant Colonel Boris Rudneva. He's a specialist in antiterrorism."

Puffing furiously on his pipe, Kirill Tarkovsky shifted uneasily in his chair and gruffly gave his opinion. "Since the *Kah Gay Beh* is picking out blocks at random, they could choose this block. We are going to have to move you, *Tovarishch* Scott." He glanced at Zoya, who, smoking a cigarette, was brushing ashes from her bathrobe. "Zoya Beliyev, do we have another hiding place for our American friend?"

"Well, there is another safe house," Zoya said, her tone pessimistic. Since she would need Tarkovsky and Tsipin's assistance in smuggling Camellion to the seventeenth-century wooden church that was, she hoped, safe, she realized now was the time to let them in on the plan.

"The two of you are familiar with the Church of Our Savior between Taria and Yakutsk?"

There was a tense pause as Tarkovsky and Tsipin eyed Zoya skeptically.

"The church is hundreds of years old and is a state monument," Tarkovsky replied doubtfully. "But—"

"The caretaker is a member of our *Charodeika Otdel,*" Zoya said evenly. "It isn't likely that Colonel Rudneva and his men would search the church. But it has been the target of many searches over the years. Because of this there are numerous secret rooms that were built during the days of the czars. The priests used them as protection from roving bands of bandits."

"How can I hide there if the authorities know about the rooms?" Camellion asked, concerned.

"I'm coming to that," Zoya said. "Yuri Gagarin, the caretaker, says he is positive that the police do not know about all the hidden rooms. He told me that he has found several of the secret crypts himself, one only several months ago. He didn't tell the authorities because he thought the rooms could be useful to us some day. That day has arrived, Arnold Scott. The sooner you and your equipment are in the Church of Our Savior, the safer you and we will be."

"Getting him to the church will not be easy," Tsipin ventured thoughtfully. "All of us have jobs. We can't take off any time we want, and starting next week, I will be on a seven-day-a-week schedule."

The Death Merchant drew a deep breath. "Sergei Tsipin, is the militia stopping any vehicles on the road, especially at night?"

"We haven't had any orders to that effect," replied Tsipin, running a hand through his thick curly hair. "But who can say when the *Kah Gay Beh* will issue such a directive? I can tell you this: Starting tomorrow, there will be twice the number of militia police cars on the streets at night."

His words didn't fill Zoya with cheerful thoughts, and one could almost see the wheels of gloom turning in Tarkovsky's mind.

"Chort vozmi! We can't move you out of here and into the church the same way we moved you in!" Tarkovsky said in a voice of defiance mingled with martyrdom, his gaze stabbing holes in Camellion. "It was a terrible chance we took after we met you and the driver of the Vanda. Later, when we had to come here through the backyard with those two boxes at three o'clock in the morning—another terrible risk! But now, with the *Kah Gay Beh* suspecting everyone—and didn't you hear what Sergei Tsipin said? Twice the number of police cars on the streets after dark!"

"We have no choice," Zoya said tersely. "There is no other way to get him out."

"I think there is." The Death Merchant tried to sound casual and confident as he got to his feet. "We can leave here, say, in the middle of the afternoon. We don't have to slink around at night." He sat down on a chair. "The weekend is only several days away, and—"

"I can get word to Yuri Gagarin by Friday afternoon," Zoya interrupted, brightening.

"And a lot of moving and trading back and forth is done on Saturdays and Sundays," Camellion finished. "Kirill Tarkovsky, do you own a car?"

Tarkovsky nodded slowly and took the pipe, which had gone out, from his mouth.

"All you have to do is show up here at, say, one o'clock on Saturday afternoon," the Death Merchant said. "You can either use the alley or park out in front of the house."

"And in broad daylight, we walk out with those two boxes that're downstairs?" Tarkovsky stared deprecatingly at Camellion. "Why, they look like crates of small arms!"

"We're not going to take the boxes," Camellion explained. "There's an old trunk down in the cellar. It will hold everything that's in the boxes. All you and I will do is carry out the trunk, and not from the cellar, but from the house. We'll also"—he looked around the shabby room—"carry out a few of these lamps to make it all appear normal. Who's sitting around watching? Who's going to keep track of how many men went into the house?" He turned toward Zoya. "I'll give you more than enough rubles to replace the lamps—tomorrow, when I give you food money."

Camellion didn't show his surprise when Tarkovsky agreed with him.

"It could work," the man said, now in a more cheerful frame of mind. "Except how do we get you and the trunk out of the car and into the church in the daylight? The church is a monument to stupidity and superstition, but it's still a public show-place. There will be visitors."

"Not as many as you might think," Zoya edged in. "There won't be any tourists from the West. Not even half-witted communists from other countries go sightseeing in Siberia. The only visitors would be our own people, who come to work in Ya-kutsk because of higher wages. They usually see the sights on Sunday. They're mostly young people, and none of them consider Sunday any kind of a holy day."

"I hope you're right," said Tarkovsky unpleasantly. "I don't like the *Kah Gay Beh*'s snooping around."

"It really won't make any difference how many people are visting the church," Zoya went on. "The caretaker's house is to the rear. Next to the house is a garage. Neither the house nor the garage can be seen from the road or by the visitors. Who's going to notice your driving into the garage? Even if someone did see you, why should they be suspicious? No one is looking for trouble, and there's not been a single word in the newspa-pers about what happened at the hospital."

Tsipin addressed the Death Merchant. "The Russians, as a people, mind their own business, especially in public. No one will pay any attention to the car, much less report it to the militia."

"What about the weight of the trunk?" Tarkovsky asked.

"Maybe eighty kilograms," Camellion said breezily. "Weight won't be a problem. The size could be. It's a storage trunk. We'd have to remove the front seat to get it into the rear."

"Size isn't a problem either," said Tarkovsky. "I'll use one of the vehicles from work. A runabout minibus should do nicely. We'll be able to shove the trunk through the rear door." He pulled a green cardboard container of tobacco from his pocket and began to fill his pipe. "I'm only sorry that the plan to free the mental patient failed. It is sad, *Tovarishch* Scott. You made the dangerous journey to the Soviet Union for nothing."

The Death Merchant decided that now was the time to tell

Tarkovsky and Tsipin that by no means was he about to fold his tent and slink back to the United States.

"Tovarishch Kirill Tarkovsky," Camellion said very formally, "to be accurate, you should have said you were sorry that the *first* plan to free the target failed."

He did not get the reaction he had expected. Zoya, who already knew he was going to make another attempt to black-bag Dr. Georgi Ulomov, remained silent. Yet there were no stares of disbelief from either Tarkovsky or Tsipin, the latter of whom said, with a cynical expression on his face:

"We did not think you were the kind of man to give up so easily. We were also thinking that the *Kah Gay Beh* would never imagine that we might make a second strike at the same mental hospital. Then again, it might."

Tarkovsky blew out a small cloud of blue smoke. "You will have to make that attempt within the next few weeks, or your last chance will be gone. All seasons but winter are short in Siberia. There is no gradual moving of one season into another. In a few more weeks the trees will stand naked. Almost overnight the cold will arrive, and we'll get up one morning and see our first foot of snow."

The Death Merchant said gently, "I understand that the Yakutsk–Okhotsk Highway is kept open even during the worst of the winter months."

"Oh, yes," Tarkovsky replied. "Even during the worst blizzards, when the *purga* is blowing its hardest, the snowplows are doing their job on that highway. It is a must. Ninety percent of all hard goods that arrive in Yakutsk come to the port city of Okhotsk."

"But the highway remaining open could not help you, *Tovarishch* Scott," Tsipin said, glancing at his wristwatch.

"I know," Camellion admitted sadly. "On either side of the road are snow drifts the size of small mountains. The truck in which we would be hiding wouldn't be able to pull off the highway so that we could leave our places of concealment." His short laugh was grim. "We could end up being hauled aboard a cargo vessel in Okhotsk and wind up in *Moskva!*"

Tarkovsky's eyes gleamed; he had made up his mind. "Listen, American, I tell you this: I will help in any way I can. When the time comes for the second attempt, I will go with you if you want. I swear that to you. I will, naturally, be here Saturday between one and two in the afternoon."

"I would also like to go with you," announced Sergei Tsipin, thrusting his head forward. "Even getting killed is better than living in this land and knowing that your future will be just as bad as the present."

Camellion studied the militiaman for a moment. "It would be very dangerous, and you could get killed," he said, thinking that young men can never really conceive of their own deaths. He tried a new tack to gain insight into the motives of the two men. "I must admit that, in view of the risks and the small rewards, the determination of you both surprises me. Statistically, most people would want to play it safe."

Relighting his pipe, Tarkovsky was too busy to reply.

Sergei Tsipin smiled. "It is difficult for you to understand because you do not live in the Soviet Union. Tell me, have you ever heard the story about the fat dog and the hungry wolf?"

Camellion admitted that he had not.

"The fat dog was in the woods one day and met a thin, hungry wolf. The dog said to him, 'Come home with me, and you will always be well fed. Never again will you be hungry.'

"The wolf thought this was an opportunity of a lifetime, and he agreed.

"On the way, the wolf noticed that the hair around the happy dog's neck was worn very thin, and he asked why this was.

" 'It's because I wear a collar,' the dog told him.

"The wolf was shocked. 'But why do you have to wear a collar?' he asked.

" 'I must wear a collar because my chain is attached to it,' the dog replied.

" 'Do you mean you are chained most of the time and are not free to run?' the wolf asked.

"The dog admitted this was so, but he pointed out that, in return for being chained, he was always fed promptly.

"The wolf looked at him for a moment, then ran back into the woods. He is still there. At times he is hungry, but he is *free*."

Tsipin's smile had been replaced by a grim look. "We Russians are even worse off than the wolf, *Tovarishch* Scott. We are chained by a ruthless dictatorship, we are not free, and we are not well fed. In helping you free the man you came after, we are helping ourselves. . . ."

After Kirill Tarkovsky and Sergei Tsipin, each carrying his own cased chess set, left the house, Zoya picked up the present that Tsipin had brought her. It was a bra, not the floppy, ugly Soviet kind with no support and no adjustments, made for big-teated country girls, but a Czech one, white and trimmed with blue and red flowers. While Zoya hurriedly tossed the brown paper to one side, Camellion glanced around the shabby room. It was furnished with an assortment of chairs and tables that looked as if they had been taken from different attics.

All very normal—for the USSR! The Russians had a strong public persona, but in their homes and private lives, they were unpretentious. They didn't worry about appearances—being freshly scrubbed, having perfumed breath, and keeping up with the Joneses. In the Soviet Union, a person could be seedy, sweaty, have a face full of acne, be as homely as mortal sin and still be accepted. One could only conclude the dichotomy was an integral part of the Russian character.

However, this was not the case with the communist nobility, the small select group that ran the Supreme Soviet, the ministers of the Politburo, officials of the KGB, and so on. They got the *kremlevsky payok*—the Kremlin ration. They got luxurious food—*free!* They bought imported items from their own special stores and lived more like Westerners than Russians.

"See. Isn't it pretty?" As happy as a little child on Christmas morning, Zoya held up the brassiere for Camellion to look at.

"Da, that it is." Unexpectedly, the Death Merchant felt a huge wave of compassion rising within him, not only for Zoya but for all the Russian little people, who were chained but not well-fed dogs of the Soviet system. They were all doing a hundred miles an hour down a dead-end street!

However, it was the mission that was important; everything had to revolve around it. An intelligence agent, while in a nation of the Other Side, is constantly checking and reevaluating his security. For the tenth time that day, Camellion automatically reappraised his position. Other than Zoya, only three members of the Sorceress network knew about him. Very soon two more members would know that a foreign intelligence agent was being protected by the *otdel*—Yuri Gagarin, the care-taker of the Church of Our Savior, and Maxim Chenko, the seventy-one-year-old retiree who was a message "runner." Should Zoya or any of the other five be picked up for any reason and subjected to intense interrogation, sooner or later that member would talk. Everyone confessed to the KGB, guilty or not. *And so would I—if they grabbed me and prevented me from self-termination!*

Unabashedly, Zoya took off her bathrobe and tossed it on the daybed. Wearing only bra and panties, she turned her back to Camellion, undid her bra, dropped it on top of the robe, slipped into the Czech bra, and fastened the three clasps in back. Turning, a big smile on her face, she shoved her hands under her ample breasts and shifted them into a comfortable position within the snugness of the bra.

Not immune to the charms of even a female pig farmer (or a roll in the hay, even if the hay was in the Soviet Union), the Death Merchant reflected that Zoya did have a nice body. Each breast was a good handful, and while her hips were a trifle too wide, her stomach was firm and flat, her navel so deep it could hide half a tongue. For a Russian woman, she did have slim legs, and shapely, too, not too thick in the calves and thighs. Nor was she unattractive facially either.

Camellion cleared his throat. "How soon will Alexey Perchany be back from his truck run to Okhotsk?"

"How do I look?" A pleased-with-herself Zoya stepped closer until she was only three feet from Camellion. "Oh, Alexey! His run takes three days, from the time he leaves Yakutsk and gets back. Then he has a day off and makes another run."

"Uh—they—you look all right to me," Camellion complimented her truthfully. "I should say the bra is a nice fit."

Zoya frowned and became serious. "You know, Sergei would like for me and him to become lovers. The poor boy. He is much too young and inexperienced. I prefer an older, worldly man."

She then explained that she had known Tsipin for five years. He had been one of her English students. At one time she had taught English to young people so that they could sing foreign tunes in English. Russian, she pointed out, being a polysyllabic language, was incompatible with a musical framework built on the terse rhythms of English.

" 'I'll kiss your lips' requires only four syllables in English," she said, "but eight syllables in Russian." Suddenly she changed the subject. "I know why you asked about Alexey Perchany: You must time the second attempt to free Dr. Ulomov with Alexey Perchany's being available with his truck."

Without putting on her robe, she sat down on the bed and crossed her legs.

"That's about the size of it," Camellion said. "The way things are now, the only way I'm ever going to get my hands on Dr. Ulomov is to use brute force. That means a quick transfer to one or two cars, then to Perchany's truck. At least innocent civilians won't be killed. Every person on the staff of any SPH is always a member of the KGB."

For a short moment, there was silence, except for the loud snoring of Zoya's grandmother coming from behind a closed bedroom door across the room. At least eighty-five, the *babushka* went to bed with the chickens, slept like a baby, and got up with the sun.

"And if you fail in the second try?" Zoya's voice was as soft as her eyes, and there was a certain kind of huskiness to it, one with which Camellion was familiar.

I'll tell her I'm married, love my wife, and can't be unfaithful!

He shrugged. "Then I'll be dead and it won't make any difference."

Zoya leaned back on her elbows, her sultry gaze probing him, asking, hinting.

She said in a velvet voice, "It must be lonely and uncomfortable for you below." She patted the daybed. "There isn't any reason why you shouldn't spend the night up here, in comfort."

Oh, yes, there is! Camellion would have liked to, but he wasn't about to make love to a woman whose grandmother was only twenty feet away. And he didn't relish the idea of getting up before dawn. But the main reason didn't have anything to do with the sunrise.

It's those damned hairy legs!

Chapter Five

It is always easier to hate something than it is to understand it. However, the Death Merchant and Zoya Beliyev didn't hate Kirill Tarkovsky when he didn't arrive at one o'clock Saturday afternoon, and they did understand why: Something had happened. But what? Zoya couldn't phone. No one in the Soviet Union trusted phones, which the KGB monitored at random.

Everything had been ready. In the middle of the night, from 0300 hours to 0400 hours Saturday morning, Camellion had carried the trunk upstairs to the small kitchen, then transferred the contents of the two special equipment boxes—the AN/URC, makeup lab, the two SMGs, handguns, ammo, and other junk—to the trunk, in the process going up and down the steps (and a short ladder) so often that he was feeling like a yo-yo by the time he had completed the task.

The job had also included taking apart the special boxes and unscrewing the stainless-steel clamps from the wood. He had then placed the wood flat on the wide shelves and replaced the jars of home-canned blackberry jam, peach preserves, and other goodies. Because they lived so close to the land, Russians in Siberia ate better than their European counterparts. Meat, too, was more plentiful.

The Death Merchant, holed up in his small room beneath the floor of the cellar, spent a miserable Saturday afternoon and evening. His Sunday morning wasn't so great either. All he could do was sit and wait helplessly, a prisoner of his own mounting anxiety.

Zoya and Nadezhda Alliluyeva Tolbukhin, the grandmother, had to suffer the same emotional purgatory as Camellion . . . even worse. The trunk was sitting there in their kitchen, right out in the open, although they had covered it with a tablecloth. To complicate the matter, Zoya had met with Maxim Chenko on Friday morning and had given him a message to take to Yuri

Gagarin, and so Gagarin, too, was also undergoing his own private hell of doubt.

The least worried of all, as far as her own safety was concerned, was Nadezhda Tolbukhin. She had lived a long, productive life and death held no terrors for her. She did not possess one iota of information about the Sorceress network. She only suspected that her granddaughter was working against the State. She never asked questions and always looked the other way. Zoya had not told her who Camellion was, or why he was there. She had only said, "Grandmother, he is not even here. He will hide in the room that Grandfather Vanya built during the days of the Stalin terror."

Secretly Nadezhda Alliluyeva was grateful that someone of her blood was fighting the regime that had destroyed her family. Her husband, one of her younger sisters, and two brothers had died in Stalin's slave-labor camps.

Kirill Tarkovsky arrived at 1:07 Sunday afternoon, parking a white-and-green Zaporozhets minivan, with a sliding door on each side, in front of the house.

"Where have you been? What went wrong?" Zoya demanded angrily after Tarkovsky had come into the house. With her was Camellion. He had come upstairs before dawn, presuming that Tarkovsky would arrive sometime on Sunday.

"We had an accident Friday afternoon on the job, and I had to work Saturday," Tarkovsky said, perplexed to find Zoya and Camellion so distressed. He blinked first at Zoya, then addressed the Death Merchant. "I'm here now, so what is the problem? Have you changed your plans, *Tovarishch* Arnold Scott?"

"*Nyet.* Nothing has changed," Camellion said, hoping that his normal tone of voice would help Zoya to control her explosive temper.

"Comrade Gagarin expected your arrival yesterday," Zoya said in a more temperate voice. "He knows you are to arrive in a van, though. We can only hope that everything will work out successfully on his end."

"First I want to give you a new set of identity papers," Camellion told Tarkovsky, "and a handgun."

Tarkovsky's mouth formed a tight line, indicating resistance to the idea. "Why can't I use my own papers? They are genuine."

Convinced that the only virtue of the stupid is that they never live long, Camellion said tolerantly, "Suppose we're stopped by the militia. The first thing they'll want to see is our papers. They'll have to notice the trunk. Suppose they demand we open it, and we have to shoot our way past them. Do you want them to know your real name, and where you live and work?"

Tarkovsky saw the logic of Camellion's reasoning and didn't argue when the Death Merchant told him his new name would be Leonid Dudintsev.

"Let's do it," Camellion said. "Zoya, you carry the floor lamps."

With Camellion at one end of the trunk and Tarkovsky at the other end, they carried the trunk downstairs, out the front door, down the dirt walk, and to the minibus. Zoya followed, each hand wrapped around the metal column of a floor lamp. While Camellion and Tarkovsky placed the trunk in the rear of the van, Zoya unscrewed the lampshades. She handed the shades and lamps to Camellion, whispered, "Good luck," and returned to the house. Tarkovsky closed the van door and locked it. He made sure the door on the opposite side and the rear door was locked, then made his way to the driver's seat and sat down next to the Death Merchant. In a little while Tarkovsky was driving the minibus toward the Myasnitskaya Nev, one of the main thoroughfares of Yakutsk.

The Death Merchant, checking a 9 mm, eighteen-shot Steyr auto pistol, was fascinated with Soviet traffic rules. Everyone drove as if he were just learning to drive. Left turns were illegal. A driver went past the street he wanted, made a legal U-turn, then came back. But more often than not the legal U-turn areas were few and far between. This meant that, depending on where a driver wanted to go, he might have to drive ten blocks in order to get to his destination only four blocks away. Camellion and Tarkovsky would not have to go so far out of their way. Myasnitskaya Avenue led straight to the highway that led toward Taria.

Now and then they passed a militia patrol car coming from the opposite direction, or else one passed them going in the same direction. Thirty-five km per hour was the legal speed, but the law did not apply to the militia.

They were almost across the city when a problem arose. Traffic, which had been slowing down for several blocks, came to a stop.

"I'm going to see what's holding up traffic," Tarkovsky said.

"Careful," warned Camellion.

Tarkovsky first reassured himself that the .45 ACP 9-shot Astra A-80 pistol Camellion had given him was snug in his belt, hidden under his jacket. Only then did he get out of the minibus and look up the road to see what had stopped traffic. In a few minutes he was back in the vehicle and shifting gears, for traffic had once more begun to move, though very slowly.

"There's been a wreck at the intersection ahead," said Tarkovsky, his jaw muscles quivering in frustration. "Several cars hit a truck carrying produce, and there are vegetables all over the road. The militia is routing the traffic in this lane onto a side street."

"How much time will we lose?" Camellion had the feeling he was about to hear the sound of one hand clapping.

Tarkovsky snorted in disgust. "An hour and a half, maybe more. We'd have to take a jigsaw route. The thing for us to do is swing off onto a side street after we make the turn. We're close to Boris Godunov Way and there are a lot of cafés there. We can kill the next hour drinking tea. I could use a few shots of vodka about now—if it's agreeable with you, *Tovarishch* Scott."

Mentally Camellion reshuffled the cards in his deck of security. His own papers identified him as Venyamin Khanpira, an engineer who worked in a wire and cable factory. Unless they looked through the windshield, pedestrians on the sidewalk would not be able to see the trunk and the lamps.

"How safe will the van be?" Camellion asked. "Zoya told me that a lot of thievery goes on in Yakutsk."

"Mostly all of it is at night." Tarkovsky pushed gently down on the gas pedal to move ahead at the speed of an elderly turtle. "The reason is that, while we have more food in Siberia than the rest of the country, we lack hard goods—furniture, rugs, decent clothing, radios, television sets and electronic goods, in fact, anything that has to be trucked in from the port city of Okhotsk. We call such scarce items *defitsitny*—deficit goods."

"All right, we'll park," Camellion said. "A cup of hot mint tea would go good about now."

Half an hour later Camellion and Tarkovsky were walking into a café on Boris Godunov Street, in the oldest section of Yakutsk. Most of this area resembled a maze, with zigzag streets and crooked alleys and buildings that were ancient before the Bolsheviks executed Czar Nicholas II and murdered his family. The minivan was parked half a block behind them.

To the right of the café's door was a large rectangular window that needed washing. Inside the main area were eight square tables, each one covered with a flowered cloth. Five of the tables were filled. The Death Merchant especially noticed one young couple and their daughter, a scrubbed-fresh little girl not more than two years old. A big white bow ribbon in her hair, she was sitting on her mother's lap, eating ice cream. *Another plus for the pig farmers,* thought Camellion. They loved children and lavished affection on them without being indulgent.

The kitchen had been built into the northeast corner of the room. Here rabbit was fried or roasted and shish kebab—spiced and skewered lamb—was prepared. A massive wooden coat rack sat on the west wall, toward the front. Farther up was the cashier, sitting behind his counter, an abacus in front of him. Finally, toward the northwest, was a counter with five stools. Three men sat there. Behind the counter, serviced by a young woman, were shelves filled with bottles of wine, liquor, and glasses. On one side of the shelves was an ornate samovar trimmed in silver and gold; on the other side a restaurant-type coffeemaker. Cups and saucers were also on a rear shelf. Underneath the shelf was an ice-cream freezer.

Only one man was sitting at the shorter four-stool counter facing the north wall, in which there was a door to the rear room.

There were no menus, either on the tables or posted on the wall. One went up to the sleepy-eyed cashier, who had turned on the radio behind him and was listening to propaganda lies from Radio Moscow, asked him what was being served that day, and paid. The cashier then wrote down the order on a piece of paper and handed it to the customer, who took it to the waitress who filled the order. Larger orders of rabbit and lamb were phoned to the kitchen by the cashier. They were brought from the kitchen by one of the cooks. The entire system was one of Soviet efficiency.

The Death Merchant sat down at an empty table toward the center of the room, and Tarkovsky—Comrade Leonid Dudintsev—went after a cup of mint tea and three shots of vodka mixed in a glass of kefir, which was similiar to buttermilk. A man who loved meat the way Romeo loved Juliet, Camellion had suggested that they order some of whatever was frying in the kitchen, the tantalizing aroma tempting his stomach. Tarkovsky, however, had pointed out that there wasn't time, that by the time they loafed in the café, walked back to the minibus, and retraced their route to the Myasnitskaya Nev, an hour and a half would have gone by. "It could be an hour or more before the kitchen would even have our order prepared," Tarkovsky had said.

Tarkovsky had just returned with the glass of tea and the glass of kefir and was sitting down when Camellion, whose back was to the east wall, saw two jeeps pull up and park. Apparently it was "coffee break" time. As three of the brown-uniformed militiamen got out of the first jeep, their driver and the four in the second jeep opened paper sacks, pulled out newspaper-wrapped sandwiches, opened them and began to eat. Well, this was the Soviet Union! It figured that many militiamen would brown bag their lunches.

Laughing and talking, the young militiamen placed their order and went to the counter by the north wall and sat down. The Death Merchant and Tarkovsky played it cool and continued to listen to the propaganda bullshit coming out of the radio, all of it directed at the mean old United States whose "anticommunist cure of Reaganism was a dangerous drug that is ruining not only the American people but all the peoples of the world." But one could "fight" this "danger" by "listening to the truth of the Soviet Union, whose only desire is for peace throughout the world."

Camellion and Tarkovsky, half finished with their drinks, remained on full alert, both tensing at the sight of the next two men who walked into the restaurant. In their thirties, they were well dressed for Russians, one man in a light-blue suit of West European cut, the other in cream-color slacks and sport coat to match. Tarkovsky, his back to the north side door of the kitchen, let his gaze wander to Camellion, telegraphing his suspicion. The Death Merchant didn't have any doubts: The two were KGB. He was proved right when the men walked over to the couple with the child and the agent in the blue suit asked to see their papers. The other couples pretended not to notice, but from where Camellion and Tarkovsky sat, they could see that the two secret police agents were examining the documents very carefully. One was actually holding up the pages of one passport to the light, evidently checking the paper's watermark. The Death Merchant knew why: Moscow Center had reasoned that whoever had splattered all the KGB personnel at SPH UZh-15/5 had gained entry with expertly forged KGB ID and was still in the general area.

Satisfied, the two agents returned the papers to the couple and moved to the next table, the table west of Camellion and Tarkovsky. The elderly couple merely handed their papers to the older of the KGB men. The Death Merchant and Kirill Tarkovsky would have liked to leave. They didn't dare. Anyone leaving a closed-in area where the KGB was inspecting papers was immediately suspect.

Sighing, Tarkovsky leaned back in his chair and unbuttoned his coat. Camellion finished his tea and let his own jacket fall open. *Yes, sir! Hang in there like smell on a skunk and you'll get more trouble than sticking your head into a beehive. Well, my mother's only child never did have too much sense!* Camellion reached into his jacket pocket and pulled out his papers. Carefully, Tarkovsky took out his and placed them on the table.

Finished with the elderly man and woman, the two KGB men moved the five feet to Camellion's table.

"Kah Gay Beh," the younger of them said. *"Likoi estv'eni prosi stven, pozhaluista*—KGB. Your identification papers, please."

Vladimir Nakodka, the older agent in the light-blue suit, glanced several times at the Death Merchant as he examined his passport, *propiksa, poryidok,* and *spravka.* Camellion pretended to be unconcerned.

Finally Nakodka returned Camellion's papers with a curt *"Spasibo."* Dmitri Skels, the other agent, continued to study the passport and other documents of "Leonid Dudintsev"—Kirill

Tarkovsky. It was evident that all was not well when Skels nudged his partner, frowned, and said, *"Odo zund tu yutsya tskol vlastivy zhini deistvuyia raktere?* Do you see anything wrong with the seal?"

While Camellion realized that Skels was perhaps only being overly cautious, he couldn't take the risk. All Skels and Nakodka had to do was *think* something was wrong and haul them to the local KGB building for questioning. Then the fat would be in the sizzling flames.

The Death Merchant couldn't take the chance. He gave a loud "Oh!" let his eyes go wide, put his hand flat on his chest, and stood up.

"I—I have a pain in my chest," he said. "It must be something I ate this morning. I had better get a 'mineral' for my stomach."

He moved around the table, to his left, as if to go to the cashier and order a carbonated drink.

"Zund techest ini'puk, grazhdanin—You stay put, citizen!" Nakodka said sharply, putting up his right hand to prevent Camellion from moving forward. Nakodka had spoken the last words and made the last move of his life.

The Death Merchant moved with such fantastic speed that his arms were only a blur of motion. As his left arm streaked upward and out, his right arm darted sideways, his hand going to the left side of his belt, his fingers finding the eighteen-shot Steyr autoloader. Simultaneously, Tarkovsky jumped up and jerked out his .45 Astra pistol.

The fingers of Camellion's left hand, formed into a deadly four-finger spear thrust, stabbed into Vladimir Nakodka's throat, right above the knot of his tie. In only a third of an eyeblink, the Russian's thyroid cartilage was crushed, the soft tissues of his throat were swelling shut, and he was starting to gag, sway, gurgle, and die of suffocation, his eyes wide with shock and horror.

The Death Merchant was so fast that he switched off the safety of the Steyr, swung the pistol to his right, squeezed the trigger and put a 9 mm HP slug into Dmitri Skels's chest before the surprised KGB officer had time to really know what was happening, and even before Tarkovsky could get his Astra into action.

Skels was unconscious, dropping and dying, as Tarkovsky, in a firing stance, swung his Astra toward the three militiamen who had jumped up from their stools at the counter and were frantically tugging at their waist-belted flap holsters in an effort to pull their Tokarev pistols.

In contrast to the crazy-brave militia morons, the cashier, the waitress, and the customers had thrown themselves to the floor, two of the women screaming like pigs rammed with hot pokers. The mother of the baby at the table close to the Death Merchant was holding the child next to her own body on the floor, the husband snuggling up to the now crying child.

The Death Merchant's concern was the driver of the first jeep and the four militiamen in the second jeep. There had to be several PPSC-84 submachine guns in those jeeps. Should the militiamen, even without chatter boxes, ever get inside the café, Camellion knew that he and Tarkovsky would have as much of a chance as an icicle in a blast furnace. He didn't have time to go to the door. He swung to his left, saw that the driver of the first jeep and the other four cops in the second jeep were piling out, and began firing, the thunder cracks of the Steyr blending in with glass falling to the floor from the window and with the booming of Tarkovsky's Astra.

The driver of the first jeep and two Russians from the second vehicle jerked and went down, each with a 9 mm hollow-point slug in his body. But two of the men from the second jeep managed to get past the west end of the shattered window before Camellion could pop them with projectiles. *Double fudge!* In an instant Camellion sprinted across the room and flattened himself between the east side of the door and the west end of the window. The only flaw was that one of the pig farmers might use some imagination and try to fire through the window. He hoped it wouldn't be the Ivan with the SMG.

Kirill Tarkovsky killed two of the militiamen at the counter as their Tokarev pistols were clearing their holsters. The third man, having more smarts than his two comrades, had realized there wasn't time for him to open the flap of his holster. He vaulted over the counter, dropped next to the waitress, and was pulling the 7.62 mm Tokarev from its holster when Tarkovsky put three more .45 ACP rounds through the thin wood of the front of the counter. One of the big slugs zipped over the terrified waitress and struck the bottom of the ice-cream freezer with a loud *zingggggg*. A second bullet streaked sideways into the third militiaman, going in at a very steep angle and boring a tunnel downward through his liver. The third .45 bullet stabbed at an even sharper angle into his outer left thigh, ripped through the rectus muscle, and severed the femoral artery and the femoral vein. Slammed into instant shock, the man's body went limp and he slumped, his chin dropping on the outer side of the waitress's left shin.

The last two Russians from the second jeep were too concerned about what might be happening to their comrades to even think about wasting time by firing through the front window. Gesa Teleki pressed down on the latch of the door, kicked it open, and jumped to one side to make room for Josef Yefremiv, the Ruskie with a PPSC submachine gun. Yefremiv moved through the doorway, his finger, close to the trigger, hesitating. During that single second, he refrained from spraying the room for fear of hitting his comrades and innocent customers. He did exactly what the Death Merchant assumed he would do, and that cost him his life. Camellion fired twice as Yefremiv was turning to his right to see who might be against the wall. The first 9 mm hollow-point hit him in the lower chest, the second slug streaking into his stomach, an inch below his navel. Worried about the last Russian, Camellion was spinning around toward the window when he heard the loud boom of Tarkovsky's Astra. Tarkovsky had stepped back to the east wall, then turned toward the front. He had seen Gesa Teleki rear up from the outside and start to thrust his pistol through. Tarkovsky's .45 slug hit Teleki just below the nose, the bullet rocketing across the roof of his mouth, going through the back of his neck and striking a lamppost on the curb. Blood falling into his mouth and running down his chin, the dead Teleki wilted to the sidewalk.

Unknown to the Death Merchant and Tarkovsky, two other KGB officers had been working with Vladimir Nakodka and Dmitri Skels. When Camellion had fired the first shot, Evhen Koreitim and Mirzo Poluchkin were halfway across the street, three doors east of the *Veliki*—"Friendly"—Café. They had been checking papers on the south side of Boris Godunov Street and had decided to stop at the café and have a drink.

By the time Camellion and Tarkovsky had whacked out Dmitri Skels and the five militiamen, Koreitim and Poluchkin had rushed across the street and were near the east end of the window that Camellion had shot out, each with a 9 mm Makarov pistol in his hand.

Koreitim—big and beefy with a big mop of steel-gray hair— had crept underneath the window to almost its center while the quick-moving, boyish-faced Poluchkin waited by the east end. The plan was for both men to fire in unison.

Neither realized that Richard Camellion was between the front door and the west end of the window. Most of the shooting had occurred when they were still east of the *Veliki;* the last shot they had heard, when they were closing in on the window, had been from Tarkovsky on the east side of the room. They automatically assumed that the berserk gunman was not close to the window.

No sooner had Gesa Teleki crumpled to the sidewalk than Koreitim nodded to Poluchkin. Both men reared up and caught a glimpse of Kirill Tarkovsky and one of the cooks, who was standing in the kitchen's doorway and was about to throw a cleaver at Tarkovsky's back. While the cook's right arm was raised, the Death Merchant spotted him, and Tarkovsky saw the heads and shoulders of Koreitim and Poluchkin. All four fired in the same split second, none taking time to aim, except the Death Merchant who fired on pure instinct.

Oskar Akikrekst, the bearded cook, let out his last grunt of pain on earth and fell back, Camellion's 9 mm metal resting against one of his back ribs. Tarkovsky fired a hundredth of a second before Mirzo Poluchkin and Evhen Koreitim, aiming at the latter. The .45 bullet missed the KGB officer, shot halfway across the street, and struck the left front door handle of a passing Volga.

Koreitim's 9 mm slug came much closer to Tarkovsky. It buzzed within a foot of Tarkovsky's left shoulder, tore through a kitchen wall, and hit a large iron skillet, the ricochet a high-pitched whine.

The Cosmic Lord of Death was having a ball. Poluchkin's 9 mm flat-nosed slug went several feet wide of Tarkovsky—to his right—and actually struck the empty shell casing that Tarkovsky's Astra A-80 was ejecting. No one heard the *ping,* which was drowned out in the racket of four auto pistols firing almost simultaneously.

Tarkovsky darted to his left to get a clearer view of the two KGB officers outside the window, both of whom were now aware that there was a second enemy inside the café. Either one has lightning-quick instincts in a fire-fight or one hasn't. Koreitim and Poluchkin did not possess such natural talent. They hesitated.

The Death Merchant swung around, snap-aimed, and pulled the trigger of the West German–made Steyr. Tarkovsky fired. Koreitim tried to make up his mind. Poluchkin attempted to drop below the window.

Camellion's projectile tore through Koreitim's left temporal bone and scrambled his brain, killing him instantly. Poluchkin succeeded—almost. He was dropping, but he wasn't fast enough or lucky enough. Tarkovsky's slug caught him very high in the forehead, bored through the frontal bone, and cut a bloody tunnel through the very top of his brain. His mouth and eyes wide open, he collapsed beside Koreitim's corpse.

The Death Merchant yelled, "Fyodor! Out through the back!" and tore north across the room. He jumped over the corpses of the militiamen and the customers who had been sitting on the stools, vaulted over the rear counter, and stormed through the rear door into the storage room. Right behind him came Kirill Tarkovsky, who had only one cartridge left in his Astra. The Death Merchant's Steyr semiautomatic still had ten cartridges.

They raced through the back door into the narrow alley and started to run west. Camellion's plan was to go to the end of the block, turn south, walk to Boris Godunov Street, then turn east and calmly walk to the minivan. The vehicle was half a block west of the café, and Camellion was counting on the probability that no one had seen him and Tarkovsky get out and walk to the *Veliki*.

"It will never work." Tarkovsky, panting, was wondering why the American was hardly out of breath.

"It has to," countered the Death Merchant. "We have nowhere else to go. Or maybe you would have us take a taxi to the church, or get there by pogo stick!"

"Why did you call me 'Fyodor'?" asked Tarkovsky, who

firmly believed that all *Amerikanski* were slightly crazy and daredevils.

"I thought you'd have guessed. One of the customers will remember the name and tell the KGB. Do I have to say more?"

Nyet, Camellion did not. The KGB would then start looking for a man who didn't exist.

What followed became the most tension-filled minutes of Kirill Tarkovsky's life, even worse than being shot at. At least in the café, he could shoot back. On the street was nothing but pure uncertainty.

They came to the end of the alley and, as if they were out for a Sunday's stroll, began to walk south. Soon they were strolling east, seemingly as unconcerned as the dead. Eleven minutes later they got into the white-and-green Zaporozhets minivan. The Death Merchant instantly went to the rear of the vehicle and opened the trunk. Tarkovsky, his hands shaking slightly, started the engine, shifted, pressed down on the gas, and eased the vehicle into east-bound traffic.

Tarkovsky glanced at the café as he went by. There wasn't any activity in front where the sidewalk was littered with the dead. He could, however, see activity inside.

By the time Tarkovsky had gone a block and a half and was turning right onto Bisha Gor, Camellion had taken from the trunk an M-10 Ingram submachine gun and half a dozen magazines of .45 caliber ammunition for the SMG, each one holding thirty-five rounds. The ammunition was of French manufacture and was very special, of a type dubbed THV—*Très Haute Vitesse,* or very high velocity—by its designers. A THV bullet delivered the same dynamite punch as a *Holloue*—hollow—point; but unlike hollow-point slugs, which crash against hard targets, THVs had three times more penetrating power than conventional jacketed bullets, due to hardness, geometrical design, and high velocity. For one thing, each bullet was made of copper and came almost to a needle point. For another, the hollowed cavity of the pointed copper bullet could hold twice the amount of powder as an ordinary bullet. A THV bullet could go through an engine block and cut through Kevlar body armor, which could resist conventional .44 Magnum loads. In the trunk were also magazines for pistols, each filled with special THV bullets.

Camellion had also attached a sonic noise suppressor to the short barrel of the Ingram.

Kirill Tarkovsky, as worried as a Jew going through Syria on a bicycle, was fighting a rising fear. He said, "Even machine pistols will not be of help if the *Kah Gay Beh* finds out about this bus."

"You're right," Camellion admitted, thinking that the national emblem of the Soviet Union should be a fly. *If they used a fish, it would drown.* "If the KGB closes in on us, a tank wouldn't be of help. That isn't why I took the machine guns out of the trunk."

Tarkovsky knew what Camellion meant, although he didn't like to admit it. If the KGB learned of the van and trapped them, they would fight it out and take as many of the KGB with them as possible before they died. There wasn't any other way. That was the way it should be. After all, reasoned Tarkovsky, all men die. And death was certainly preferable to living in a nation where poets perished in prison and honest men were psychically murdered in special mental hospitals.

Chapter Six

Thirty-five minutes crawled into the past. Obeying all traffic regulations and driving very carefully, Kirill Tarkovsky drove the vehicle back to where the accident had occurred on the Myasnitskaya Nev. The road was open, the militia having towed away the damaged vehicles. In almost no time at all, the minibus was only half a mile from the "Y," the left arm of which would take Tarkovsky and the Death Merchant to the highway that was the route to Taria and onward.

Tarkovsky was almost cheerful, and even Camellion was entertaining thoughts that no one had seen them get out of the Zaporozhets and walk to the café. If so, the KGB and the militia would have only an ice-cold trail. Nonetheless, he remained by the window in the rear door and continued to monitor traffic. He could see nothing out of the ordinary and was positive that another vehicle was not following them.

"We'll be turning off onto the highway shortly," Tarkovsky announced. "We'll then be only nine kilometers, or six of your American miles, from the Church of Our Savior. I don't think we'll have any more difficulty."

"I sincerely hope you're right," Camellion replied, thinking that Tarkovsky had become enthusiastic only because he had not considered the complete project. Reaching the church would not solve the major problem of how to organize and carry out the incursion into SPH UZh-15/5, free Dr. Georgi Ulomov, and escape with him to the east coast of the Sea of Okhotsk.

Another worry for Camellion was that his only link with the outside world was the AN/URC-101 SATCOM shortwave in the trunk. Should it be destroyed, he would be unable to contact the CIA. Nor would the Agency be able to transmit the time of pickup to the radio station in Otaru, Japan. The bottom line was that the *George Washington* wouldn't have the date, the time, and the coordinates for the pickup from the beach.

They came to the turnoff and left Yakutsk behind them. Traffic began to thin, though it had never been thick, not to a westerner.

There were no suburbs outside of Yakutsk, no small knots of dwellings and small businesses. There was only an occasional *izba* built by the old Siberians, some of the cottages old before even the days of Stalin's grandfather.

This was still another feature of the Soviet Union and particularly of Siberia: the stark contrast. There was never any blending, and the Death Merchant often compared the Soviet Union to a painting done in only black and white, with a total absence of color.

Only ten minutes ago there had been streets and buildings and people. Now the minibus was on a road that moved through virgin country, the fields and shrubs and undergrowth wild and untidy, totally free of man's wrecking hands. It was tough country, Siberia, dangerous country, hard on human beings. People often suffered a form of nervous breakdown peculiar to Siberia, especially during the darkness of winter, and it occurred not only among the Russians but also among the tribal peoples and others who had to endure prolonged inactivity in a snowbound wasteland.

A scattering of dirty white clouds warmed their backs, and the air was fresh and clean, smelling of pines and cedar, but soon raindrops wearing ermine coats would fall and the snow would claim control of the land. Another clean cutoff! Summer and fall, all rolled into one season, would vanish overnight, and winter would begin to reign for many long and dreary months. It was a fact of Siberian life that forced the Death Merchant to arrive at only one conclusion: He had to hit the hospital and grab the scientist within the next four days. *I've got to have the prize by the time Alexey Perchany makes his next run to the east coast! I have got to make the impossible possible!*

Camellion heard Tarkovsky's loud, husky voice. "Comrade Scott, are you going to stay in the back until we reach the church? I think we would know it by now if the *Kah Gay Beh* were wise to us. I doubt if we would have gotten out of the city."

"How many cars do you see ahead of us?" Camellion asked.

"Two. A small truck on the side; it, too, is going east. It's far ahead. There's an automobile on the opposite lane. It will pass us in a few minutes. What do you see, Comrade?"

"The road's empty, but I'm going to remain back here."

Camellion continued to watch the road, now and then glancing at the fields and woods on either side. In some of the fields were *chiti'igodi*—"hay houses"—enormous stacks of bailed hay, some as much as twenty-five feet long, twenty feet wide, and ten bales high.

Their luck took a dip toward death four miles northwest of the church. A few hundred feet ahead of the minibus was an intersection, the road that crossed moving from the southwest to the northeast. It was Tarkovsky who first spotted the two olive-green militia vehicles half a mile to his right.

"Militia!" he shouted over his shoulder. "A Volga and a jeep, to the southwest. But who knows if they're after us?"

It was then that the driver of the Volga turned on the siren and it began its screaming "ah-ou-ga, au-ou-ga."

"They want us!" Camellion yelled back. "And not because we might have a broken taillight. Give it all you've got."

By then the minibus had shot past the intersection and Tarkovsky was pressing his foot down hard on the gas pedal, but he and Camellion knew that the little four-cylinder Zaporozhets could not outdistance a Volga, and especially a jeep. Obviously someone had seen them and had connected them with the shootout. This was definitely not going to be a good day.

The Death Merchant turned, hunkered down, and stared through the front windshield. A thousand feet ahead, the road turned rather sharply and moved past a thickly wooded area, the trees appearing to be almost to the edge of the concrete. Russians, pig farmers that they were, loved woods. There almost had to be a side road into the woods, a lane, a couple of tire tracks, something.

"Listen, Tarkovsky. After you go around the curve, turn into the woods at the first opportunity," Camellion said. "The instant you make the turn, stop and let me out. I'll jump from the rear door. Then you take the van to where it can't be seen from the road."

"An ambush is the only chance we have," Tarkovsky said in a worried voice. "Do you think it will work?"

"Why not?" Camellion smirked. "Age and experience and treachery can overcome youth and skill any day of the week—and twice on Sunday. Today is Sunday."

The Zaporozhets began to go around the curve at 61 mph, rocking on its springs. Watching through the rear window, the Death Merchant saw that the Volga and the jeep had executed the left-hand turn onto the highway and were only a third of a mile behind, coming up fast.

Camellion had to give credit to Tarkovsky: He was a good driver. He was soon racing the minivan around that part of the curve where the road went right up to the forest. By the count of a slow ten, the vehicle was out of the line of sight of the Volga and the jeep.

"Up ahead!" yelled Tarkovsky. "I see an opening. Get ready to jump, Scott!"

Knowing that Tarkovsky was becoming excited—*He forgot to say "Tovarishch!"*—Camellion prepared himself, his right hand around the butt/magazine of the M-10 Ingram, his left hand on the horizontal latch of the rear door. He had already jammed a spare magazine for the Ingram into his belt.

Tarkovsky turned left—so fast into the weeded lane that the minibus swayed and tilted, the tires almost spinning on the ground that cried desperately for rain. Then he stopped.

Camellion pushed up on the latch, threw open the door, jumped to the ground, and raced to a clump of bushes only twenty feet from the highway. Immediately Tarkovsky gunned the van and headed it into the woods, the uneven ground making the rear door swing back and forth.

In spite of Camellion's often referring to the Russians as "pig farmers," he never once underestimated them, not for an instant. They were not Einsteins; neither were they morons. They had a lot of practical common sense and were brave fighters.

Waiting behind the bush, he never expected the Volga and the jeep to come tearing around the curve hellbent for leather. Within twelve seconds he was proved right.

The Volga had slowed considerably, coming around the curve at a cautious 40 mph. A hundred fifty feet behind it was the jeep, the man beside the driver and the two men in the rear seat holding AKR submachine guns.

Directly ahead of where the curve ended, the highway stretched straight for almost a mile, and the Russian militiamen in the Volga didn't have to do much brainwork to know that the terrorists' minibus had turned off into the woods. To the right of the highway there was only an open field.

Camellion would never know whether the Volga would have turned off into the woods or have pulled off the highway and parked. He would never know because when it was directly across from the bush and only twenty-five feet away, he reared up and raked it horizontally with the Ingram—from the left front of the engine to the left taillight, directing the stream of fire at a height just below the handles of the two doors. *PHYYYTTTTTTTTTTTTTTTT!* The silencer gave a long, deep whisper, and *presto!* there was a row of twenty-one holes across the left side of the Volga, which rolled to a halt, even though the driver had his foot on the gas pedal.

Five .45 THV copper projectiles had shot through the engine, turning two of the cylinders into junk. The other sixteen THVs had not increased the longevity of the three members of the militia and the KGB officer. The copper-points had poked through the door and the driver as easily as if the metal and cloth and flesh and bone had been soggy tissue paper. The special French slugs kept right on going and struck the other man on the left side of his body. Being taller than the driver, the KGB officer was sitting higher, and the two bullets banged all the way through his body, zipped through the right side door, and continued on their impersonal way. Neither man had time to cry out or even think of his mother.

Neither did the two men in the rear, three slugs hitting the man on the left and four striking Paul Raske, who was on the right. When the Death Merchant had triggered the Ingram, Raske had been bending over to pick up an AKR submachine gun. Three of the slugs that ripped through his seatmate bored through Raske's left side. A fourth projectile smacked him in the side of the head with such force that his skull exploded. There was a loud pop that no one heard, and pieces of ripped flesh and bits of bone and bloody brain were suddenly all over the floor, the rear of the front seat, and the right side of the dead dummy to the left.

The Volga sat there on the highway, its engine smoking, black oil dripping to the pavement. In only five and a half seconds, it had been turned into a morgue on wheels.

The Death Merchant still had a problem. The jeep was still 150 feet behind the demolished Volga and its bloody cargo of corpses, but because of the bend in the road, Camellion could see only the front of the jeep and part of its left side. The Russians had two options: They could try to jump from the jeep and seek refuge in the fields on either side, or the driver could try to back up. The Death Merchant didn't intend for them to do either. As far as he was concerned, the pig farmers were already dead meat.

The hell with death! And what protection was a damn bush! Camellion sprinted to the right and began to trigger the Ingram after he had moved twelve feet, holding the rounded bottom of the hot silencer on top of his left forearm to stabilize the SMG, which he had switched to full automatic—
PHYTTTTTTTTTTTTTTTTTTTTTTTTTT!

The two troopers in the rear seat were trying to get out of the jeep while the two men in front were standing and starting to level AKR submachine guns at the Death Merchant. The man next to the driver even managed to get off a burst, a dozen full-metal-jacket 5.45 x 39 mm projectiles burning air close to Camellion. Close was not good enough. A miss by a millionth of an inch might as well be a mile, or a light-year.

The rule that "If you don't succeed the first time, try again" didn't apply to the four troopers. The tidal wave of .45 THV slugs washed all over the jeep and drowned the four Russians in a flood of copper death. The termination had taken only twelve seconds. The two who had been in the rear lay on the road, pools of blood spreading beneath them. Impact had knocked the driver back to the rear seat. The man who had been next to him was draped over the right side door. A ton of TNT could not have made him more dead.

Camellion, looking over his handiwork, pulled the empty magazine from the Ingram and shoved it into his belt. He pulled the full clip from his wasteband, shoved it into the feed-well of the SMG, pulled back on the top knob, and sent a

cartridge into the firing chamber. After glancing up at the sky
—the clouds were still there—*Damn sunshine!*—he turned, ran
thirty feet into the woods, and yelled, "Tarkovsky, let's get out
of here."

"What kept you?" Camellion demanded as he climbed into
the Zaporozhets and sat down. "It took you almost three minutes! I was standing out there exposed like a bump on a log."

"God damn it! What do you think I was doing, just sitting in
this van waiting? Suppose they had taken your life?" Tarkovsky
gave the Death Merchant a dirty look as he started to drive out
onto the highway.

"All right. So what were you doing?" Camellion muttered
while wondering why Soviet-built cars didn't have automatic
shifts.

"I was behind a tree fifteen meters in back of you. If you had
not killed the ink souls and they had killed you, I would have
shot it out with them and have taken as many of them into
death as I could."

Camellion was surprised. "Shoot it out! With what? You had
only one cartridge left in the Astra!" He looked at the straight
stretch of highway ahead. "And why do you call them 'ink
souls'?"

"With this, Comrade Scott!" With his right hand, Tarkovsky
reached underneath his jacket and pulled out a German
Walther P-38 pistol. "My father brought it back from Germany.
He was a soldier. The pistol has been a prized possession in my
family. I have kept it and the two spare magazines of ammunition oiled and free of dirt and grime. I had the weapon tied to
my left leg."

He turned and gave Camellion a quick grin. "An 'ink soul'!
In Siberia an ink soul is the worst insult you can call a man. It
means 'bureaucrat,' especially one from the big cities on the
other side of the Urals. The bureaucrats in *Moskva* are the biggest ink souls of all."

Camellion gave a low chuckle. Now he had another name for
Courtland Grojean—ink soul! He then asked, "How far are we
from the Church of Our Savior?"

Tarkovsky thought for several moments, his eyes on a white
Topikek T-14, a car similar to a Zaporozhets sedan, only larger.

"Three of your American miles," Tarkovsky said. "We should be there shortly."

The white Topikek and its driver sped by. "That poor comrade is going to get a shock when he comes to the militia vehicles. *Da,* he will keep on going and report nothing. No one likes to become involved with either the militia or the *Kah Gay Beh.*"

"Well, someone does!" Camellion reminded him in a gruff voice. "The someone who tipped off the police about us! I'd sure like to know how we were made!"

Tarkovsky didn't answer, his eyes on a black Zhiguli in the distance. Instantly he was on guard. Not a working man's car, Zhigulis were often used by KGB officers and lower officials of the Party.

"*Tovarishch* Scott, do you see the vehicle approaching us?" Tarkovsky asked sinisterly, as if contemplating total destruction.

"It doesn't have to be the KGB," Camellion said. "I could be wrong, but I don't see how we could be so unlucky as to have them come at us twice in a row."

Wrong! It was the KGB, and Camellion and Tarkovsky were that unlucky. Filled with four men and traveling at 60 mph, the Zhiguli passed the minibus on the opposite lane, and from the expressions on the faces of the driver and the man next to him, Camellion and Tarkovsky could see that they were definitely not friends. One man on the left rear even turned and was still staring after the Zhiguli shot by.

"The militia in the Volga and the jeep gave our position!" Tarkovsky said angrily. "All we can do is shoot it out with them—and so close to the church too!"

"Don't increase your speed!" Camellion snapped at Tarkovsky, who was watching the other car in the rearview side mirror. "That's what they expect us to do. They'll turn around and come after us. When they're close enough, I'll blast them with the chopper from the rear door." He pushed himself from the seat.

"But I think—"

"Don't think. Do what I tell you." Camellion moved to the rear of the van, his mind a jumble of pure worry. A single well-placed burst from an automatic weapon would stop the minibus as easily as a shotgun could ace out a frog. He wasn't concerned about enemy slugs wrecking the AN/URC. In the trunk, it was safe in its armored case. It would take a THV bullet to penetrate the outer shell. And why worry about the transceiver? Should the slobs in the Zhiguli get that close—*We'll have had it in spades!*

Camellion got down by the rear door that Tarkovsky had closed and latched and began to unscrew the silencer from the M-10 Ingram. With the silencer attached, the little music box would be too cumbersome within the confined space of the minibus. The black Zhiguli, 125 feet behind them, had spun around and was hot-dogging it toward the van. The man next to the driver was leaning out the window, a Vitmorkin machine pistol in his right hand.

Waiting by the side of the oval window to his left, the Death Merchant was positive the KGB officers could do only one of two things: try to run the Zaporozhets off the road—easy enough to do with a big Zhiguli—or open fire when they were close enough. It was fifty of the first and fifty of the second. The KGB had to know that the two terrorists were extremely dangerous. Hadn't they murdered twelve men in Yakutsk? And evidently they had either killed the militiamen in the jeep and the Volga or given them the slip.

Camellion looked at the rear-door window. A foot in diameter, it was round, shaped like a port hole. The glass swung inward. Camellion thumbed up the latch and opened the window, pulling the glass toward him and pushing it back against the left side of the door. Because the opening was so small, he would have time for only one quick burst. If he missed—*Well, not even I can win all the rounds.*

It was then that Kirill Tarkovsky did the worst thing possible: He speeded up the minibus, on the rationale that it was foolish to waste time—get it over and done with! The highway was still a straight stretch of concrete ribbon, and Tarkovsky jammed down on the gas, taking the vehicle up to 70 mph.

The Death Merchant didn't bother to yell something stupid like "What are you doing?" or "Why did you speed up?" There wasn't time. The Zhiguli, which had also increased speed, was approaching rapidly.

Never taking his eyes off the Zhiguli, Camellion yelled, "Stay as low as you can! One of them has a Vitmorkin. I can't fire until I'm positive I can smear all of them!"

Camellion was only a second from placing the short barrel of the Ingram on the rounded bottom rim of the open window when the man with the Vitmorkin cut loose with a short burst. There were four *ping-ping-ping-pings* as four FMJ projectiles tore through the metal of the door. Two more slugs came through the open window, missing Camellion's nose and chin by only inches. Three slugs stabbed through the front windshield, leaving three holes from which radiated an array of spider web cracks. A fourth and a fifth bullet rocketed under the dash and would have struck the engine if they hadn't struck a cross-brace on the frame that held the motor in place. The sixth 9 mm went through a space of the steering wheel, and it, too, stabbed through the windshield. It was this sixth bullet that caught Kirill Tarkovsky. It tore deeply through the innerside of his upper right arm, halfway between armpit and elbow. There wasn't much pain, only a sharp sting as the metal burned through the triceps muscle and clipped the cephalic vein.

Tarkovsky let out an involuntary cry of pain and jerked on the wheel, causing the minivan to sway dangerously. By one of those side jokes of fate, the Vitmorkin bullet that clipped Tarkovsky saved his life and that of Richard Camellion a micromoment later. If Tarkovsky's jerking of the wheel had not swayed the minivan, some of the projectiles from the machine pistol's next burst would have struck him in the back and caught Camellion in the neck and head. As it turned out, the stream of slugs cut through the top of the minivan's rear door. Nine pieces of high-powered metal passed over Tarkovsky's head and tore out eighteen inches of the top of the windshield, which by now was so full of spiderweb cracks that Tarkovsky could hardly see to drive.

Emin Viipuri, the driver of the Zhiguli, couldn't be sure if Anton Cheklitt's machine-pistol slugs had hit the driver of the Zaporozhets. Fearing that they might have killed the driver and that the van, careening from side to side, might be out of control, Viipuri let up on the gas and started to drop back instead of going around the minibus.

"*Nyet, nyet,* fool!" shouted Major Cheklitt. "Go around him, so that I can rake the front of the car!"

It was too late, but Cheklitt didn't know it. Emin Viipuri had made a fatal mistake, and the Death Merchant was quick to take advantage of it. He shoved the barrel through the rounded window and squeezed the trigger—*BBBBBRRRRRRRRRRRrrrrrr-rrrrrrrrrrr!* The Ingram SMG chattered loudly, a stream of metal death pouring from the muzzle of the stubby barrel. Three of the *Très Haute Vitesse* pointed copper slugs chopped into the engine and wrecked it. There were loud grinding sounds as cylinders and crankshaft came to a sudden halt within the engine block. The other twenty-four THVs dissolved the windshield and turned the heads and the upper torsos of Anton Cheklitt and Emin Viipuri into a crimson mess of flesh and bone that, splattering all over the front inside of the Zhiguli, looked as if it had been churned out of a meat grinder. The two KGB officers in the rear suffered the same fate.

The Zhiguli's engine had stopped running, but the momentum of the large car carried it forward. Out of control, with only a laughing Cosmic Lord of Death perched on the steering wheel, the Zhiguli began to race wildly back and forth across the highway, at times almost running off the concrete onto the narrow shoulder.

Richard Camellion had heard Kirill Tarkovsky give a yell and realized he had been hit by a bullet. The right arm of Russian's jacket was soaked in blood, which was dripping to his upper right thigh. Even so, Camellion could see that the bullet had not broken the bone. Tarkovsky's right hand was still on the wheel.

The pleasant smell of burnt gunpowder thick in his nasal passages, Camellion shouted, "I got him! Slow down, pull over, and stop! The Zhiguli is out of control!"

Tarkovsky, not thinking clearly because of the pain, turned slightly to his right, reduced speed, and jammed on the brakes, tires screaming in protest. The sudden stop threw the Death Merchant forward. The trunk, full of equipment, slid forward. The long round cylinder that was the silencer rolled forward.

This mistake on Tarkovsky's part—the sudden slamming on of the brakes—pulled his and Camellion's bacon out of the fire. Just as Tarkovsky turned the minivan and stabbed his foot down on the brake pedal, the Zhiguli shot by, its right side so close to the left side of the minivan that the bus's left rearview mirror was ripped off. As the Zaporozhets began to spin around, its front end going to the right, the Zhiguli tore to the right in front of the van and kept right on going. It charged off the road, rocketed across the shoulder, struck a log fence facing the field, flipped over on its left side, and came to rest on its top. There it rested, upside down, its four wheels spinning slowly.

The minivan turned completely around until its front end was facing the west.

And they call this "experience"! Camellion got up from the floor and crawled the rest of the way to the front seat.

"Move over. I'll drive," he said to Tarkovsky. "First, keep your head down. I'm going to get rid of the windshield."

A quick burst from the Ingram sent the glass, crisscrossed with a million spiderwebs, flying outward.

"How badly wounded are you?" Camellion asked as he was settling into the driver's seat.

"It hurts, but it's not serious," Tarkovsky said in a strained voice. He was pressing his left thumb into his right armpit, against the pressure point of the brachial artery. "It's still bleeding. I can tell it's not from an artery."

Feeling lower than a well digger's butt in a deep well, Camellion started the minivan, turned it around, and headed it down the road. The side road to safety was only ten minutes away.

"The road we must take cannot be more than three kilometers away," Tarkovsky said weakly. "Remember the words of Zoya Beliyev. She said the road to Yuri Gagarin's house was a hundred and twenty meters east of the sign."

"All we need is to have the wrong person see us make the turnoff," Camellion said mechanically. He glanced at the speedometer; the needle was right on 73 mph. He chuckled to himself. He was breaking the law, speeding. Not that it made any difference. Any police they might meet would not be thinking of speeding, once they saw the van.

In only a few hops and jumps in time, the minivan covered a mile and a half, at which point three vehicles, one right after the other, passed on the opposite lane—two Volgas and an East German–built motorcycle. A veritable parade—for a Soviet highway!

The last half mile went by very quickly.

"There's the sign," Tarkovsky said, a note of hope in his voice.

The Death Merchant slowed slightly as they approached the white sign on which was printed, in black Cyrillic letters: CHURCH OF OUR SAVIOR MUSEUM. BUILDING BEGUN IN 1709 AND COMPLETED IN 1721. And in smaller letters: *Follow the road.*

The brick road was next to the sign. It led south, a sixth of a mile to the church, which the Death Merchant and Tarkovsky could see in the distance. An ugly thing, the Church of Our Savior was a trilogy in wood gray-black with age—an unadorned bell tower and two sections of onion-shaped domes, four domes in clusters on top of one massive tower, two domes together on top of another high structure. These domes weren't the magnificent, colorful domes of St. Basil's Cathedral on Red Square in Moscow, these were of wood discolored with age—"a boil on the green countryside!" Sergei Tsipin had said during the meeting.

Camellion sped by the sign and began to watch the area to the right. Only four hundred feet later was the opening of the road.

Tarkovsky grunted in pain and discomfort. "We might get out of this mess in one piece yet, if no one sees us enter the garage." He glanced at Camellion, as if seeking assurance. The Death Merchant did not reply.

The road moved south through a long grove of pine trees that served as a wind- and snowbreak—a plus for Camellion and his companion. Moving within the grove, the minivan couldn't be seen from either the east or the west. On either side were fields, here and there a *chiti'igodi.*

Then the grove ended. The road did not. It began to curve sharply to the southeast, prompting Tarkovsky to say nervously, "I don't like this! We're moving away from the museum-church and the house!"

"This has to be the road," Camellion insisted. "We don't have any place else to go—except to hell!"

Unexpectedly, after twisting five hundred feet almost due east, the road made a sharp turn that took the minivan south, then another even sharper turn, toward the southwest. A few hundred feet, then straight west. Tarkovsky relaxed. Camellion increased speed. In another three minutes they were approaching Yuri Gagarin's house.

Made of logs, the house and its front porch faced the east and was several hundred feet from the wide rear of the church-museum. Between the museum and the house was a row of tall elms. More elms and pines served as wind- and snowbreaks to the south, west, and east of the house. A gray cat, resting on the porch railing, stared suspiciously at the minivan as Camellion turned and started to drive slowly past the house. There it was: the garage. It also was made of logs. The two doors—standing wide open—were made of rough boards. Southwest of the garage was a small ramshackle barn, its south side fenced in. A cow was within the fence, munching hay from a trough. Outside the fence were half a dozen chicken coops. Dozens of chickens, watched over by five strutting roosters, hunted and pecked for food.

Compared to Soviet city dwellers, Yuri Gagarin was well-to-do.

The Death Merchant drove straight into the garage. He shut off the engine, got out of the van, then hurried outside and pulled the doors shut. Then he went back to the Zaporozhets, got back inside on the driver's side, and turned to Tarkovsky, who was pushing down on the handle of the right side door. "How's the arm?" Camellion's voice was as hard as his eyes.

"The bleeding has stopped," replied Tarkovsky. "All we can do now is wait. I'm going to stand by the door. I'll feel better if I can look out."

The Death Merchant nodded, picked up the M-10 Ingram from the floorboards, and started to climb in the back. He would feel better when the chatter box had a full magazine of THV slugs.

The sun was only a pale red ball and sinking fast by the time Yuri Gagarin pulled open one of the garage doors and slipped inside. In the near darkness, he found himself confronting the Death Merchant and an Ingram SMG and Kirill Tarkovsky, who now had a fully loaded Astra pistol in his right hand.

"Comrade, you had better be *Tovarishch* Yuri Tomaskavitch Gagarin," Camellion warned, concealing his surprise. Zoya had not given any personal data on Gagarin, and Camellion and

Tarkovsky had expected the caretaker to be an elderly man, or at least one well into middle age. But Gagarin couldn't have been more than thirty-five. He was tall and rather awkward-looking, his eyes dark, with heavy brows over sensitive, intelligent eyes.

"I am Yuri Tomaskavitch Gagarin," the caretaker said firmly. "I demand—"

"And you are the caretaker of the museum-church?" interjected the Death Merchant.

"I am. Who are you men and what are you doing in this garage?"

Camellion lowered the Ingram SMG. "Names are not important." He then gave Gagarin the code phrase that Zoya Beliyev had given to Maxim Chenko, who had then conveyed the words to Gagarin. "We come from the Freedom House."

Gagarin didn't bat an eye. "What is a 'Freedom House'?"

"It's a house controlled by Zoya, a house that fights tyrants of all creeds and colors."

Gagarin relaxed, reached into his shirt pocket, and pulled out a pack of Fet Frumos. "I expected the two of you yesterday," he said, taking out a cigarette. "When you did not arrive"—he paused long enough to light the cigarette with a kitchen match—"I knew something had gone wrong. I did not believe that the police had closed in. We have been much too careful."

Only then, as his eyes became accustomed to the darkness, did Gagarin notice that Tarkovsky was wounded. "So! There was difficulty! How bad is the wound, Comrade?"

"Bad enough, but I'll survive, provided I can get it bandaged," replied Tarkovsky with a deep sigh of tension.

"We will take care of your wound shortly, Comrade," said Gagarin. While not a heavy man, he had cheeks that puffed out. His facial appearance gave the impression of a gerbil scared stiff that it would run out of food for the winter.

The Death Merchant, concerned that Tarkovsky might put up an argument in the next few minutes, brought Yuri Gagarin up to date on what had happened, beginning with the terminations in the *Veliki,* going on to the Volga and the jeep full of militia, and ending with the running KGB gun duel.

His eyes wide with astonishment, his smile one of delight,

Gagarin counted rapidly on his fingers. "Good! Good! That is several dozen of the swine that you killed."

"We didn't have time to take a body count," Camellion said. "I consider it an accident of fate that we even got here. But we're here, with a shot-up car in your garage. How do we hide it? And don't tell me the KGB won't search this place and your house."

Tarkovsky said quickly, "Zoya Beliyev told us that there are secret rooms in the church that even the *Kah Gay Beh* does not know about. Those pigs will search the church also, Comrade."

The Death Merchant moved closer to Tarkovsky. "I don't have to tell you that you're stuck here the same as I. Return to Yakutsk is impossible. Not only are you wounded, but the minibus is shot full of holes."

"The car is also minus a windshield," added Tarkovsky. "You are right, Comrade. My only concern now is our safety and what we will have to do before this week is over." He added in a lower tone thick with implication: "There is the matter of Zoya Beliyev. It will not take the police long to consider me a possible link to the killings."

"The KGB will have to work on a possible connection between you, the missing van, and the terminations," Camellion acknowledged, delighted that Tarkovsky might be thinking along the same lines of security as he. *Let's see if he carries it to its logical conclusion.*

"The *Kah Gay Beh* will associate me with the killings within a matter of days," Tarkovsky said practically. "They will then question all my friends and associates. That means that they will question the comrade who came with me to Zoya Beliyev's house. They will question every member of the chess club that he and I and Zoya Beliyev belong to."

"Please get to the point, Comrade," Yuri Gagarin urged. "I take it you mean that Zoya Beliyev and the other comrade must be warned?"

"More than that! They must come here and vanish from society, or they must be killed!"

"Killed!" Gagarin drew back, amazed at Tarkovsky's bluntness.

Yes, he carried it to its logical conclusion.

"The other comrade knows why this American came to Siberia," Tarkovsky said with cold logic. "Should he be made to talk, he will tell the *Kah Gay Beh* everything he knows. So would Zoya Beliyev. She knows the names of the members of each cell. Should the *Kah Gay Beh* become suspicious of her and force her to confess, she would tell everything she knows. The entire *otdel* would collapse."

Yuri Gagarin looked at the glowing end of his cigarette. "The *Kah Gay Beh* will search every house and building in this area, but they will not find the two of you in one of the crypts below. It is too cleverly hidden. As for the Zaporozhets"—he moved the fingers of his right hand gingerly over the rounded edges of the bullet holes in the rear door—"did you not see the *chiti'igodi* in the fields? There are large ones in the field in back of this place, and it is almost dark. We will drive the van to one of the hay houses and then reassemble the hay house over and around the vehicle. The trick will be not to have any bales of hay left over. Irana, my wife, will help us."

Tarkovsky was horrified at the idea. Camellion was none too happy about it, but he knew that the scheme was the only one possible. Where else could they hide the minivan?

"Right out there in the open!" exclaimed Tarkovsky. "How can we dismantle a hay house without running the risk of someone seeing us?"

"We can't," Gagarin said. He dropped his stub of a cigarette and ground it out with the toe of his foot. "But it is not likely. There will not be a moon tonight. It will be pitch dark out there in the field." He shrugged, then went on, talking more rapidly, "We really do not have a choice. There isn't any other place in which we can hide the vehicle. First, we'll go to the house and clean your wound and bandage your arm. We will then hide the van. After the van is safe, we will go to the church."

"We have a trunk filled with equipment. It's in the vehicle," the Death Merchant said. *Where else could the trunk be!*

"So? We could hide fifty trunks in the crypt."

The Death Merchant got down to brass tacks. "Listen, it is imperative that I get a message to Zoya Beliyev," he said urgently, a kind of exasperation growing in him. "She can get word to the other man. Can you arrange it?"

"Tomorrow Irana is going to Yakutsk," Gagarin said patiently. "Once a week she takes eggs, butter, milk, and cheese to one of the free-barter markets. It has already been arranged for her to meet the comrade who carries messages."

"Comrade Maxim Chenko," muttered Tarkovsky.

"It was last week that Zoya Beliyev arranged to have my wife meet Chenko tomorrow," said Gagarin. "It is her way of knowing the two of you arrived safely. How Comrade Beliyev will contact your friend"—he looked steadily at Tarkovsky—"is her concern!"

"And our concern!" Camellion said curtly. "Our safety depends on her safety and on the other man's keeping his mouth locked."

"We cannot control her action, Comrades," Gagarin said, his tone one of resignation. "We can only hope. In the meanwhile, we must sleep in bed with a time bomb."

"I suppose that beats bedding down with a frigid woman," Camellion said, debating whether he should ask Gagarin the question. "The difference is that a woman can't explode in your face."

With typical Russian frankness (in a closed circle), Kirill Tarkovsky asked the question that had been churning in Camellion's mind:

"Comrade Gagarin, why is it that you, a young man, are only a caretaker? You are an intelligent man. Surely you could do better, even in this prison of a nation."

"I was wondering when one of you would ask me that question." Gagarin sounded as if he were enjoying some kind of grim, private joke. He proceeded to explain that he and his wife were from Moscow, and that he was more than a simple caretaker. He was also an expert antiquarian who specialized in the restoration of frescoes and other works of art. For four years he had been restoring the art in the Church of Our Savior. It was his "sentence"!

"Let me explain why I said 'sentence,' Comrades. You see, Irana and I are Jewish. Some years ago, when world attention was focused on the plight of the Soviet Jews, we applied for permission to emigrate to Israel. The permit was refused."

A few weeks after the government had refused the emigration permit, the Soviet Institute of National Art, History, and Artifacts "released" Gagarin from his duties in the Moscow area, and he was told that he was being transferred to Siberia. Of course, he didn't have to accept the transfer 2,300 miles away, but . . .

"If I had not accepted, we would have starved," he explained. "I would have become a nonperson—and how can a man do any kind of job if he does not even exist?" He uttered a short laugh. "And so I came here to the Church of Our Savior. It's not as good as being able to leave the country, but it's better than living in *Moskva*. We have more food here, more meat, vegetables, butter, eggs, cream, cheese. All we need. The rest we barter for clothes and other *defitsitny*. But in *Moskva*'s eyes, we are still Jews—*pyaty punkty,* which makes us less than human beings."

"Comrade, you should have had more sense than to apply for a permit to leave the country," Tarkovsky said roughly.

The Death Merchant was curious. "Why are Jews referred to as 'five pointers'?"

"*Pyaty punkty?* Because it is point number five in the passport where nationality is listed. Ridiculous, isn't it? It is as if your American government considered Roman Catholics a distant nationality. But we must hurry. We have much work to do."

Chapter Seven

Three members of the militia, two carrying AKR assault rifles, were several hundred feet east of where the Zhiguli had turned over and was still lying on its top. Three more uniformed militiamen were stationed several hundred feet to the west. They, too, were on the highway, standing around two wooden A-frame instant barricades with reflective orange stripes. On each barricade was mounted a halogen flasher beacon, its red light revolving 360 degrees.

Mounted on six jeeps, emergency worklights illuminated the general area around the wrecked Zhiguli and the wrecker that was angled across the road, its driver and his helper waiting for militiamen to remove the corpses from the vehicle.

The stiff breeze was chilly. Above was the black bowl of sky dotted with the blue and white of stars.

Standing by the right side of the wrecker, a disgusted Colonel Boris Rudneva watched Captain Bodgan Konstantinn walk toward him. The Center in *Moskva* was already furious over the invasion of SPH UZh-15/5. This latest slaughter would no doubt make even Party Secretary Gorbachev himself demand action. Heads would roll, and Rudneva was afraid that one of the heads would be his.

"Major Cheklitt was among the dead, Comrade Colonel," Konstantinn said unemotionally after he reached his boss. "They made the identification from his papers. It was terrible. As you know, his head was blown off. He and the other three men were butchered by that special ammunition the terrorists used. I think what happened is that—"

"I know what happened," Rudneva said sharply. "The militiamen we found in the jeep and in the Volga spotted the van and gave chase. The damn fools then drove into an ambush. The van was moving east when Major Cheklitt and the others, returning from the Special Psychiatric Hospital, passed the van, turned around, tried to stop it, and were killed by the terrorists. We have proof from the skid marks on the highway."

Konstantinn agreed with a vigorous nod and said, "We do know it was the same two men who murdered four of our people and the militiamen at the café in Yakutsk. I can't understand why—" He didn't finish.

"What were you going to say?" Rudneva, keenly feeling the loss of Anton Cheklitt, did not trust Bodgan Konstantinn. At one time Konstantinn had been in the *Glavnoye Razvedyvatelnoye Upravleniye*, the Chief Intelligence Directorate of the Soviet General Staff. He had then transferred to the *Kah Gay Beh*. But was the son of a bitch still sending reports to the *Geh Eh Ru?*

Of medium height, bony, and with rounded shoulders, Konstantinn coughed and pulled a handkerchief from his pocket. He was allergic to hay.

"I was going to say that I can't understand why a passing motorist didn't report the three wrecked vehicles. If a militia road patrol hadn't found them, we would still be wondering what had happened to them."

"These damned Siberians!" Rudneva said bitterly. "We can be grateful that the manager of the State butcher shop reported seeing the two men getting in and out of the van. He is a very patriotic citizen. Why, he was even working on Sunday, his day off, mopping the floor. It is citizens such as he that make the Soviet Union the greatest among nations."

"That is all very true, Comrade Colonel," Konstantinn said very properly. Privately he thought that the manager of the butcher store was a brainwashed idiot. Imagine! A sap working on Sunday. Or else he was working to score points. No matter what his reasons for working, he had done his duty by reporting the two men. He had been in the front of the butcher shop, had taken a break, and was looking out the small side window when he had seen two men park a white-and-green Zaporozhets minivan. The two had gotten out and walked east. At the time he had not attached any importance to the incident. Later, after he had heard a lot of gunfire down the street, he had stayed close to the window, awaiting developments.

"I didn't dare go out onto the sidewalk," Ilyich Markirov had excitedly told the militia. "After the shooting stopped, I saw the same two men get into the minivan and drive off. They went east. One appeared very nervous, the one with short blond hair. The other man was tall and had short dark-brown hair. I began to ask myself: Why didn't the two men return from the east? Why did they come from the west? It did not make sense. I decided to report the incident to the police."

Colonel Rudneva said, "I want this entire area searched. That includes every building in and around Taria. Start the search tonight, Captain. That damned minibus can't be hidden under the floor of an *izba*. Another thing: Don't count too heavily on anyone named 'Fyodor' having information or being one of the terrorists. That name was only mentioned to give us a false lead. As good as those two were, one of them would not forget and mention the real name of the other."

Konstantinn finished blowing his nose. "What about the church? Do we search it too?"

Rudneva was instantly on double alert. "What church?"

"The Church of Our Savior. It's a museum," Konstantinn said. "The office in Yakutsk tells me there are a lot of secret rooms in it. It's only three or four kilometers from here."

Rudneva turned and studied Konstantinn, his face without expression. "Comrade Captain, since when does the *Kah Gay Beh* not search a church? I am surprised that you even felt the need to ask!"

Captain Konstantinn stroked his mustache before answering. "These Siberian peasants are a religious lot. Even under the best of circumstances, they're contemptuous of the law and consider the authorities oppressors, particularly the *Kah Gay Beh*. Should we stir them up now, in view of the other trouble. . . . I thought it best to ask you first."

"Search the damn church," Rudneva said in a voice that was almost a snarl. "Search it from top to bottom, and search every building connected with it. The hell with any priest who might object. Let his idiot god protect him."

"There aren't any parasite priests at the church," Konstantinn said. "Two come from Yakutsk every Sunday; they leave after the four masses. Only the caretaker and his wife live there."

"Search his quarters," Rudneva snapped. "It's half-past eight, and the sooner you start, the better. Return to Yakutsk and get ten militiamen and five of our own people. Comrade, be very careful. The two men we're looking for—and we know there are more than two—are extremely dangerous. I want every man in body armor as protection against that hellish ammunition the terrorists are using. Report to our own *Kah Gay Beh* Central in Yakutsk every hour."

"*Da,* Comrade Colonel. I will use extreme caution." Konstantinn drew himself up to his full height, saluted, then turned and motioned to his driver. Both then walked quickly to a jeep.

Another KGB officer hurried over to Colonel Rudneva from the command car, a Zhiguli, which had a long radio-phone whip antenna on the right rear fender.

"Colonel Rudneva. General Nikoley Proskurov is on the line. He wants to speak to you, sir," the man said.

"Thank you, Lieutenant." Rudneva hurried toward the car. He was convinced that he had made the right decision by sending Anton Cheklitt and the other three officers to SPH UZh-15/5 with fifty pounds of a special substance known as nitrophenylpentadienal, or NPPD. NPPD was a chemical tracking agent that could be applied to an object or to the skin. If the latter, the chemical would bind to the protein in the skin. The subject could then be followed with a high-intensity "sniffer," which, in a sense, worked on the same principle as a radio beam. Only instead of tracking electromagnetic radio waves, the sniffer focused on the invisible radiation given off by the NPPD.

Cheklitt, the other KGB officers, and members of the hospital staff had forced the patients of the hospital to dip their hands and feet in liquid NPPD. For a full thirty days, the patients would not be permitted to wash their hands and feet, or take a bath.

Rudneva had decided that the American agents had not invaded the mental hospital as part of any terrorist action. They had gone there to free a certain patient. Something had gone wrong, and they had been forced to flee. Feliks Vartanyan, his assistant, and members of the front office staff had been gunned down as part of the Americans' escape—if indeed all were Americans. One or two could have been Soviet traitors.

After reviewing each patient's file, Rudneva had become certain that the target of the American agents was Professor-Dr.

Georgi Ulomov. He was the only patient of importance at the hospital. At one time Raoul Wallenberg, the Swedish diplomat, had been in SPH UZh-15/5, but he had been transferred and had since died.

Ulomov was a scientist, a specialist in climatology. The rest of the patients were poets, writers, artists, and an assortment of other personalities who were minor in their fields and unknown to the outside world.

Rudneva had reported his analysis to KGB headquarters in Moscow and had recommended that Ulomov be moved at once, preferably to a hospital in the Moscow area. The Center had refused on the grounds that should Ulomov be moved, the terrorists might leave the region and escape. It would be more practical to leave Ulomov where he was, in the hope that the enemy agents would make another attempt to free him. It was absolutely imperative that the American agents be found. Of equal importance were the Soviet traitors helping them. They had to be found, tried, and shot as an example.

The order from the Center in Moscow had been firm: Rudneva was not to let anyone know that the target might be Ulomov, even the other KGB officers helping him. There would be a change at the hospital: The orderlies would be replaced by KGB men. Business would go on as usual. But the next time the American agents made an attempt to grab Ulomov, the ending would be different. The Center had also made it clear that Ulomov was Colonel Rudneva's responsibility. *Nothing had better happen to the scientist.* His services were still needed.

Coating the patients' hands and feet with NPPD had been Rudneva's idea. Nothing would happen to Ulomov. In case something did, Rudneva would be able to track him. Realistically, there could be only one route of escape—straight east to the coast. And that is where General Maxim Nikoley Proskurov, the boss of the Chief Border Guard Directorate, came in. . . .

Chapter Eight

It was another crappy day in the workers' paradise. It was also chilly but dry in the crypt—and eerie, the light from the two candles only adding to the enigma of the ancient chamber, the same flickering glow throwing shadows over the face of Zoya Beliyev, who was listening intently as Yuri Gagarin explained how close he and the "two other comrades" had been to catastrophe only three days earlier.

"We first hid the minivan in the hay house," he explained, moving his hands as he talked. "The comrade with the wounded arm could not help, but the other comrade and I and my wife did the job. It took us several hours. I then brought them and their trunk to this secret room. We had to lower the trunk on a rope, and that, too, was difficult and required a lot of time. I knew that the *Kah Gay Beh* would descend upon Irana and me at any time, so I brought clean cloth and a bottle of antiseptic down here. There simply was not time for Irana to clean and bandage the comrade's wound."

"But the police didn't discover anything—obviously!" said Zoya, her lips curling in a satisfied smile.

"I was returning to the house from the church when two cars and four jeeps pulled into the yard in front of the house. It was the militia and the *Kah Gay Beh*. They searched everything—the house, the barn, and the garage. They even poked around the chicken coops."

"And they searched the church," said Sergei Tsipin, wide-eyed.

"Oh, yes! They—"

Only half listening to the conversation, the Death Merchant felt it was ironic that monks of the Russian Orthodox Church—dead for two hundred years—had saved his life. Their ingenuity in constructing the secret rooms beneath the Church of Our Savior deserved gold stars. A stone trapdoor in the floor behind the high altar could be opened by releasing a tiny catch concealed in one of the confessionals. Beneath the trapdoor was a square shaft, then down twenty-nine feet on a ladder to a low, narrow passage that stretched for sixty feet to the north. Twenty-three feet to the north was another trapdoor concealed in the floor; beneath it was the first occultated room. A cleverly hidden door in its south wall opened to another room. At the end of the sixty-foot passage was a door concealed in the stones of the north wall. The outer stones of the door were so finely cut that, when the door was closed, the edge of a razorblade couldn't be inserted. Beyond the door was a large crypt, behind its west wall a smaller catacomb containing the sealed sepulcher of four monks. In the north wall was still another hidden door, beyond it another vault filled with broken stones. The Soviet government knew about these five rooms. The KGB knew. What the KGB didn't know was that Yuri Gagarin had discovered two more tomblike rooms. In the floor of the rubble-filled chamber was a trapdoor that opened to a shaft. Ten feet below and at the end of the shaft was a large chamber. Beyond the south wall of this chamber was the last and final space. It was to this room that Gagarin brought the Death Merchant and Kirill Tarkovsky.

As a measure of precaution, Gagarin—when he left—had piled more stones over the trapdoor of the shaft in the debris-filled room. The KGB had searched the rooms they had known about. They had not, however, suspected that they had been duped.

Another joke of fate was that it was Yuri Gagarin who had helped solve the Death Merchant's problem of how to get in and out—with Dr. Ulomov—of SPH UZh-15/5. The Death Merchant had decided on a scheme, but he couldn't implement it, because he didn't have enough pentolite for the job.

It was the next day—Monday—during a conversation with Gagarin that Camellion learned that the caretaker-antiquarian and his wife did not intend ever to be taken alive by the KGB.

Gagarin had spoken without emotion, his low voice and choppy sentences sweeping away all the vestiges of hope that he and Irana had once had for a better life.

"To live in the Soviet Union is to live in hell," Gagarin had said. "It is a special hell for Jews. Since the destruction of the

Temple and the defense of Masada, what have we had? Our lot has been blood, massacre, and destruction. It is the same with the modern Israelis. They live in an armed camp and know they are only a step away from annihilation."

A Russian philosopher—but he's speaking truth!

The Death Merchant had leaned back against the wall and said, *"Zehu hakoach hapoel lemaan hatsedek hanitschee—* There is a power that works for ultimate justice."

Surprised that Camellion could speak Hebrew, Gagarin had smiled very bitterly.

"Even if such a power exists, its slowness cannot give faith to the average man. But we Jews are a people apart; we know the heart of all misery. Another thing is that while a real Jew may be susceptible to anguish, he is inaccessible to despair. Some would say that makes me and Irana hypocrites."

Gagarin had then said that should the KGB ever come to his house to arrest him, either he or Irana would somehow manage to go into the kitchen, reach behind the refrigerator, and touch the ends of two copper wires together. The house and everyone in it would be destroyed, exploded into nothingness by the twenty-two kilograms of Titvuytol that he had concealed in the walls and under the floors of the four-room house.

The Death Merchant had done a double-take. Twenty-two kilograms of TVL, which was Russian TNT! Where had Yugi Gagarin obtained an incredible fifty pounds of TVL? he asked.

With some of his earlier briskness, Gagarin explained that he had obtained thirty-one kilograms—or seventy pounds—of the powerful explosive by dealing with *fartsovshchiki,* black marketeers. First he had traded his car, an old Moskvich, for a cow, a television set, and four wooden chairs. Later he had traded the TV set to a coal miner, who worked in one of the shaft mines north of Yakutsk. In return, the miner had given him the TVL, which miners used to blast coal from seams.

"What have you done with the other nine kilograms?" Camellion had hardly been able to contain his excitement. "Do you still have it?"

Sure. Buried in glass jars under the chicken coops.

Camellion had been blunt. He needed that twenty pounds of explosive, and he explained why. Would Gagarin give it to him?

Gagarin had not hesitated. Yes, he would.

But in spite of Gagarin's willingness to help Camellion and thereby assist the American CIA, he was not an admirer of the American government and its people. He considered the American government naive in world politics and filled with self-serving men. American society was too materialistic, American people worrying more about a new car than their nation's own security.

As Gagarin went on with his description of the KGB search, the Death Merchant went into a deep reverie, then became aware that Gagarin was saying. "Oh, yes. They searched the church. And they kept asking if I had seen or heard anything unusual during the afternoon. Not once did they come right out and ask if I had seen a white-and-green Zaporozhets minivan. As if it were a secret that could be kept forever." His laugh was gleeful. "If those agents had only known the trouble we had with the trunk. We had to lower it with rope and tilt it sideways. It was worse than hiding the van in a hay house."

Kirill Tarkovsky's expression grew mischievous. "I often find it incredible how the *Kah Gay Beh* seems to think that by not printing anything or putting it on the air, no one will know about it."

"That's true," Gagarin commented, showing big teeth. "Already the news of what happened yesterday on the highway is making the rounds. Even in world news the *Kah Gay Beh* underestimates the average citizen. This comrade"—his gaze moved to the Death Merchant—"and I were discussing his nation yesterday. He asked me how I could be so knowledgeable about the United States when ours is a closed society in which we hear only news favorable to those scum in the Central Committee. I told our American friend that if *Moskva* tells us that something is black, we know it must be white. We always believe that the opposite of what we are told is closer to the truth —and it usually is."

Everyone laughed, except the Death Merchant, who continued to rub a handkerchief back and forth over the cocking slide of a Steyr auto pistol. He wanted to get on with the planning of the strike, an operation that was only twelve hours away. However, Camellion knew it was best that Zoya and the others relax by getting the small talk out of their systems.

On Monday afternoon, Irana Gagarin had taken his message

to Zoya Beliyev and had given it to Maxim Chenko in Yakutsk. In the message Camellion had explained what had to be done. He stressed that the attempt to free Georgi Ulomov would have to be made Thursday morning—or not at all. The temperature was dropping with each day, and the KGB was getting too close. In another five days the peasants would begin taking hay into their barns, and the hay houses would disappear. Among them would be the *chiti'igodi* hiding the Zaporozhets minivan.

How could the van's exposure be handled? The Death Merchant had arrived at a solution. Late Wednesday night, the bales of hay would be removed from around the minivan. Early Thursday morning, an hour before Camellion would attack the hospital, Gagarin would drive the vehicle several miles from the church and park it in some wooded area. He would then make his way back to his house across fields. At two o'clock in the morning, it wasn't likely that anyone would see him.

Much of the success of the plan rested on Zoya. She would have to contact Sergei Tsipin and three other members of the network. Three people would be needed to drive the escape vehicles. Should the members not have cars, they would have to beg, borrow, or steal them. Alexey Perchany was due back from the east coast on Tuesday. Zoya would have to arrange with him to be available with his truck. Knowing the countryside the way they did, Zoya and Perchany could decide where the pickup would be, but it would have to be within ten miles of the hospital—sixteen kilometers.

Tuesday had dragged by, with the Death Merchant feeling lower than a gagging maggot and doubting if the strike could be pulled off successfully. In such a closed society as the Soviet Union, he was severely limited in the organization methods he could use and because he couldn't check and evaluate group coordination. The tight security within the Sorceress web was another handicap, in that he couldn't evaluate the people on whom he had to depend, the people in whose hands he would be putting his life. Conclusion: So much depended on various favorable circumstances meshing together that the odds were against success.

There were so many possibilities. Suppose the three driving the cars lost their nerve at the last minute. Suppose even one didn't show up and wasn't in position on schedule. He couldn't blame them. What he was asking them to do was tantamount to suicide. Zoya had arrived at Gagarin's house Wednesday afternoon, and she had said that the three would either steal or borrow cars. Borrow? How could they return a vehicle that might be filled with bullet holes—provided any of the drivers were alive to return it?

Another giant *suppose* involved Alexey Perchany and his truck. The big rig could break down. Or his driving schedule might be changed. He could be given another route other than the Yakutsk–Okhotsk Highway. Or the State highway control system might assign another relief driver to Perchany's tractor and trailor rig. Perchany's regular relief driver, Pytor Angara, was a member of Sorceress. But should Perchany be stuck with another driver: *With Perchany's crazy-brave determination, he'd kill the guy at the proper time. Alexey is the type to go down with the ship—even if he were the captain of a barge!*

Damn it! Even with the best of planning, just getting to the hospital would require an extra amount of Fate's good fortune. The three members of the net who would drive from Yakutsk to the pickup and transfer points would need even greater luck. Even if only one vehicle ran into a militia patrol car and was stopped, the entire plan would fall apart like a house built of soggy newspapers.

I'll force success! His jaw set, the Death Merchant stuffed the handkerchief into his pocket and shoved the Steyr GB D.A. auto pistol into its shoulder holster. Refusing to think of failure, he turned his attention to Zoya Beliyev.

"Zoya, show me the pickup points again; it's time we got down to business," he said. "And can you give me any kind of assurance that your three people will be where they're supposed to be at the proper time?"

Her eyes narrowing, Zoya looked at the Death Merchant, then pulled a folded sheet of paper from the left outside pocket of her brown corduroy jacket.

"Let's move over by the larger candle, Comrade Scott," she suggested. "We'll have more light."

Once they were by the candle in its tall iron holder, Zoya got down on her knees, unfolded the paper, and spread it out on the large, flat stone on which the candle and the holder rested. The

Death Merchant got down on one knee. The others clustered around him and Zoya.

"I can only tell you that the three cars will be waiting, unless something unforeseen happens," she said with typical Russian fatalism. For several moments her gaze remained on Camellion; she then moved her finger to one of the three red *X*'s marked on the carefully drawn map and explained that the first car would be waiting only 500 meters—1,500 feet—southeast of the mental hospital.

"It will be the same car that comes to Comrade Gagarin's house to pick us up," she said. "After you and Dr. Ulomov reach the first car, it will go southwest on a side road—"

The first vehicle would go two kilometers down the road and meet the second car at a turnoff. The second car would proceed for three kilometers and meet the third vehicle in a patch of woods. The third car would drive the remaining distance to where Perchany and his tractor-trailer would be waiting.

"Alexey will be at this point, Scott." Zoya tapped the map with her finger, then looked up at Camellion, who was thinking that while Time was a great teacher, it always killed its pupils. He was also speculating about the risks Zoya and the others would be taking. He had already suggested that Tarkovsky go to the coast and board the *George Washington*. It didn't seem reasonable that Zoya and the others would take such fantastic risks without some kind of protection from the long arm of the KGB.

"We'll cross the Kolga River in Perchany's rig," Camellion said.

"If all goes as planned—*da!*" she said. "A part of his regular route crosses the Kolga. I mean from where he leaves in Yakutsk, at the loading dock, to where the actual Yakutsk–Okhotsk Highway begins. We will not have to worry about anything once we're hidden in one of the trailers. Should the *Kah Gay Beh* see the truck, they will not be suspicious. All the trucks that go east on the Yakutsk–Okhotsk Highway take the same route."

"We?" Camellion looked steadily at her, the tip of his tongue moving slowly over his lower lip.

Zoya blinked in some confusion. Kirill Tarkovsky and Sergei Tsipin glanced uneasily at each other.

"We," Zoya repeated. "You and Dr. Ulomov, and Comrades Tsipin and Tarkovsky and I." From Camellion's expression, Zoya realized that she was giving Camellion brand-new information. "You didn't know? Your superiors did not tell you that our going with you to America was part of the deal?" There was some alarm in her eyes.

Damn Grojean! Now I have to ride herd on an entire group of pig farmers!

"*Nyet,* I wasn't told," admitted the Death Merchant. "I was going to ask how all of you intended to protect yourselves after I broke out Ulomov."

"Does it make a difference—I mean, to you?" Zoya asked.

"We will follow your orders, *Tovarishch* Scott," Tsipin inserted quickly.

"You didn't mention the three people who'll drive the cars," Camellion said to Zoya. "What about them?"

"They will use another route of escape, one that will take them to northeast China," Zoya said. "But please do not ask me any more about their route."

The Death Merchant stood up, indicating he was finished looking at the map. "I don't care about the details of their route," he said. "I'm thinking that going to the United States by way of northern China seems to be the long way around."

"They're not going to the United States," Zoya said hesitantly. "They don't like the United States and its do-nothing government that permits cults to brainwash young people."

Afraid that Zoya's remark about the U.S. might anger Camellion, Tarkovsky interjected, "I think that Comrade Scott is too worldly to think that every Russian who might despise the Kremlin wants to go to the United States."

Camellion smiled. "Frankly, I couldn't care less where the three go. *(The U.S. is better off without them!)* Right now my only concern is getting out of Mother Russia with Dr. Georgi Ulomov. There are a number of little side problems that will make the job difficult. For one thing, we'll have to take the shortwave radio with us. I'll contact my people just before we meet Perchany and his rig. We'll take the radio with us into the trailer. And the five of us in a hollowed-out space in the trailer is another problem. I assume that Perchany will see to it that we have water and empty jars in which to urinate?"

"Comrade Perchany is attending to that. It is not a problem," Zoya replied. She finished folding the map and looked at Camellion, who had sat down on a stone that was part of the base of a mausoleum containing some long-forgotten monk. Neither Zoya nor any of the others knew it, but Camellion dreaded being confined in the trailer with her and the rest of the group. He had an absolute horror of urinating in front of a member of the opposite sex, even with his back turned. Better to face an entire division of KGB trash.

Tarkovsky said, "Thanks to Sergei, we have more than enough weapons—and even grenades." He turned sideways and presented Tsipin with a warm smile. "Your stealing three assault rifles and that small crate of grenades is good for at least fifty years in a gulag, should you ever be caught. But you know that."

Tsipin patted the 7.62 mm Tokarev pistol in his waistband.

"I'll never be caught, not as long as I have one bullet left."

The Death Merchant addressed the group. "There are two more items we need. A change of clothing for Dr. Ulomov, including socks and shoes, and three gallons—or rather eleven liters—of gasoline."

"I have the spare clothing," Yuri Gagarin said.

"We have sufficient petrol for the cars," Tarkovsky said. He glanced at Zoya, who nodded.

Tarkovsky, scratching his upper lip, frowned. "Why only eleven liters?"

"For bathing. . . ."

Everyone stared at Camellion. . . .

Chapter Nine

The Death Merchant was wise enough to know that if a man could wave a magic wand and have half of his wishes granted, he would succeed only in doubling trouble. Still, wouldn't it have been nice if he could have made a wish and had a totally dark sky? No such luck. The moon, in its first quarter, hung in the sky—watching. Worse, it seemed that even the Siberian weather was against him. The first low rumble of thunder—from the northwest—had come when Camellion and the other three were getting into the Moskvich, which Semyon Gluzman had driven from Yakutsk to Yuri Gagarin's house behind the Church of Our Savior.

Joy and happiness was not bubbling within Camellion and the other people in the car. In the first place, they had to travel over twelve miles before Gluzman would reach the wooded area that would make Special Psychiatric Hospital UZh-15/5 accessible to the Death Merchant and his deadly talents. In the second place, there were five people in the Moskvich, which, though large for a car that ordinary Soviet citizens could buy, was extra crowded and uncomfortable since grenades, three AKR assault rifles, a large can of gasoline, and the AN/URC-101 SATCOM transceiver were on the floor between the seats.

Camellion and the others were not even thinking of comfort. For the moment they had only one worry: that a militia patrol car would stop them and demand to know what they were doing on the highway at two o'clock in the morning. The militia almost never patrolled after midnight, but the possibility was there. Whether the militia or the KGB, whoever tried to hail down the Moskvich would die quickly in a blast of slugs from automatic weapons.

Luckily, Gluzman didn't have to drive through Taria. Instead, he turned onto a side road five and a half miles west of the village and headed north, saying as he made the turn, "We are only eight kilometers from where we'll turn into the woods."

Forty-two years old, with a short beard and a pleasant face, Gluzman was a Jewish engineer who had come from the Ukraine to Siberia four years earlier.

Camellion liked the civil engineer, who, soon after he had arrived at Yuri Gagarin's home, had laughed and said he had borrowed the Moskvich from a friend. The Death Merchant had not made any comment at the time. Sensing what he was thinking, Gluzman had then said, "No doubt our American comrade is thinking I am throwing dust into the face of a friend and treating him very treacherously. Is that not so, *Tovarishch* Scott?"

"The thought did skip across my mind," Camellion had told him.

Gluzman had smiled. "You see, the 'friend' is the chairman of the Communist Party in my district. Let *him* explain to the militia and the *Kah Gay Beh* why it was that I, the Recording Secretary of the Party in his district, fled and possibly assisted in an attack on a mental hospital. We'll be far away by then—or dead."

The Moskvich was soon moving into an area where the branches of trees draped over the twisting, turning road. There wasn't any conversation. Everything had been said. The only thing left now was the end result—success or failure.

Mentally, Camellion rechecked the equipment he would use. Other than the MAC/Ingram M-10 and eight magazines of ammo for the little SMG, he carried two 9 mm Steyr autoloaders in shoulder holsters (three spare clips for each pistol) and six grenades. Three were Mk3A2 American offensive grenades; three were M14 thermite canisters. He had other instruments of death. One was a Ruger assassination pistol that fired .22 Magnum bullets. The nice part about the weapon was that it had a noise suppressor built around the barrel. Of even greater importance were the thirteen one-pound packages of explosives, each composed of some pentolite and the TVL Camellion had obtained from Yuri Gagarin. Stuck into each package was a detonating charge that could be triggered by remote control. Camellion would take ten of the bundles with him in a canvas bag, carrying it by means of a shoulder strap. The three other units of explosive would remain in the vehicle.

He did have two other weapons, weak when compared with the Ingram and the Steyrs, yet still deadly—two eight-inch long Devil's Darts. Very slim, each Devil's Dart—a sleeve dagger—was made of 440c stainless steel and had a sandblasted appearance, including the triangular blade. The darts rested in leather holsters, side by side, between his shoulder blades, held in place by narrow straps over his shoulders and around his chest and back.

There were several disadvantages. Lacking walkie-talkies, he would not be able to communicate with the Moskvich. Nor would he be able to wear night-vision goggles when he approached the hospital-prison. The general-purpose Cyclops, with its long IR tube, was too bulky. The small hand-held IR night-sight device would have to do.

"We are close to the woods," Gluzman finally said, his voice lower than it had been earlier. He reached into the seat beside him with his right hand, picked up a flashlight, turned it on, held it close to the handdrawn map attached to the dash, and took a quick look.

"Another half kilometer. I am sure. We must first pass a crossroad." He switched off the flashlight, then the headlights of the vehicle, and turned on the parking lights.

"We're on schedule," Zoya whispered, looking at her wristwatch.

Camellion picked up the pocket night-vision scope from his lap, turned it on, and looked through the eyepiece. The 25mm/f1.4 lens, increasing background light by five hundred times, did the rest. Several hundred yards ahead was the east-west intersecting dirt road.

"Everyone here knows what to do," Camellion said as he turned off the scope. "If Tarkovsky doesn't see me ten minutes after I blow the walls, he'll rush back to the car. All of you then get out of the area as fast as possible."

The Moskvich was soon past the crossroad. Five minutes more and Gluzman was carefully turning off the road, to the left, the front bumper knocking aside weeds and small bushes, the tires crushing grass on the powder-dry ground. Now the ride became bumpy, a mild torture for Sergei Tsipin, whose hemorrhoids were acting up.

There was another low rumble of thunder, prompting Kirill Tarkovsky to say, "The rains this time of year tend to be heavy. A good shower would turn this ground into mud."

Tsipin gave him a sideways look of disapproval. "If the rest of us were as pessimistic as you, we would go home, Comrade!"

"I only stated a fact," Tarkovsky insisted. "We can't assume only the good and not speculate on the bad. The American Scott will tell you the same thing."

Right on, brother! We're "assuming" that the two other vehicles will be in position. We are also "assuming" there aren't any KGB waiting outside the hospital!

"Tarkovsky's right," Camellion said matter-of-factly. "We're not monks who came here to renew our faith. We're on a dangerous, high-level operation, but we do have one thing in our favor. The KGB doesn't expect us to be suicidal and *attack* the installation. That's our big edge—and surprise."

Zoya sighed. "I guess Yuri Gagarin has parked the minivan by now and is on his way home. I hope—" She stopped when Gluzman parked the Moskvich under the branches of an old oak.

The target was only 1,500 feet away—northwest.

Getting out of the car with the four Russians, Camellion, dressed in black, pulled a black nylon face mask from his jacket and slipped it over his head. After he put on black, thin rubber gloves, he walked forward, along the right side of the car, and took the bags of explosives and grenades from Tsipin. The MAC/Ingram and the pouch of magazines were next, and the special hip holster filled with the silenced Ruger. Camellion put the straps of the bags over his shoulders and strapped on the Ruger as Tarkovsky pulled out the three AKR assault rifles and handed one to Tsipin and one to Gluzman. He kept the third for himself.

It was Tsipin who reached into the backseat, pulled out and handed to the Death Merchant the last item needed for the assault on SPH UZh-15/5—a twenty-five-foot length of strong but thin nylon-Textite rope that Camellion had brought into Siberia with him. At one end of the rope—knotted every fifteen inches—was a hook that, under ordinary circumstances, was used to handle bales of hay. The horizontal wooden handle had been removed and that end put into a heavy vise and bent into a ring through which the rope had been inserted and fastened.

The Death Merchant clipped the coiled length of rope and the hook to a special belt he wore, then for only a moment did his eyes dart over the shadowed faces of the four Russians.

"Let's do it," was all Camellion said. The MAC/Ingram in his right hand, he turned and started walking toward the northwest. Tarkovsky followed.

Lying on his belly, Tarkovsky next to him, Camellion peered through the small night-vision scope at the hospital complex and its walls two hundred feet away. This area, southeast of the hospital, was partially wooded and slightly higher than the ground on which stood the KGB funny farm. Camellion saw that he would have to cover the last 150 feet in the open, without cover of any kind. In the darkness, however, it wasn't likely that anyone would see him, unless the guards in the two towers were scanning the countryside through NV devices. One watchtower was in the front south wall. The second tower was in the center of the rear north wall. A mile north of the hospital complex were the lights and the barbed wire of the gulag, the concentration camp. At this hour of the night—0250 hours—the guards in the towers would be dozing, if not sound asleep. At each corner of the walls was a double spotlight, the beam of one light pointing downward, striking the ground outside the complex, the beam of the other pointed inward illuminating the area inside the installation. But there were dead spots, dark sections outside the walls untouched by the light—not by accident or consciously poor design. Knowing the KGB as he did, Camellion realized that the lights were more for show than for security. Not for a second had the KGB ever considered the possibility that the mental hospital would ever be attacked.

"Comrade Scott, I must say it," whispered Tarkovsky. "You are crazy if you go inside that place. You will never come out alive."

Camellion gave an almost inaudible chuckle. "I'll come out, and I'll come out with Dr. Ulomov, if he's in there. See the center of the east wall, where the lights don't hit? I'll be coming through that wall. Remember, give me ten minutes after you hear the explosions. Here, you'll need the night-vision scope."

"Idi s Bogóm—Go with God!" whispered Tarkovsky.

As silent as a shadow, the Death Merchant moved out and headed toward the east wall. There wasn't any need to linger. Either the guards in the towers would see him or they wouldn't. He ran straight to the blind spot in the center of the east wall, took out a package of explosive, noted that it was marked number one, and placed it firmly against the wall, after turning on the detonator. He moved south rapidly, thinking that success or failure really didn't matter. Both, like life and living, were illusory, as vaporous as Man's search for peace. In only a short time—on the scale of history, ten years is far less than a second —the world would be plunged into the darkness of death and destruction, of blood and violence and barbarism. The living would envy the dead, and the long night of horror would begin.

But tonight I'll give the pig farmers my own brand of savagery!

He rushed through the glow of the light on the southeast corner of the walls and dropped the number-four package of pentolite and TVL. Turning, he sprinted north. In rapid order, within the next ten minutes he turned on the detonators of bundles number seven, eight, ten, and five, and placed them by the west end of the north wall, by the west wall (two packages), and the southwest corner. He then reversed his course. He turned, ran silently along the side of the west wall, spun at the northwest corner, and headed east. He turned again at the northeast corner, again rushed through a glow of light, and stopped when he came to the dead spot in the center of the east wall. There he unsnapped the coil of rope and its hook, wondering if the same dead areas existed inside the walls. Yes, of course. But there would be other lights inside the compound, especially around the actual hospital building.

The ease with which Camellion had planted the six packages of explosives had not caused him to let down his guard, not for a single second. What had Sergei Tsipin said about Colonel Boris Rudneva? Uh-huh. Rudneva was a specialist in antiterrorism. *If Rudneva is any good at his job, he'll know that the first attempt was not a random act of terrorism. He'll deduce we were after a specific target. Well, now, could he be making it easy for me?*

Camellion tested the hook at the end of the rope. He looked up at the top of the twenty-foot, mustard-color wall. The hook couldn't go over the wall. It had to catch on the top of the east edge. He measured the distance, then swung the rope and the hook. A miss. He succeeded on the third try. The hook caught, hung there, and Camellion pulled on the rope, forcing the icepick point into the mortar between the stones on top.

The Death Merchant, having had plenty of practice over the years, climbed the rope as easily as the average man walks up a flight of stairs. He flattened himself on the four-foot-wide top, pulled up the rope, and looked out at the buildings within the compound. He had been right. Certain areas inside, by the walls, seemed as black as the inside of a sealed mine shaft. There were also lights on three steel poles, illuminating much of the complex. One of the poles was between, and to the rear of, two of the buildings east of the administration building. The second pole was farther to the north and to the west, by the southeast corner of a storage building. The third lightpole was north, and at the end, of the east wing of the hospital building. Camellion could not see a single human being.

Camellion listened. Other than low thunder, there was only the stillness of the night and a chilly wind blowing over hell. Camellion could sense death in the air. His lips, behind the face mask, formed into an ironic smile. *Yes, indeed! Welcome your neighbor into your fallout shelter. He'll come in handy if you run out of food. . . . Do it, you damn fool!*

He moved the hay hook to the west edge of the wall, jammed it down firmly, and tossed down the knotted line. In seven seconds he was on the ground, inside the compound, and "whipping" the line to free the hook. Twice he had to give the rope a very hard ripple to dislodge the hook and make it fall.

Protected by the darkness in the blind spot, he re-coiled the line and fastened it to his belt, making sure the hook was on the outside of the rope. Now to plant the remainder of the explosive.

Camellion unclipped the M-10 Ingram from the ring on his belt, pulled back the cocking knob, and shoved on the safety. He pulled the Ruger with its built-in silencer from its holster and thumbed the safety to *F*—fire.

Conscious of the risk he was taking and aware that the enemy could be anywhere in the shadows, he crept west, the Ruger in his right hand, the Ingram SMG in his left. He passed the rear of the generator house and moved to the back of the long storage building, where he pulled out explosive package number two and placed it toward the center of the north, rear wall.

Satisfied with his progress, he moved north along the side of the building. In spite of the three big lights on poles, the bright light could not reach the rear of the storage building and the north side of the three-story structure north of it. From its design, the Death Merchant sensed it was living quarters for personnel, perhaps for the doctors and nonuniformed KGB. The building was between the west end of the storage building and the east end of one of the hospital wings.

He was almost to the northwest corner of the storage building when he heard humming from the west side. Someone was walking in his direction humming a Russian tune. Camellion stopped and waited. The humming stopped, but he could hear boots crunching on the hard ground. The KGB guard, his AKS-74 assault rifle on a strap over his right shoulder, turned the corner and started walking in Camellion's direction—but while the Death Merchant was in the shadows, flattened against the side of the building, Oskar Muldokav was ten feet out.

Muldokav spotted the extra-dark shadow that was Camellion a shave of a second before the Death Merchant squeezed the trigger of the Ruger auto pistol—*phyyyt, phyyyt!* Camellion's aim was deadly. The two .22-caliber Magnum hollow-point projectiles struck Muldokav in the chest, the second slug cutting through the mitral valve of his heart. The pig farmer was dead meat before he had fully crumpled to the ground.

Camellion dragged the corpse into the darkness by the side of the building, then rushed to its northwest corner and looked south toward the front of the complex. The area ahead was brightly lit from the pole between the KGB guard headquarters building and the living quarters, the two stucco structures east of the administration building.

The Death Merchant considered the risks. He couldn't have it both ways. He couldn't plant a package of blow-up-bang stuff behind each building unless he stuck his head in a noose. But would he be able to pull his head out of the noose? He did some rapid calculating. The distance to the two buildings was 75 feet, with 25 feet between the buildings. Round trip: 175 feet. And three to four seconds to throw a detonator switch and drop a package of explosive. Round trip: three to four minutes. *Do it!* He thumbed on the safety of the Ruger, then did it. He raced forward, knowing that if he ran into any KGB guards, he'd have to take the show off the road. The snarling of the Ingram would awaken the entire complex. He'd be able to get out by exploding the east wall, but he'd have to leave Dr. Ulomov behind.

He saw no one. No guards came unexpectedly around corners or out of building doors. He dropped one package of pentolite/TVL in the rear of the guard headquarters building, behind a garbage can, noting that it was number nine. He placed package number three on the windowsill in the rear wall of the guards' living quarters, after which he ran back north and darted to the northwest corner of what he presumed was the living quarters of the higher KGB and the hospital's physicians and their families. Once more he pulled the silenced Ruger, switched its safety lever to *F*, and proceeded to move in the darkness along the rear of the building.

Fifteen feet out, the area was not in darkness, the light coming from the spotlight on the pole on the north side of the hospital's east wing. The light couldn't reach the back wall of the living quarters because the northwest corner of the building blocked the light.

The Death Merchant sensed trouble, and he got it in the form of three KGB guards who came around the northwest corner, the one in the center of the trio carrying a lantern-type flashlight that was turned off.

Camellion's mouth became a tight, hard line. Terminating the three was not the problem. Where they would fall was. They would fall in the area that was lighted, in which case they could be seen by the guard, or guards, stationed at the east end of the hospital. *Unless I wait and don't fire until they reach the darkness. They'll have to walk another twenty feet.*

He began backtracking in the darkness along the rear of the building, the three KGB guards, talking among themselves, suspecting nothing. They paused when they were several feet inside the darkened area, one lighting a cigarette. Another man took a small bottle of vodka from his pocket and took a drink, then passed it to the second man. The third guard declined a drink, and the three continued on their way. The pig farmer with the lantern-flash turned it on and started to sweep the wide beam back and forth.

Phyyyt. The first .22-caliber hollow point caught the KGB boob with the flashlight in the mouth and blew out the back of his neck. He dropped the lantern and was falling backward when Camellion fired four more times, the silenced Ruger pistol whispering. The second Russian went down with an exploded heart and a slug that had angled through his right lung and rested against the innerside of the scapula. The third guard took the last fall of his life with slugs that had cut through the thin zygomatic bone of his face and had tickled the pons, the brain stem. He, too, had become as useful as a parachute on an ocean liner. The lantern-flash lay on its side, its beam pointing northeast. Another *phyyyt. Ping!* The beam went out.

Dead was dead. Camellion didn't bother to inspect the corpses. He ran to the northwest corner of the building and looked out carefully toward the west. There was half the target —the hospital. Built in the form of a Greek cross, the building was laid out with the operations section in the center. The two horizontal "arms" and the two perpendicular "arms" of the cross were the four wards, each wing having room for thirty-two "mental" patients.

The end of the east wing was only thirty-one feet southwest of the Death Merchant. Two guards patrolled back and forth in front of the steel door in the center of the wall. When one man was facing the north, the other man, moving in the opposite direction, was facing the south. Fudge and damn it! The door would be locked from the inside, and Camellion doubted that either of the guards had keys. There was, however, a telephone in a box attached to the side of the building, to the left of the door. The guards were able to gain access to the inside; they could phone and have someone open the door.

The problem was how to take one of the guards alive and in good condition. He had to sound normal when he used the phone. And the action would have to be fast for the east end of the wing was bathed in light.

The two guards reached the end of their walk, turned, and started back toward each other. Camellion's eyes never left them—*You're both going to gargle with razor blades! Don't feel bad! We're all the mega-dead!*

He switched the Ruger to his left hand and, with his right hand, reached behind his collar and pulled one of the Devil's Darts from its narrow holster. Yeah, a risk. If he didn't throw the dart just right, just so, if one guard wasn't dazed enough— *For me to get to him, I might as well go home. I could still use the Ruger to put him to sleep forever, but what good would it do? The door would still be locked.* Holding the Devil's Dart by the tip of the pencil-slim handle, he tested its weight.

Once more the guards reached the end of their short route, turned, and headed back toward each other. Camellion waited until they had met in the center and started walking away from each other, then he pulled the trigger of the Ruger. *Phyyyt.* The bullet hit the guard walking north just above the nose. The slug tore through his skull, bored a tunnel in the frontal lobe of his brain, and instantly turned off his life. No sooner had the guard's body given its first jerk from the impact of the metal than Camellion threw the Devil's Dart with his right hand, snapping and twisting his wrist. His aim was accurate, as was his method of throwing. The kill-dart streaked across the space, the small knob at the top of the handle hitting Daniil Pisarvev low on the back of the head. The world turned black around the Russian and he sank to his knees, as helpless as a baby. By the time his mind cleared and he had the strength to get to his feet, he found himself staring up at a man in black wearing a black face mask. He also found himself looking at the black muzzle of a silencer, which was only half an inch from his nose.

"Get up and go over to the phone, you stupid *chernozhopi,*" the Death Merchant told him in a voice that was pure ice. "You are going to tell them to open the door. Don't get cute or I'll blow your head off—move!"

The back of his head pounding, Pisarvev got to his feet and moved over to the telephone in the open box, trying to watch Camellion from the corner of his eyes.

"Wait!" warned Camellion. "I know there's a code word. So tip them off all you want, but you're going in ahead of me. Walk me into a trap, and you'll get the first bullet—from me! Get on that phone and tell whoever answers that Comrade Colonel Boris Rudneva and two of his aides are out here, making an inspection. Do it!" For emphasis, he jammed the muzzle of the silencer into the small of the guard's back.

Pisarvev knew total death when he saw it. He took the phone off the hook, waited for acknowledgment, then said, "This is Comrade Daniil Pisarvev. Comrade Colonel Boris Rudneva and three of his men are out here. Open the door. Sunset-rise. I repeat: sunset-rise."

He took the phone from his ear and, holding it, turned and looked fearfully at the Death Merchant.

Camellion motioned for Pisarvev to hang up and move to the door.

" 'Sunset-rise' had better be the right word," warned Camellion in a whisper. "If it's not, we'll be in hell within minutes."

"It w-was the code word for the day," the Russian managed to croak.

"How many will open the door, and how are the rooms laid out?"

"One orderly will open the door. There is a hall in the center, just beyond the door. There is a dormitory to the right and rooms to the left of the hall."

There was a clicking sound from the door. Standing to one side of Pisarvev, Camellion jammed him in the side with the Ruger and whispered, "Open it."

A nervous Pisarvev had pulled the door half open when Camellion chopped him across the back of the neck with a powerful left sword-ridge hand, then, with his body, shoved the unconscious man out of the way. Camellion finished opening the door and triggered the Ruger—twice—with such speed that he didn't have a chance even to get a good look at the white-clad orderly, who was actually a lieutenant in the counterintelligence department of the First Chief Directorate of the KGB. Both .22-caliber bullets hit the man in the stomach, the impact and shock of metal through flesh starting to double him over by the time Camellion had darted inside and was moving past him. . . . Seeing that the lieutenant was still conscious, Camellion did him the favor of easing his agony by slamming him across the head with the silencer.

Camellion closed the door and snapped the lock. He then shoved the Ruger into its holster, took the MAC/Ingram from its ring, and switched off the safety. The .22 Magnum bullets were powerful, but in no way could they be compared to the 9 mm *Très Haute Vitesse* cartridges in the Steyr pistols and the big .45 THV slugs in the M-10 Ingram SMG.

Holding the Ingram like a pistol in his right hand, Camellion moved down the hall, which was lighted only by nightlights on the side walls. From the dormitory and a few of the rooms, he could hear patients snoring. And he could see, fifty feet ahead of him, a fully lighted control center.

The Death Merchant's luck couldn't hold, and he knew it. The guards he had whacked out would be missed, and they'd be found. There were two guards lying in the light, the man he had just shot and the guard he had knocked unconscious. Other guards on patrol would have to find them.

He was only fifteen feet from the end of the hall when destiny decided to make him work for the $300,000 the CIA was paying him to get Dr. Ulomov out of the Soviet Union. Two of the KGB agents, posing as orderlies, happened to walk past the mouth of the hall and spotted him. They didn't have to look twice to realize that a man dressed entirely in black and carrying shoulder bags and a machine pistol wasn't a good and true friend of the Soviet Union.

One agent froze, his mouth falling open. The other agent reached for a 9 mm Makarov pistol in his right rear pocket and yelled, "Sound the alarm!" to the four men at the desks in the control center.

Discovery meant that the Death Merchant no longer had to creep like a night crawler in a rose garden. Now he could move with all the speed at his command. Darting forward, he pulled a Steyr pistol from a right-side shoulder holster and at the same time raised the Ingram SMG and fired. The submachine gun chattered raucously, its snarling, rapid voice out of tune with a siren on the roof that had begun to wail.

Two THV slugs unthawed the agent who had frozen, the impact of the metal in his left side almost lifting him off the floor as they pulled apart his heart and lungs and broke several ribs.

Josef Chokitensky, the second "orderly," made a fool of himself by trying to pull his Makarov and throw himself to one side —all at the same time. Two .45 projectiles popped him, one hitting his right kneecap and tearing off his lower leg. The second bullet exploded his stomach, ripped out three vertebrae, and kept right on going, striking one of the desks in the control center. And Camellion kept right on going—straight at the control desks.

There were four KGB agents at the desks and at the control boards. All were supposed to be orderlies. Stephen Klyun, who had pressed the siren button, dropped behind a desk, pulled open a drawer, and took out a Vitmorkin machine pistol while the other three agents—rattled by Camellion's lightning intrusion—started to pull Makarov pistols from rear pockets or belly holsters.

Klyun's effort amounted to chasing the wind. Camellion had seen him drop and wasn't about to see what the pig farmer might pop up with. The Death Merchant solved the problem by putting three .45 slugs through the front of the desk. One hit a stapler in a drawer, ricocheted back and forth, and got lost in the shuffle. The other two tore through the desk, bored tunnels through Klyun's lower chest and upper stomach, and continued going north. One zipped down the hall of the west ward and buried itself in the west wall. The other bullet struck Trofim Mimalsk in the right leg above the knee. While narrowly missing the femoral artery, the bullet exploded three inches of the femur bone into fragments. Mimalsk screamed and went down like a sack of wet cement. A sadist who delighted in questioning prisoners with a small sledgehammer—hitting them in just the right places—Mimalsk was getting a big dose of his own medicine.

"Drop the guns!"

Before either Ivan Basnikov or Dmitri Dolgikh could even raise their Makarovs, they found themselves confronted by the tall man in black holding a Steyr GB D.A. pistol and an Ingram submachine gun. The two KGB officers let their pistols slip from their fingers and fall to the floor. They stared in fear and hatred at the Death Merchant.

"What ward is Dr. Georgi Ulomov in? Answer—now!"

The two KGB agents felt an eerie sensation crawl along their spines. It wasn't what Camellion had said. It was how he had said it—cold, calm, unemotional. Camellion turned the Steyr to Basnikov, who was proud of his good looks. "You're the first," Camellion said. "Where is Dr. Ulomov?"

Basnikov had more nerve than common sense, more emotion than training. "Go to hell, you son of a bitch! I won't—"

Camellion squeezed the trigger of the Steyr. The weapon roared and Basnikov looked as if he had jumped backward. The 9 mm slug had hit him in the center of the chest. He fell backward across one of the desks, his eyes and mouth wide open.

Camellion turned the still-smoking Steyr toward a frosty-eyed Dolgikh. "You won't die as fast, stupid," Camellion warned him. "I'll only shoot off both your kneecaps. Where is Ulomov? Don't bother to lie. You're going to take me to him. Answer now or die now."

"He's in ward C," Dolgikh said, showing more sense than the dead Basnikov. "The ward to the north."

"How many orderlies are in ward C?"

"None. We're the entire night shift," Dolgikh said evenly. He thought of telling the man in black to surrender, then decided it would only sound stupid. All he could hope for was to remain alive—and not get demoted.

Two of the telephones by the switchboard rang. The Ingram chattered. The phones quit ringing, and the switchboard began to spit and sputter while sparks from short circuits made *spz-spz-spz* sounds.

The Death Merchant asked, "What's the purpose of the other board, the one with all the numbered switches?"

"It's . . . it's used for controlled lighting in the wards," Dolgikh said hesitantly.

Again the Ingram snarled. Now the light board began to spit and sputter and give off blue sparks.

The Death Merchant's voice was also a snarl. "You mean flashing colored lights to prevent the poor devils in here from sleeping." He motioned with the Steyr GB. "Walk two meters from the desks and get flat on your belly—hands on your head. Do it—fast."

Wondering what Camellion was going to do, the Soviet did it. So did Camellion. He reached into one bag, took out an M14 thermite canister, and pulled the ring while keeping his hand down firmly on the curved metal release handle. He got down and very carefully shoved the hellfire canister under the body of Trofim Mimalsk, who had passed out from shock and was lying on his back. Even more cautiously he made certain that, as he pushed the grenade under the small of the man's back, the weight of the man's body would keep the handle in place. Until Mimalsk moved, or someone tried to move him!

"Get up and move," Camellion ordered Dmitri Dolgikh, "and don't try to point out the wrong man. I know what Ulomov looks like."

The Death Merchant and Dolgikh headed toward the north hall. They were twenty feet inside when they heard the roaring of assault rifles from the outside, from the end of the east hall. KGB officers were shooting open the outside door at the end of the east wing.

Dolgikh led Camellion into a dormitory and turned on the lights. A pathetic sight confronted Camellion. There were fifty-three men lying on fifty-three beds. Several dozen of the patients were in canvas straitjackets and had leather masks buckled tightly over their entire faces. Only their noses were free so that they could breathe. Some men were jerking from side to side, or they would roll over either onto their stomachs or backs, or they would double up their legs. Whatever, they were constantly changing position, the need to do so the result of heavy doses of halopcridol. Some men were handcuffed to beds by their wrists and ankles. Stark naked, the body of each man was a mass of hives, red swelling piled on red swelling from doses of perphanazine frenolon. Handcuffed as they were, the patients could not scratch. They could only suffer the agony of itching.

Dolgikh led Camellion to a bed on the right side, halfway down the long room. The Death Merchant immediately recognized Dr. Georgi Ulomov from photographs Courtland Grojean had shown him. But the man lying on his left side, clad only in a short gray hospital gown and hugging a pillow, was not the same healthy-faced man Camellion had seen in the photographs. The Ulomov on the bed weighed only 120 pounds. There were heavy shadows under his sunken eyes; his face was wrinkled and his hair was white. Now and then his body jerked as if from palsy, as though he suffered from Parkinson's disease. He was fifty-six years old. He looked seventy.

Ulomov was awake but afraid to look up at the Death Merchant and Dolgikh.

"Get up, Dr. Ulomov," Camellion said in a kindly tone. "I'm breaking you out of this hellhole."

"Nyet! Nyet! You're not fooling me," screeched Ulomov in a high, weak voice. "This is only another one of Dr. Libinsky's tricks." He continued to hug the pillow.

Camellion motioned to Dolgikh with the Ingram. "Get him on his feet."

His face a mask of resentment, the KGB officer pulled Ulomov off the bed and forced the frightened scientist to stand. Ulomov let out a frightened "Ohhhhh!" when Camellion slammed the Steyr pistol against the side of the agent's head. The Russian slumped and fell across the bed.

"It's not a trick, Doctor," Camellion said. "You're going to the United States, if we're not killed getting out of here. Can you run?"

"Not too fast, but I'll try," Ulomov said, hope now in his voice and eyes. His lips twitched and now and then his head would jerk either to the left or the right. "But I've only got this nightgown and—"

"We have clothes for you," Camellion said, his eyes on the wide entrance of the dormitory. "There's no time to explain. They'll do their best to kill us, Doctor. Are you sure you want to risk it?"

"Risk what?" Ulomov's head jerked violently to the left. "My life? I would rather be dead than remain in here."

Camellion was satisfied. "Good. Watch the rear, and when I tell you to drop, do it fast. Understand?"

"Da. I will do as you say. Give me one of your pistols." Ulomov's lips quivered and his voice shook.

"Nyet, you don't need a weapon. If you're not shooting at them, they won't be so prone to shoot at you. Follow me."

The Death Merchant hurried to the door, switched off the lights, and whispered, "Stay down, Doctor." Ulomov was trembling, not from fear but from excitement, from the prospect of liberation, of freedom from the Soviet nightmare known as a mental hospital.

A few seconds before Camellion looked around the edge, he heard the high-pitched screams of agony and saw a part of the bright white-blue flash that flared from the control center. The would-be rescuers had reached the desks, and someone had attempted to move Trofim Mimalsk. The thermite canister had exploded, and four KGB officers had been doused with molten iron burning at a temperature of almost 4,000 degrees.

As the screaming continued, Camellion stuck his head out and looked south. He pulled back quickly, just in time to avoid a dozen or more projectiles from six men firing short-barreled AKR assault rifles and PPS43 submachine guns. Some of the slugs chopped into the wood at the edge of the entrance; others zipped through the opening and killed two patients handcuffed to their beds.

None of the patients in the ward seemed to notice the gunfire. None seemed to care what was happening around them. Camellion attributed their emotional malaise to suffering. They had already been through so much that nothing else mattered.

Camellion dropped to his knees and counted to five. He then thrust the Ingram around the edge of the entrance and, holding it only three feet above the floor, opened fire, moving the SMG from left to right. He had assumed correctly; he had timed it correctly. The six KGB gunmen had been charging in low and had walked right into his cloud of metal death. There were short screams and yells as the .45 THV projectiles flowed all over the Russians, the big slugs butchering them.

Camellion shoved a full magazine into the Ingram and pulled back the cocking knob. "We're going out, but first I'm going to give a present to whoever might be waiting," he said to Dr. Ulomov. He took an Mk offensive grenade from one of his bags, pulled the ring, and threw the grenade south into the hall as hard as he could. The grenade fell two feet outside the entrance of the hall, and the flaked TNT exploded, the ensuing shock wave spreading two and a half yards in all directions. Right behind the big bang came the Death Merchant and Dr. Ulomov, both of whom moved around the bloody messes that had been human beings. Camellion did stop long enough to pick up a PPS submachine gun and an AKR assault rifle, lifting the automatic weapons by their canvas straps.

"Leave it alone," he said sharply to Ulomov when the scientist tried to pick up an assault rifle. Ulomov didn't argue. He only looked surprised.

There was one very good reason why Camellion didn't want a weapon in Ulomov's hands: He didn't trust him. While he was

99 percent positive that the man was Georgi Ulomov, suppose he wasn't? Suppose he was a double? The Death Merchant now had proof that the KGB had guessed Ulomov was the target. The KGB triggermen coming straight to ward C proved that Colonel Boris Rudneva was not a dummy.

Another problem now confronted Camellion due to the arrangement of the halls. From the north, he could look directly across into the south corridor. Once he was near the end of the north hall, he would be able to see the mouth of the west passageway, but only if he stayed by the wall to his left. He wouldn't, however, be able to see the opening of the east hallway, not until he moved to the wall to his right, in which case he would be blind to the opening of the west wall. He couldn't have it both ways, and he would soon come to that section in the hall where he would have to make a choice. Through the black smoke rising from the half-burned desks and the half-eaten-by-thermite corpses, he could see that the south hall was empty—but for how long? So bottle up the west wing hall!

He had attached the MAC/Ingram to the ring on his belt and had put the PPS43 SMG over his shoulder on its sling. With the AKR assault rifle ready to spray, he inched ahead until he could see a small portion of the entrance of the west hall. By the same token, anyone in the west hall could see him. The group of Russians clustered in the mouth did see him and opened fire. Camellion jerked back to avoid the slugs that sizzled through the air and zipped into the wall to his left.

The Death Merchant placed the AKR assault rifle on the floor and took out an offensive grenade and a thermite canister. He first threw the thermite, knowing it would never reach the mouth of the west passage, but it would come close. The canister did, the thermite *whoosshhhhhhing* into a huge burst of beautiful blue-white fire that was only five feet from the entrance. Cursing, the Russians fell back. Right behind the thermite came the concussion grenade. *BLAMMMM!* It exploded and scattered some of the thermite, a bit of it splashing into the hall. Most of the molten iron hit the floor, except for five drops. Three fell on Yulian Shibelof's left cheek. Two dropped on Bulat Imikvisky's left shoulder. The thermite began to eat straight to the bone. It was the same as being touched with a red-hot poker or Satan's tongue. Shibelof and Imikvisky began to shriek in agony, to jump like wild men and beat at themselves.

"Keep down, Doctor," Camellion said. "We're going to run for it in a few minutes. If you believe in divine help, I suggest you pray!"

Now for the big surprise! He took the remote-control detonator from his jacket pocket and turned it on. The tiny green light glowed. The device was ready; so was Camellion. In rapid succession, he threw switches 1, 4, 7, 8, 10, 5, 2, 9, and 3. In rapid succession there were nine huge explosions, one right after the other, each less than a second apart, the concussions making the hospital building shake.

Camellion sprayed a short blast of slugs at the mouth of the west hall, then ran along the left wall of the north hall, stopping when he came to the end. He threw a thermite canister toward the mouth of the east corridor, then followed with an offensive grenade. *Whoooossshhhhhh! BERBLAMM!*

It's now or never! "Let's go, Doctor!"

The Death Merchant stepped out from the end of the left wall and began triggering the AKR assault rifle. He had caught the group of KGB officers in the east hall off guard. The thermite and the offensive grenade had partially disorganized them, and the nine explosions from the outside had completed the job. Without knowing it, the pig farmers had given Camellion the lag time he needed. The AKR roared, its muzzle spitting full-metal-jacket 5.45 mm projectiles. Four KGB officers yelled and, raked with metal across the middle, went down. The other six did their best to level down on Camellion, who was racing forward, ducking and weaving and swerving.

Captain Gennady Kipeka came very close to killing the Death Merchant. His stream of 9 mm Vitmorkin projectiles streaked so close to Camellion's right side that three ripped through his clothing, one coming within a sixteenth of an inch of hitting his hip. Another tore through the bag in which he had carried the explosives. Packet number six was still in the bag. Still another slug sliced between his left arm and his left side, the metal raking along the outer edge of the shoulder holster, cutting slightly into the leather.

The 215-pound Kipeka was dead 2.11 seconds later. Two of the Death Merchant's 5.45 mm projectiles punched him in the groin, cut through his intestines, and kicked him back against Vento Rodinnski, who stumbled but didn't fall. It was Aram Smerg who fell, as dead as he would ever get. Three projectiles from Camellion's AKR had blown a hole in his chest the size of a baseball. With bits of his uniform fluttering around him, he half spun around in a spray of blood, then fell on his face.

Camellion, darting to his left to escape a stream of 7.62 mm slugs from Lavrenti Belov's PPS chatter box, braced the AKR against his right hip and with his left hand pulled a Steyr pistol from its shoulder holster and thumbed off the safety. He fired twice before the brutal-looking Belov could regroup his reflexes and get off another burst, pulling the trigger twice because he knew he could also scratch out Sidor Zendrok, who, behind Belov, was about to step around him and fire. The first 9 mm THV projectile rocketed into Belov's solar plexus, went all the way through his body, and struck Zendrok low in the left side. The second bullet tore off Belov's right hand and stabbed him in the face on the right side of the nose. He went down with parts of his skull and brain dropping around him.

The Death Merchant heard the telltale roaring of a Soviet PPS chatter gun behind him and the kind of sharp, distinctive cries made by men who have been shot, but he was too busy to turn around and look. He didn't have to. He knew the firing was coming from Dr. Ulomov. *He's picked up a pig farmer's music box and is helping out! So he's not a double!*

Chingiz Akmov and Vento Rodinnski tried to throw themselves to one side before firing at Camellion. Taking those six seconds was a mistake. Camellion chopped Akmov in the chest and sent him flying backward in a fast two-step, to stumble over another corpse. Rodinnski died as quickly. One minute he was Here. The next instant he was in the Ultimate Elsewhere, his head exploded by a 9mm THV projectile.

Camellion spun around in time to save Dr. Ulomov's life. Ulomov had picked up a PPS whose magazine was half full. He had already sent three KGB men from the west hall and two in the entrance of the south hall into the constancy of eternity. Running out of ammo, he was unable to do anything about the three men who were now running out of the south hall and only seconds from killing him and the Death Merchant.

Camellion was not unable. With the smell of gunpowder and

the odor of burnt metal and flesh and plastic in his nostrils, he fired rapidly. One-two-three! The three Ruskies went down. The last man's finger contracted on the trigger of his LS-4 Skoptisch submachine gun, and as the death reflex tightened and he fell backward, the weapon spit a long stream of slugs that chopped holes in the ceiling above the still-smoking control center.

"Follow me and pick up a couple of assault rifles," Camellion yelled to the Russian scientist.

Camellion tossed aside the now-almost-empty assault rifle, unhooked the MAC M-10 from its belt ring, and raced down the east hall to the shot-apart door, which was standing wide open. Even before he reached it, he could see the glow from the fires generated by the explosion of packages number three, nine, and two.

The instant Camellion and Ulomov stepped outside, they could see red and orange flames licking at the KGB headquarters, living quarters, and warehouse, which were giving off clouds of dirty black smoke. Whipped by a breeze that had increased in strength, the smoke was not only boiling upward, it was rolling all over the ground, increasing the misery of the Ivans trying to fight the fires and slowly losing the battle.

The Death Merchant saw something else: five agents who spotted him and Ulomov when the two were halfway between the east wing of the hospital and the northwest corner of the three-story building that housed the torture hospital's medical personnel. One of the Ivans got off a stream of slugs from a Vitmorkin machine pistol while the two regulars brought up SKA carbines. The Death Merchant didn't know how close the 9 mm flatpoints came to him. He did know that one came too close to give him any feeling of comfort. *PINGGGGG!* The bullet hit the hay hook, the impact making the steel "claw" jump and jerk on the end of the nylon-Textite line.

Camellion fired on the run, moving the Ingram from left to right, raking the three Slavic saps with a short burst of .45 *Très Haute Vitesse* projectiles that slammed into them with the force of a runaway express train.

Camellion hoped that no one else had seen him and Ulomov as he and the Target—now the Prize—reached the north wall of the medical personnel building and the fragile security of the darkness. The Death Merchant had saved his last package of explosive for the center of its north wall. He didn't bother to try to conceal it. He turned on the detonator and placed the bundle firmly against the foundation, then whispered to Ulomov, who was leaning against the wall, "We're going through a hole I blew in the outer east wall. Don't quit on me—and on yourself —now. We're almost free."

"I—I'll t-try," whispered Ulomov.

Camellion took the AKS assault rifle from the scientist and slung it over his shoulder. Looking toward the east, Camellion could see that explosive package one had blown a fifteen-foot hole in the east wall, and he could visualize with a good deal of pleasure what the other bundles of pentolite and Titvuytol had done to the walls. What he saw in the window of his imagination was on the mark. The southeast and southwest corners had been blown into oblivion. Packages eight and ten had demolished half the west wall, which looked as if it had been bombed. There was a jagged twenty-foot rent in the north wall. All the gaps in the walls were surrounded by the rubble of broken stones, on both the inside and the outside of the complex.

Camellion and Ulomov ran toward the ragged opening in the east wall. They weren't opposed by any KGB guards for one logical reason: The Ivans were too busy fighting the fires, and since there had been six explosions outside the four walls, it never occurred to any of the enemy that whoever had invaded would try to escape through any wall. *Over* one of the walls, maybe. But *through* it?

In fact, Camellion had attacked so suddenly and with such speed that Captain Gennady Kipeka and Dr. Stephen Libinsky, the two pig farmers in charge, had not had time to think of anything. Kipeka was now a candidate for a six-foot-under bungalow, the kind with a roof of grass and walls of granite.

Fat and queer Libinsky, hiding on the first floor of the building that housed the medical personnel, would soon join him.

The Death Merchant and Ulomov moved through the opening in the east wall and headed southeast toward Kirill Tarkovsky, two hundred feet away. The only immediate danger was from the two guard towers, the one by the main gate in the south wall and the one perched thirty-two feet above the north wall. Guards in both towers were moving large spotlights back and forth over the north and south areas outside the walls.

They had covered half the distance to Tarkovsky's position when Camellion said, "Drop flat, Doctor. I have work to do." He pulled the remote-control detonating station from his jacket pocket by the time he and Ulomov were prone on the ground. He turned on the station. The green light glowed. *Vern Cole* *should be here! He loves to blow up buildings—and people!*

Camellion pushed switch number six. *BLAAAMMM-MMMMM!* The north side of the medical personnel building exploded into flame, the big flash illuminating the entire north side of the grounds, but only for a moment. It was during that moment that Dr. Stephen Libinsky joined Captain Gennady Kipeka. An eight-inch splinter had stabbed Libinsky in the left side of the neck. He lay in a half-wrecked room, face down in a pool of blood.

Camellion got to his feet and put away the remote-control station.

"Another thirty meters, Doctor," he said. He felt a few drops of rain on his right cheek.

He should have remained on the ground for five more seconds. If he had, the searchlight beam from the south tower would have passed over him.

"Run in a zigzag pattern!" he yelled at Ulomov. The scientist did, then stumbled and fell.

A ShKAS light machine gun began chattering from the tower, and 7.62 mm projectiles began to make *bld-bld-bld-bld* sounds as they struck the hard ground very close to Camellion and even closer to Dr. Ulomov. Suddenly there was a burst of automatic rifle fire ninety feet ahead. In the distance there was the sound of glass breaking and a howl of pain. The searchlight winked out. The ShKAS stopped firing. Kirill Tarkovsky had turned off not only the spotlight but one of the Ruskies manning it.

The assault rifle in his hands, Tarkovsky moved out into the open.

"Hurry up," he called out. "It's going to rain. We'll be stuck making mud pies!"

Camellion and Ulomov reached Tarkovsky, but they didn't

---

* See Death Merchant #65, *Mission Deadly Snow,* also published by Dell.

turn and look at Special Psychiatric Hospital UZh-15/5 until they were six feet into the woods. By then the four buildings blasted by the explosives were blazing like Boy Scout rally bonfires, the flames leaping sixty feet into the air and tinging low-rolling strato-clouds with shades of red and yellow and orange and a kind of deep purple-crimson.

There weren't any more drops of rain, but the strong breeze had turned into a half-strong wind that rose and fell, lashed the fire and smoke back and forth, and only made the situation worse for the Russians inside the walls.

"Let's get out of here and to the car," urged Camellion. "We've pulled off half the miracle. Now—"

"You mean *you* did, Comrade," said Tarkovsky.

"Now for the other half of the impossible."

Dr. Ulomov gave a little cry of pain. He had stepped on a broken branch with his bare feet. Inside the hospital and on the ground within the walls, he had been too afraid to notice his feet, which were bleeding and now had begun to hurt. Suddenly he was aware that he was wearing only a hospital gown. He felt ridiculous.

"I—I can't go very fast through these woods," he said, sounding forlorn. "Maybe—"

"No maybes, Doctor," Camellion said calmly. "We don't have time for you to tiptoe through the tulips and the tall grass."

Before Ulomov could say anything, the tall man with the black mask over his face swept him up in his arms, like a baby. Ulomov wasn't the only one surprised. Kirill Tarkovsky who himself was a strong man was too. He was amazed at the ease with which Camellion carried the Soviet scientist and ducked the branches being bullwhipped back and forth by the wind.

For some reason he could not define, Tarkovsky felt an inner chill as he watched the man who called himself Arnold Scott. Even with Dr. Ulomov in his arms, *Tovarishch* Scott kept several steps ahead of Tarkovsky. . . .

Chapter Ten

The Death Merchant was pleased to see that the security around the Moskvich was first-rate. Hidden forty feet northwest of the vehicle, Sergei Tsipin stepped out from behind an oak tree, an assault rifle in his hands, when Camellion, carrying Dr. Ulomov, and Kirill Tarkovsky passed. The four men reached the car in short order, and Zoya Beliyev and Semyon Gluzman came out of the deep brush.

With only a brief glance at Ulomov, Zoya and Gluzman opened the right rear door of the car and took out a bundle of clothing and the can of gasoline. A pair of short boots was tied to the bundle of clothing. As Camellion put Ulomov on his feet, Tsipin and Tarkovsky took up their positions: Tsipin was to monitor the lane that led in from the road and Tarkovsky was to keep an eye on the woods to the northwest.

The Death Merchant came right to the matter at hand. "Dr. Ulomov, I'm sorry, but it's necessary that we douse your entire body with petrol," he said apologetically. "I suspect that either your clothing or parts of your body have been coated with a mutagen substance. If that's the case, it would be easy for *Kah Gay Beh* technicians to track you. Should they find you, they would find us."

Understanding glowed on the thin face of the weather expert. "Whoever you are—"

"My last name is Scott."

"I believe you are right, *Tovarishch* Scott," Ulomov said weakly. "A week ago every patient in my ward was forced to submerge his hands and feet in a tub filled with a thick, colorless liquid. Since then we have not been allowed to bathe, not even to wash our hands. Petrol will render the chemical inactive?"

"Completely," the Death Merchant said, picking up the can

of gasoline. *"Grazhdanka* Beliyev, if you will turn your back, we'll get on with it."

He unscrewed the cap on the can and stared at the pathetic scarecrow, who was one of the world's leading authorities on climatology and weather modification. "The gasoline won't make your feet feel any better, and they'll burn worse after you put on socks and boots. So will the rest of your body. But it's better to have that kind of short discomfort than to be captured and taken back to a mental hospital."

"Do what must be done," Ulomov said resignedly, and as Zoya turned her back to him, he began pulling his hospital gown over his head.

Camellion did more than splash gasoline all over Georgi Ulomov's body. He also made sure that the man washed his hands and arms as well as his feet with a handkerchief the Death Merchant gave him. Ulomov winced with pain as he scrubbed the soles of his feet and worked the cloth over and between his toes, the gasoline finding its way into cuts and abrasions.

It took sixteen minutes for Dr. Ulomov to "bathe" and dress in rough peasant clothes and for Gluzman to drive the Moskvich out of the wooden area onto the side road. The ride was far from comfortable, especially for Sergei Tsipin in the backseat. Ulomov was sitting on his lap. Next to them, his feet on the armored case of the AN/URC tactical transceiver, was Kirill Tarkovsky, worried that, because of the lack of space, he would be hampered if they were chased by the militia and the KGB and he had to fire out of the left rear window.

Even when they were two miles south of the mental hospital, they could still see the red-orange glow in the sky from the burning buildings, the light flickering against the low clouds adding to the general tension and to the strange sensations that had taken possession of the Russians. Never had they been able to smell the air and the countryside with such intensity. All their physical senses had been heightened to a new awareness. Never had they been so wide awake, so *alive,* their intensification conveyed to Camellion by their movements and expressions. The Death Merchant was not a stranger to the process: It was the excitement of intense danger, of standing toe to toe with the Cosmic Lord of Death. None of the Russians knew it, but they were experiencing the unreality of reality, the impossible that had become possible, that which is common to every soldier going into battle: They were living from moment to moment, from heartbeat to heartbeat, because they realized that they were close to Death and accepted it. Only Camellion was immune—and bored, as usual. He had shaken hands with Old Rattle Bones many, many times and harbored no illusions about being in the Here one moment and in the Ultimate Elsewhere the next. It was the normal scheme of all physical matter. Without death, life would be meaningless. In eternity there are no goals to reach.

"The next car had better be in position, or we'll have had it," Tsipin said. He couldn't understand why he was sweating so. The temperature was only fifty-eight degrees.

"We'll still have three kilometers to go after we reach the second car," muttered Tarkovsky. "Oh, God! It's starting to rain!"

"I don't dare go any faster," Gluzman said, as if defending himself. "The damned road is too narrow."

This time the rain was more than a light sprinkle. While it was not a downpour, enough water was hitting the outside of the glass so that Gluzman had to turn on the windshield wipers.

"The rain will not interfere that much," Zoya said quickly, knowing what was on everyone's mind. "Not after we transfer to the second vehicle and get out of the woods. The rain is not too heavy. It will take awhile for the ground to become muddy."

Camellion, watching the rain hit the road ahead of the car, wasn't convinced. "Perchany and his tractor-trailer aren't exactly lightweight. His rig could bog down very easily, even after a light rain."

"How far must we go? What is our final destination?" Dr. Ulomov found the courage to ask.

"Zoya, where is Perchany parked and waiting?" Camellion's tone was blunt. "And don't tell me it's 'most secret' for reasons of security. At this stage of the game, if we run into the militia —I don't think we will, unless by accident—we're all dead, or all alive—except for anyone who might become wounded."

"What do you mean, Scott?" Tsipin asked, jumping in.

"If anyone is wounded seriously, he—or she—will have to be

left behind. He would have to be put to sleep forever by us. That includes me, if I'm wounded. There are no exceptions."

Silence, a heavy silence. Finally Zoya said, "We're meeting Comrade Perchany at a State trucking inspection station. I know that surprises you, Scott."

"Not really," Camellion lied for tactical reasons. "I would only like to know the arrangements after we get there."

"A State station sure doesn't make me feel any better!" Tarkovsky said. "We should have sent the *Kah Gay Beh* an invitation!"

"I thought you would have guessed, Kirill Tarkovsky," Zoya said. "It was arranged with the two men at the station as part of *na levo*." She looked at Camellion. "In English, you would call it being in on 'the take.' "

Camellion nodded. "You're talking about bribery. The *baksheesh* of the Arabs, or what the Mexicans refer to as *mordida*."

"Exactly," said Zoya. "*Na levo* is a built-in, permanent feature of our society, although *Moskva* won't admit it. *Na levo* takes in everything from petty bribery and black marketing to wholesale thieving from the State and deals involving *samizdat*, the underground, or the 'underworld' as you would call it in America."

"It only proves that the Soviet Union has more goods than any other country!" joked Gluzman. "People have been stealing from the State for sixty years, but there are still plenty of goods left to swipe."

"Comrade Perchany will be parked in the small concrete lot behind the building at the inspection station. The two men at the station will look the other way while we get into one of the trailers. I sense you do not like such an arrangement, Scott?"

"No, I don't," Camellion said. "I suppose it's the best that you and Perchany could do?"

"It was, and Perchany is positive that he can trust the two attendants at the inspection station. Before this day he has smuggled goods for them into Okhotsk. This time he will carry eight kilograms of heroin for them to Okhotsk. Of course, he will not turn over the drug to anyone there, since he will be going with us on your submarine."

"Scott, do you have any specific plan in case we meet the militia?" Tarkovsky asked.

"We'll have to do the best we can," Camellion said evenly. "For now all we can do is remember the tea kettle. It's always up to its neck in hot water, but it continues to sing. I really don't think we'll be bumping into any militia or KGB, unless it's by accident."

Zoya inhaled loudly and turned in the seat and stared at the Death Merchant in dismay. "By accident! After what you did back there! You wrecked the entire complex! I can't understand why we haven't already met two or three carloads of guards!"

"Join the club. I consider it an act of God that we even managed to get to the woods and that I wasn't stopped by the *Kah Gay Beh* on my way to the hospital," Camellion said sheepishly. He gave a deep sigh of boredom and weariness. "I hadn't discounted the possibility of Colonel Rudneva's having men hidden outside the walls. Apparently he didn't think such precautions were necessary. He should have considered the chance of a one-man strike."

"Who would?" said Kirill Tarkovsky. "But what does that have to do with their not chasing us?"

"No one is ever more surprised than a revolutionary rebeled against," Camellion said. "I created so much confusion at the hospital, and it happened so fast, when they least expected it, that I doubt if anyone took time to consider the direction I might have taken in escaping. For that reason, if we do run into a—"

Camellion stopped and stared ahead. The short turnoff road to where the second car was waiting—or was supposed to be—was only four hundred feet in front of the Moskvich. It was the headlights twelve hundred feet ahead that grabbed their attention and made the adrenaline flow faster.

"Whoever it is, they're approaching from the southwest," Semyon Gluzman said, his voice nervous and excited. "The car up front might be the driver we're supposed to meet. He could have been delayed for some reason and is just now getting here."

There was a loud click from the backseat. Tarkovsky had shoved a full magazine into his AKR assault rifle, pulled back the cocking knob, and sent a 5.45 mm cartridge into the firing chamber.

"Take a good look," Camellion said. "Those lights are too far apart to be on an automobile. They're on a jeep. It's the militia coming at us. Tarkovsky, take five grenades from the crate and put them in your pockets. As soon as we get out, put them in the center of the road, one next to the other."

"If the militia spots Comrade Tystsevich in the other car, and—" Zoya stopped when Gluzman braked the Moskvich, and Camellion said:

"Gluzman, after we're out, back up, not more than twenty kilometers per. Tarkovsky and I will do the rest."

Zoya said quickly, "The other car we're supposed to meet can't be more than ten meters back from the road. There isn't room."

"We can't do anything about that now," Camellion told her. "Tarkovsky and I have to rush it. The militia boys can't see this far, not yet, except for our lights. In another few minutes it will be too late."

Camellion got out of the car on the right side, the Ingram SMG in his left hand. Tarkovsky moved out into the rain from the rear left, his hand wrapped around an AKR. As soon as Gluzman had backed up, Tarkovsky took the five RGD-5 Soviet grenades from his jacket pockets and placed them in a line on the center of the road. Moments later he and the Death Merchant were down in a clump of weeds, thirty-five feet from the road, the rain pounding on them. Soon they would be soaked and more uncomfortable than they already were. The militia jeep, its driver having slowed, was only six hundred feet to the southwest.

"They saw the lights of our car," Tarkovsky said, heavy concern in his low tone. "Look! They've turned on spotlights and are raking the sides of the road. Damn it, Scott! If the other car we are supposed to meet is where it should be, it can't be more than forty-five meters southwest of us. Those dolts in the jeep will have to see it! I hope the driver has enough sense to get out of there!"

His eyes calculating, Camellion watched the approaching jeep move ahead, several militiamen in the rear seat continuing to move hand-held spotlights and point the beams into the foliage. These goons weren't about to drive into an ambush— *They think!*

Camellion smiled. "Give me the night-vision scope. We're going to move farther back off the road."

Tarkovsky dug into an inner pocket, pulled out the small scope, and handed it to Camellion. The Death Merchant stared through the eyepiece of the infrared scope. Although the rain struck the outside of the lens at the opposite end, he could see the five grenades on the road clearly. The location of the grenades firmly established in his mind, he got to his feet. He shoved the night scope into his pocket and picked up the Ingram submachine gun.

Tarkovsky followed the Death Merchant, who had turned and was going deeper into the brush.

This area, unlike the woods close to the hospital, was not densely populated with trees, and the trees that were there weren't large. However, small fir and spruce trees offered excellent cover. Camellion stopped behind two firs, in a position that allowed him to see through the trees and clearly see the grenades, which he estimated to be eighty feet away. He stared through the night-vision scope and again fixed the position of the five grenades in his mind. He put the scope in his pocket and held out the Ingram to Tarkovsky.

"Here, take the MAC and give me the AKR," he said. "The AKR has the range."

Tarkovsky wasn't going to argue with a man who had single-handedly destroyed a KGB special psychiatric hospital. He accepted the Ingram and handed over the AKR to the Death Merchant, who was watching the approaching jeep. He had accustomed his eyes to the darkness, but he could barely see the vehicle through the trees. The vehicle—a six-man model—was moving no more than 12 mph, two of the men methodically working the beams over each side of the road, three other militiamen waiting with automatic rifles. The jeep was still too far away for Camellion to fire.

Tarkovsky released the safety of the MAC/Ingram. "If the other car is in place, they almost have to find it. Those damned spotlights are digging sixteen to eighteen meters inward."

The Death Merchant waited, the theme of Tchaikovsky's *Pathetique Symphony* jumping around in his thoughts. Only a Russian mind could have produced such hauntingly beautiful music. Then came the remembrance of his last meeting with

Courtland Grojean. The Fox had mentioned Moammar Khadafy, the psychotic dictator of Libya. *KILL KHADAFY!* Impossible? The impossible only took a little longer. . . .

The bright-white beam from the left spotlight found the front of the Zhukovki-1 sedan. The jeep stopped instantly, and three militiamen raked the vehicle and a wide area around the car with full magazines of PPSC SMG and AKS assault rifle projectiles.

BLAMMMMMM! FMJ slugs found the gas tank and the Zhukova-1 exploded, the flash—only several hundred feet southwest of Camellion and Tarkovsky—briefly illuminating the general area.

"They're not taking any chances," Tarkovsky muttered, wiping water from his chin. He glanced uncertainly at the Death Merchant, who had lifted the assault rifle and was looking down the point of the crossline sight.

The jeep started forward once more, this time picking up speed. The militiamen were convinced that they had eliminated the immediate danger and that they could now investigate the vehicle that was slowly backing up. By the time the driver spotted the short row of grenades in the middle of the road, it was too late. He was braking and yelling a warning when the Death Merchant squeezed the trigger of the AKR and a stream of 5.45 mm projectiles struck the grenades.

An RGD-5 Soviet grenade is nothing more than a tin can filled with twenty-eight ounces of TNT with a primer/detonator fitted into the head. It's a crude grenade that, although ineffective against tanks, can be deadly against thin-skinned vehicles.

The 140 ounces of TNT exploded with a terrific roar when the front of the jeep was only six feet away, the savage concussion upending the vehicle as if it were a child's toy. The six militiamen, stunned and numbed by the explosion, were tumbling out of the jeep when Camellion and Tarkovsky's slugs began tearing into them. The jeep exploded into a dirty red ball of fire, parts of it flying upward and outward. Upside down, what remained of the jeep crashed to the road and crushed the bodies of two of its former occupants. They didn't feel a thing. They had already been slug-stabbed into eternity. Somehow another man had been thrown clear and was unhurt. He got up and managed to stumble half a dozen feet before Camellion rained slugs on his parade and exploded his head with several projectiles. Another man, trying to get up, fell back dead, two of Tarkovsky's .45 THV Ingram slugs having torn his chest to streamers of bloody flesh. Lying on his face, the last man was eight feet to the side of the burning junk and was barely moving as AKR projectiles stitched him from skull to ankles and left him butchered, the rain quickly diluting and spreading his blood.

The Death Merchant and Tarkovsky hadn't taken any spare magazines with them. Out of ammo for the AKR and the MAC/Ingram, they pulled pistols—Camellion, a Steyr, Tarkovsky, his Walther P-38.

Soaked to the skin, they left their positions and hurried through the rain, which was now falling harder. Now and then there was a peal of thunder and lightning zigzagged ominously across the sky. They were halfway to the road and the burning wreckage of the jeep when they heard a voice, to their right, call out to them in Russian.

"Comrades! Wait! Please!"

Camellion and Tarkovsky spun around. Coming toward them from between trees and bushes to the southwest was a gangling shadow of a man, stumbling through the weeds and grass and brushing aside dripping pine and fir branches. The man soon reached Camellion and Tarkovsky, both of whom saw that he, like them, wore rough, ill-fitting clothes and was soaking wet. Unlike them, he did not carry a weapon.

"I am Boris Tystsevich." The man, in his sixties, was so terrified he could hardly speak. "I was waiting close to the road, expecting Comrade Zoya Beliyev and her people. I suppose you are with her. When I saw the militia jeep, I moved deeper into the trees and waited. I came forward when I saw you explode the jeep and heard your weapons firing."

"You are safe now, Boris Tystsevich," Tarkovsky said. "But I think you'll have to depend on your own resources. We don't have room for you."

"Come with us, Tystsevich," said the Death Merchant. He didn't give a damn what Tarkovsky might think and had a good feeling when he saw a hopeful expression blossom on the face of the skinny newcomer.

As soon as Gluzman and the others in the Moskvich saw the jeep explode, Gluzman started to drive forward. It took only a few minutes for the car to reach the Death Merchant and his two companions. Tarkovsky went around to the left rear and got inside.

Camellion pulled open the front door on the right side and, without getting in, leaned down low and explained the situation to Zoya and the three others in the car. They couldn't transfer to the Zhukova-1 because the militia had blown it up. "And Tystsevich here needs a lift."

Zoya moved over on the seat and leaned out so far that some of the rain struck the flowered scarf around her head.

"Comrade Boris Tystsevich, haven't you made arrangements to move south with the others?" Zoya asked, worried.

"Those arrangements are no longer valid," Tystsevich said, sounding as pathetic as he looked. "I was going to drive to the point of contact after I delivered you and your party. Without a car, I cannot get to the contact area. Once I do not return the car, and the *Kah Gay Beh* learns it was I who borrowed it from Professor Malgovsky, I will be as good as dead."

Camellion looked down the road, then snapped, "Boris Tystsevich, get in the car on the other side. Sit on Tarkovsky's lap. Go on! Get going!"

Tystsevich went around to the other side of the car, opened the door, and started to climb in, feeling like a poor relation because of the way Tarkovsky glared at him.

"See here, Scott! This is against my better judgment," Zoya said sternly. She moved over to make room for Camellion, who was getting into the Moskvich. "I would also like to help Tystsevich. Yet he knew the risk he was taking, the same as we did."

"It's against my better judgment too," admitted the Death Merchant. "But he risked his life to get the car to the area. He deserves better treatment than for us to pull out and leave him standing in the rain. Anyhow, he's here, so shut up about him." He inserted a full magazine into the feed-slot of the Ingram SMG. "Gluzman, drive straight to the truck inspection station where Alexey Perchany is waiting. Do you know the location of the station?"

"Yes, but—" Gluzman glanced at Zoya Beliyev.

"What!" Zoya turned and stared in disbelief at Camellion,

who had just sent a round into the firing chamber of the MAC/ Ingram. "We're supposed to meet a vegetable truck in the woods only a short distance from here. But—" she paused. "I suppose with this rain. . . ."

"Exactly. It's not dew pounding down out there," Camellion said. "You told me yourself, back at Gagarin's place, that you had covered every possibility with your organizing, and that included the possibility of rain—right?"

She nodded slowly. "Misha is probably not even there. I instructed him and Tystsevich that if it rained and it appeared that their vehicles might become stuck not to chance it, but to drive away."

"Scott is right. It would be stupid for us to go into any area that could be turned into mud," said Tarkovsky, who could be angry one moment and practical the next. He was not a man to carry a grudge—one of the things that Camellion liked about him.

Mollified by the Death Merchant's tough realism, Zoya settled down and presently asked, "Scott, when are you going to contact your people on the shortwave? We can't stop in the middle of the road and park."

"And we can't pull off to any place that is hidden, not in this rain," said Semyon Gluzman.

"I'll use the radio at the inspection station," Camellion replied as he wondered if the rain had loosened any of the "moles" fastened to his body. Or if the rain had wet the T-14yB. If so, would the neurotoxin be absorbed into his body? *Then, I'm a dead Richard Camellion!* "The two men at the station won't be able to say anything to the authorities, because they're up to their eyebrows in smuggling."

"It is still a risk," Zoya said in a small voice. "Only a fool wouldn't suspect the truth, once they saw your radio."

"In that case, I'd have to put them to sleep forever," Camellion answered. "But I don't think we'll have to use the radio at the station. On the way into Siberia, I studied the interior of the trailer. I believe there's a way we can use the AN-URC transmitter from inside it while the rig is rolling. How about Pytor Angara? He'd better be Perchany's relief driver."

"Perchany said he would be," replied Zoya. "Angara will go with us to the submarine."

The group lapsed into silence, an explosive, tension-filled silence broken only by the *flub-flub flub-flub* of the windshield wipers moving back and forth and an occasional growl of thunder.

The Death Merchant and the tiny band of Russians were three miles from the inspection station when they saw lights in the distance. Another vehicle was approaching them at a high rate of speed.

Chapter Eleven

There are only two kinds of opposite awareness: Things seem to be what the world says they are, or they are known for what they really are. Lieutenant Colonel Boris Rudneva knew the situation for what it really was: The destruction of SPH UZh-15/5 was a catastrophe of the first magnitude. So was the escape of Georgi Ulomov.

Rudneva also considered it inexcusable that Lieutenant Ivor Gryaznoi had not notified him by phone until after a full forty-three minutes had passed from the time the guards heard the first shot from the hospital.

"Comrade Colonel Rudneva, we did not have time to notify you," Gryaznoi had reported. "We were too busy fighting the fires—for what good it did us."

Still in his pajamas, Rudneva had snarled, "Where are Kipeka and Dr. Libinsky? Why didn't one of them phone?"

"They are both dead. Colonel, sir, the warehouse, our headquarters, and our living quarters have been burned to the ground. The building of the hospital personnel has been wrecked. We have not yet counted the dead. Bodies are scattered all over the place."

There had been worse news. "Comrade Colonel, we can no longer function as an installation. The personnel and the patients will have to be moved to the work camp. I need your authority to do this, before I can confer with Comrade Major Gusbichev, the commander of the corrective labor camp."

Not having any choice, Rudneva had given his permission.

Captain Bodgan Konstantinn put down the phone and turned from the desk to Rudneva, who was standing at the window staring out into the gray and gloomy wet dawn, his hands clenched behind his back.

"Colonel, the helicopter will land on the roof at 0800," Konstantinn said.

Rudneva nodded and continued to stand at the window, his melancholy thoughts revolving around the conversation he had had with Major General Fedor Eristiv Chistka, the head of the First Chief Directorate of the KGB. After talking to Lieutenant Gryaznoi, Rudneva had telephoned Chistka in *Moskva*.

General Chistka had been furious and had screamed at Rudneva, "You god damn idiot! You're supposed to be a specialist in counterterrorism! How could one or two men have gotten inside the hospital complex, much less freed Ulomov and escaped with him? What the hell are you and your people doing in Siberia? Didn't you have your special units hidden around the outside of the hospital?"

"Comrade General, as you will recall, we agreed not to position men outside. It was part of our plan to let the traitors get inside with the American agents. And—"

"Damn it! There isn't any evidence that there are CIA agents in Siberia! How could I report such nonsense? How would that make our security look, especially counterintelligence?"

Rudneva had gone on doggedly, "Comrade General, it was you who insisted that I use extreme care to keep the people of Yakutsk and in other cities and towns from knowing what was going on."

"I know what I said," Chistka retorted. "What other measures have you taken since Ulomov's kidnapping? Understand me, Rudneva! Ulomov wasn't 'freed.' He didn't 'escape.' He was kidnapped!"

Rudneva had told Chistka that he had ordered the militia to intensify spot checks of all trucks and other vehicles on the Yakutsk–Okhotsk Highway. He also explained about the nitrophenylpentadienal, the NPPD chemical tracking agent that had been used to coat the hands and feet of Dr. Georgi Ulomov.

"At this very moment there are four chemical technicians in four different vans combing the area," Rudneva had said. "We'll find Dr. Ulomov. When we do, we'll find the American agents and the Soviet traitors. It's raining hard in this part of Siberia, but water will not remove NPPD."

Rudneva's report had not filled General Chistka with any enthusiastic confidence. "You are still convinced that the traitors and the CIA agents leading them will take Ulomov to the east coast and attempt to escape by submarine! Well, aren't you?"

"I am convinced that's what they will do, Comrade General." Rudneva hated being forced into reaffirming his sincere belief, for he realized that he could be wrong. If he were, General Chistka would be the first to use the mistake against him.

"And why not south, Rudneva?"

"It's a matter of distance, of logic. The south is too far. All they could look forward to would be the northern coast of China. How could they get into China the way we have the border guarded not only with guards but six divisions of crack troops? They can't head north and the west is out. I don't think they want to go to *Moskva*. But it's less than five hundred kilometers to the east coast, to the Sea of Okhotsk."

"It's only logical if you're right, Rudneva. You have started it. It is only right that you finish it. Is there anything else you need?"

"Comrade General Chistka, I should appreciate it if you would confer with General Nikoley Proskurov. I want border guards moved into position along the coast of the Sea of Okhotsk, thirty kilometers to the north of Okhotsk, thirty kilometers to the south, and I should like to be put in command of the troops for the next two weeks."

Just as Rudneva turned from the window, the phone on the desk rang. Captain Konstantinn picked up the receiver, said, "Yes, this is Colonel Rudneva's office," listened for a moment, then said, "I'll inform Comrade Colonel Rudneva."

Rudneva knew at once, from Konstantinn's expression, that the news was not good; nonetheless, he said, "Was it one of the tracking vans?"

"No, sir." Konstantinn replaced the receiver on its cradle. "It was the militia. One of their patrols just found a wrecked jeep and six dead militiamen on a side road not far from the mental hospital. Nearby they found a Zhukova-1. It had been blown up. Apparently the militia patrol found the car and attacked but were ambushed by the terrorists who had been inside."

Sucking in his lower lip, Colonel Rudneva sank to a chair, uncertainty shooting around like electricity in his mind. If the terrorists and Dr. Ulomov had used the Zhukova-1, where were they now? How could they get to the east coast? Surely they knew that all vehicles on the Yakutsk–Okhotsk Highway would be stopped!

Rudneva wrenched his mind away from the black blanket of depression and got to his feet. There was only one answer: Seal off the coast so tightly that no one would be able to get out to the sea.

Or in from the sea.

Chapter Twelve

There was no room to jog in the rear of the first trailer behind the Vanda diesel tractor that Alexey Perchany was driving. It was not that the Death Merchant and the six Russians were packed together like sardines in a flat can. However, peace and contentment cannot be found in what amounts to an eight-by-seven "closet" whose only "doors" were wooden cases filled with ballbearings and gears of various sizes.

Add to this mixture the uncertainty of not knowing how long you might remain alive and having only water to drink and a few sausages each for a journey that would last fifteen to eighteen hours—depending on the weather—and the situation was miserable and depressing.

The group had plenty to worry about. Security was full of rips and gaps. Besides the two men at the inspection station, the men who had loaded the trailers in Yakutsk were privy to what they considered a black market operation. It was they who had arranged the space in the rear of the trailer. The crates that were supposed to fill the area would be sold on the black market, and the loaders would also get their share of the pie. If anything went wrong and the KGB learned of the operation and forced a confession from one of the loaders . . .

For illumination, there were two battery-powered lanterns. Only one was burning, the beam turned toward the wall of chained crates so as not to create glare. There were four large wooden buckets with lids for the elimination of body wastes.

Sufficient air was not a problem. At the front end and in the rear were ventilation vents on the sides of each trailer. There was also a tightly sealed hatch in the rear roof of each trailer. When the trailers were loaded with vegetables, chunks of ice could be dropped through the hatches into containers that resembled long cages made of very heavy wire, each container stretching horizontally across the inside top and fastened to the roof by bolts. The hatch could be opened from inside the trailer but could be locked only from the outside.

There hadn't been any difficulty after Camellion and the members of the *Charodeika Otdel* had reached the State inspection station. Perchany had parked the rig to the rear of the station building, and Camellion and the others, except for Ulomov and one of the station men, had gone to work moving crates and making a narrow passage, on the left side, to the secret space in the rear. Though the boxes weren't large, they were heavy with gears or ballbearings. But since fear always produces energy in extra amounts, it only took a bit more than forty minutes to clear the way to the rear of the trailer and for the Death Merchant to run the small cable through the right air vents. The cable was for Perchany or Angara to tug to notify the trailer inhabitants that things looked safe. It took another fifty minutes for Perchany, Angara, and one of the station employees to seal the "passage" to the rear. The Death Merchant had made certain of two things: that the hatch on top was unlocked and that he had several large screwdrivers and a set of socket wrenches.

By dawn, the tractor and its two trailers were twenty-one miles east of the inspection station. With each second it was farther and farther from Tarialag. The Death Merchant and his group considered themselves very lucky. Three different times, as they had been unloading and then reloading the trailer, militia jeeps had sped by on the wide highway, sirens screaming, blue-and-red strobe lights revolving. From the highway the militiamen could see only a part of the cab and half of the second trailer. No matter how much of the rig they might see, there wasn't any reason for them to be suspicious. It was a common enough sight to see State-owned trucks parked around an inspection station. In the Soviet Union, these stations were the equivalent of the American truck stop. There drivers could eat, rest, take on fuel, and get their vehicles checked.

It had been 10 P.M., during the evening of the same day, that Camellion used the AN/URC-101 transceiver to contact the CIA station in northern Japan. It had not been difficult for him to run the antenna cable—half the size of a pencil in thickness —from the transceiver through one of the ventilator slots on the right side of the trailer. From the outside of the slot, the cable stretched to the right side of the tractor and ended in the satellite dish—which wasn't a concave reflector but a nineteen-inch square framework of aluminum to which numerous wires were attached. On one side was the handle. Angara held the handle, his right arm extended through the window, the "dish" pointed upward toward the bleak night sky.

Perchany would jerk on the antenna cable to signal that it was safe for Angara to hold the dish and for Camellion to turn on the set and transmit. This could occur only when the rig was on a very long stretch of straight highway and Perchany could see ahead and behind for miles.

Four times Camellion had sent the time of arrival out into the airwaves, frequency-hopping over 2300 MHz channels, the time when he and the Russians would be on the beach waiting for the commandos from the *George Washington. We will be on the beach in nineteen hours,* Camellion had told the CIA, estimating from the time the rig had left the inspection station.

He did not have to give the coordinates of the location on the beach. The pickup locale would be the very same spot where, weeks earlier, he had come ashore—sixteen miles south of Okhotsk. The location made Alexey Perchany and Pytor Angara the men of the hour. They were the only ones who knew how to get there.

Tarkovsky was on his hands and knees, doing his best to hold his body steady. Standing in his bare feet on Tarkovsky's back, Camellion jammed the socket wrench into his belt. The nut was now loose enough for him to turn it off the rest of the way with his fingers. On either side of him, Tsipin and Gluzman were standing, their arms above their heads, their hands pushing against the bottom of the ice container. Beliyev held the lantern, angling it so that light from the side part of the beam shone on Camellion's work area.

The nut turned free of the bolt, and Camellion stepped down to the floor. "Let's take a break," he said. "We have only two more nuts to go."

"Scott, it's a waste of time to take the ice cage down." Zoya lowered the lantern. "If the militia or the KGB finds out that we're back here, what chance would we have? We'd have to crawl out of the hatch one by one."

"I suppose we'd have about as much chance as a snowball dropped into a bucket of boiling water," Camellion said, looking up at the container. He had removed all but two nuts, one at each end, which he had loosened. Without Tsipin and Gluzman holding the cage up against the roof, it rocked back and forth from the movement of the trailer, making creaking sounds.

Standing up, Tarkovsky arched himself forward to take the kinks out of his back. "Once we have the cage on the floor and tilt one end against the back wall, we'll at least be able to use it to crawl up to the hatch. That would beat hoisting each other up to the opening."

Tsipin gave a giggly laugh. "Who would lift the last person up? I say that one chance is better than no chance at all."

Boris Tystsevich, sitting on the floor with his knees up against his chin, said in a low, strained voice, "I hope the two men at the station got rid of the Moskvich in time. It's been reported missing by now, and the police might have connected it with what happened yesterday. There are so many uncertainties. . . ."

With her foot, Zoya Beliyev pushed at the small wooden box containing the heroin syrup. "Those two crooks at the station don't want to get caught. We can be sure that they drove the car down the highway and parked it in some out-of-the-way place. Anyhow, there isn't anything we can do about it, not here, not now."

Camellion glanced around him. "Let's get at the last two nuts. I want us to have easy access to the hatch above."

He hadn't said anything to the others, but he was positive that the worst was yet to come. Common sense demanded that—

The entire area around the beach will be crawling with border guards!

Chapter Thirteen

A mile and a half from the pickup area on the beach—17½ miles south of the port city of Okhotsk. 2400 hours—two hours before the scheduled rendezvous.

The rig had been stopped four different times by the militia during the previous hours, each time the militiamen asking to see Alexey Perchany and Pytor Angara's internal passports and their work orders from the Central Trucking and Transport Commission. The militia also made them open the two rear doors of the two trailers and remove a dozen or so crates.

Except the fourth time. The fourth time, there had been three jeep loads of militia and one jeep filled with KGB border guard officers. This time, Perchany, Angara, and eight militiamen had unloaded half of the second trailer. They had then reloaded it and moved on to the first trailer, the one directly behind the cab.

Almost afraid to breathe, the Death Merchant and the Russians with him could hear enough of the conversation outside to know what was happening. Weapons in their hands, they waited and listened as Perchany, Angara, and the militiamen began to move crates from the rear of the first trailer. There could be only one solution. Once one or two crates from the last row—in front of the Death Merchant and his people—were removed, the hollow space would be discovered. All Camellion and his group could do then would be to push over the rest of the crates and come out firing while Tarkovsky—waiting on the ice to open the hatch—would start lobbing grenades to each side and to the rear of the trailer.

Perchany, Angara, and the militia stopped the unloading only two rows of crates away from the hollow space concealing the Death Merchant and his group. Then the crates that had been removed were put back and the chains between the doors and the last row of crates replaced and tightened. The doors were closed and locked and the drivers permitted to continue the journey to Okhotsk in the dark, overcast night.

Now, five hours and twenty-six minutes later, Perchany had driven two miles off the regular highway route and was moving the big Vanda over what could have been a road but wasn't. It was a very large area of granite rock on which lay—scattered here and there—a thin layer of topsoil, which nurtured short grass and weeds. As the granite outcroppings neared the beach, the soil gave way to sand. And then there was no rock, only sand, and finally the waves.

Perchany had told Camellion and the others that when the ride became very bumpy and when they could hear great black-billed gulls, they would be very close to the pickup area. The truck slowed to only 20 mph, and the ride became very uncomfortable as the big wheels rolled over uneven slabs of granite. There was no screeching of gulls, for it was night and the birds had their bills tucked under their wings and were fast asleep.

Every single bit of Richard Camellion's luck ran out when the truck was a bit over a mile and a half away from the beach. Coming from the direction of the highway—sirens and strobe lights off—two six-man jeeps and a Zhiguli raced after the Vanda and caught up with it. One of the jeeps pulled fifty feet in front of the tractor, the driver jammed on the brakes, and rubber burned on rock. Four of the militiamen jumped out, pointed AKR assault rifles at the cab, which was slowing down, and yelled, *"Stop or we'll fire!"*

As Perchany applied the brakes to the large rig, the second jeep jerked to a halt to the left side of the cab. The black Zhiguli stopped to the right, between the first and second trailers. All six militiamen from the jeep on the left side jumped out, rushed over, and pointed rifles at Alexey Perchany, who was pretending to be terrified. The four militiamen from the other jeep ran to the right side and covered Angara with their AKRs. The three KGB officers—two from counterintelligence and one from the Chief Border Guards Directorate—hurried over to Perchany's side of the cab. One of them stepped up on the rung-step and jerked open the door while a militiaman opened the door on Angara's side and snarled, "Get out of there and keep your hands in sight!"

Inside the "dead" space of the first trailer, the Death Merchant and the group of Russian revolutionaries realized that every single cow patty had hit the big fan. This was not a simple spot-check on the highway. What excuse could Perchany give for being so far off his route and so close to the beach? The jeeps' arrival also proved to the Death Merchant that he had been right: Rudneva had deduced that the "terrorists" would head for the coast and be picked up by submarine, although it might be an ordinary patrol that had happened to stumble across the tractor and trailers.

Because the militiamen had not spoken in soft, gentle whispers, Camellion and most of the others had heard every word that they had said—and were saying. It was all very clear to Camellion, who had used the tilted ice container as a ladder, climbed to the top, cracked the square hatch cover, and was listening to every word. An Ingram SMG was in his right hand. Six RGD grenades were in his pockets. Another was in his left hand.

"What are you and your truck doing here? Why did you leave the main highway?" demanded Captain Lenordi Byhairin, the KGB counterintelligence officer who was attached to Colonel Rudneva's special unit. "And don't tell us you got 'lost.' And before either of you say anything, remember Article 181 of the RSFSR Criminal Code concerning responsibility for deliberately giving false statements."

Perchany, standing only four feet from Byhairin, fcigncd extreme nervousness, his mouth half open, his eyes wide. So did Angara. A hunched-over man with a sad face and a Pinocchio-like nose, he faked high fear and confusion.

"But, Comrade, didn't you see it?" Perchany asked to Byhairin. "Surely you must have seen it streak down out of the sky and dive toward the sea?"

"We saw it. We both did. We both saw it!" Angara said excitedly.

Byhairin frowned. "Saw what? And what the hell do you mean—something streaked out of the sky? We haven't seen any planes in this area."

"Oh, no, Comrade," Perchany said quickly. "What we saw was round and as large as a house. We could see it clearly in the darkness because of the flashing red-and-yellow lights in rings around it. I tell you, Comrade, whatever it was could not have been of this world."

"It's a lot of nonsense!" sneered Lieutenant Paul Norvorzhev, another KGB officer. "We want to know right now why you two left the highway and came here."

"Comrade, we are telling you why we came to this spot," Pytor Angara said, whining submission in his voice. "We came here to find the strange craft. The way it came down, it had to have landed very close to here. Comrades, you must have seen the round thing!"

"Let's see your passports, your *spravki,* and your orders from the trucking commission," ordered Byhairin, "and let's not hear any more nonsense about flying saucers. Be quick about it."

"Certainly, Comrade," replied Perchany and Angara. They reached into their jackets, pulled out their *kharakteristiki* and *spravki,* and handed the papers to Byhairin. Perchany also produced his manifest and special movement orders from the State Trucking Commission, and said indignantly, "We are honest, patriotic citizens. Yet *Cu'z Bógom*—my God! We are chased and being made to submit to this indignation as though we were criminals. Why, there is a jeep on our left side, a jeep only fifteen meters in front of the cab, and"—his voice rose in volume—"a car on the right between the trailers. What is so terrible about wanting to see a strange craft that has landed?"

The Death Merchant, about to push open the hatch, smiled. Perchany had done a good job of tipping him off about how the enemy was dispersed. No fools, Perchany and Angara knew that the KGB and the militia were not about to let them go on their way, not before every crate in both trailers had been removed. More likely the KGB would take the truck and drivers to KGB headquarters in Yakutsk.

Camellion clipped the Ingram to the ring on his belt. The men in the jeep in front of the cab were the number-one danger: They would have a clear field of fire at the hatch. The rest of the pig farmers would not be a problem. *I'll only have to be careful not to hit Perchany and Angara.*

Camellion pulled the pin from the grenade and clamped his left hand tightly around it, holding down the handle. With his right hand, he unclipped the Ingram SMG from the ring and looked down at the Russians in the trailer staring up at him. "Zoya, turn off the light," he whispered. "I don't want the glow showing when I open the hatch." As soon as she turned off the lantern, he started to push the stubby barrel of the Ingram against the inner side of the square hatch cover in the ceiling.

Captain Byhairin was returning Angara's passport, and Norvorzhev was beginning to put together why Perchany had itemized the positions of the vehicles around the tractor and trailers when the Death Merchant threw back the hatch and stood up tall on the ice container, so that half of his body was outside of the opening.

Every second of lag time was with Camellion, who tossed the RGD and was swinging the Ingram to the right and squeezing the trigger as the grenade exploded only seven feet from the side of the jeep parked in front of and parallel to the cab. There was a terrific BERUUUMMMM! A flash of fire, and the jeep tilted dangerously but did not turn over. Neither did the two militiamen. They only slumped dead from the concussion that had hemorrhaged their brains.

During those few micromoments, Perchany and Angara, having known what was going to happen, dropped to the ground. In contrast, the militiamen and the KGB agents jerked their heads toward the Ingram chattering from the top front of the first trailer.

In only a few seconds the four militia troopers on the right side of the cab were blown away by the Ingram's THV .45 slugs, tiny pieces of their uniforms fluttering down around Angara, who was trying to roll underneath the cab.

On the left side of the cab, Alexey Perchany was rolling under the rig as slugs from the chattering Ingram chopped into the six troopers and the three KGB agents. Byhairin's head seem to jump six inches from his neck. It had. Three .45 THV slugs had almost decapitated him. He fell with his head held by only a strand of flesh and flopping like a football, bouncing back and forth between his shoulder blades. The blood spurting from the stub of his neck splashed all over Lieutenants Norvorzhev and Josef Perikiriv. Both men were stone dead, their upper chests having been ripped open by the axelike *Très Haute Vitesse* projectiles.

Two of the militia troopers gave short, sharp cries of agony as .45 slugs sliced through their uniforms and stabbed into their flesh. A third fell backward with his face erased and his exploded head flying all over a fourth man who had almost dropped to the ground in time. Two of Camellion's slugs missed him. The third smacked him in the top of his peaked uniform cap and opened up his skull—exactly the way a balloon explodes when hit by a pellet gun.

The last two troopers did manage to drop to the ground and escape the Death Merchant's tornado of .45 metal—for all the good it did them. Perchany had pulled a Tokarev auto pistol and had pumped two 7.62 mm slugs into each man.

As quickly as the firing had begun, it stopped, and there was a crashing high-tension-filled silence broken only by the Death Merchant's feet hitting the top of the cab as he jumped from the roof of the trailer, a Steyr pistol in his left hand, the almost-empty Ingram in his right. By the time he had jumped from the roof of the cab to the ground, Perchany and Angara were getting to their feet.

"All of you inside the trailer—out! And bring the shortwave with you!" Camellion yelled to Zoya and the other Russians. Then he said to Alexey Perchany, who was pulling a Vitmorkin machine pistol from the bloody corpse of Perikiriv, "We'll drive the rest of the way in one of the jeeps. We'll make better time. The truck's usefulness is over."

"Why not the Zhiguli?" Perchany's thickset face broke into a deathhead's grin. "We could go the rest of the way in style."

"And we could get our heads blown off!" Camellion said. He glanced at his wristwatch. "Right now it's only an hour before the scheduled linkup with the American commandos from the sub. You can bet your last drop of vodka their commander sent scouts. They could mistake us in the enclosed Zhiguli for Soviet officials. In the jeep, the commandos will be able to see us through night-vision devices and know we're not KGB."

He glanced at the truck. Sergei Tsipin was jumping from the trailer to the cab and Kirill Tarkovsky was coming through the hatch saying, "Pass the radio up to me, Zoya."

With Perchany hunched over the wheel, the crowded jeep bounced along over granite slabs covered with patches of sand, soil, pebbles, and vegetation. With each second the sound of the breakers grew louder, for along this section of the coast of the Sea of Okhotsk there were enormous rocks piled haphazardly at the edge of the shore, natural formations of sandstone and oligoclase, which were exfoliated and striated, some, at the water's edge, rounded by wave action. For a stretch of twelve miles along the twisted beach, there were only four areas where it was possible to come ashore. The jeep's destination was one of those areas, a section of beach only 150 feet wide, between jagged rocks over which waves smashed dangerously. Yet along that 150 feet there were no rocks, and the water rolled over smooth sand—perfect for a boat landing from a surface craft or a submarine.

Perchany stopped the jeep in almost the exact same spot where he had parked the tractor and trailer weeks earlier, a fifth of a mile southwest of where the Death Merchant and the commandos had come ashore.

"The militia or the *Kah Gay Beh* border guards could be observing us at this very moment," said Kirill Tarkovsky, getting out of the jeep. He hoped his warning would spark a deeper caution in *"Tovarishch* Scott." What kind of caution? All the group could do was go to the area and wait. And hope.

The Death Merchant pulled the small night-vision scope from a pocket of his jacket. He hated the clothes he was wearing. The pants were of rough wool and scratched the skin, and since they had gotten wet and dried, they irritated him more than ever.

"The KGB could be watching from a distance," he said. "I doubt it. More likely, they have sound detectors scattered around, in which case Colonel Rudneva—if he came to this section of Siberia—knows there's been a shootout."

"You're saying a force of border guards could be here in a short while," Tarkovsky said.

"Exactly." The Death Merchant began to survey the entire area through the scope. There wasn't anyplace where the enemy could hide—*Not behind us! In front is a different matter.* Ahead were rocks and boulders, some as small as a marble, others as large as a pickup truck. However, it wasn't likely that any troops would be behind any rocks—*Or the KGB would have had to know in advance the exact location of the pickup. Do it!*

"Let's move out," Camellion said to the group. "Perchany,

you and Comrade Angara lead the way. Tarkovsky, you take up the rear. Dr. Ulomov, stay with me. Comrade Tsipin, whatever you do, don't leave the shortwave behind. It's of advanced design, and we can't allow it to fall into KGB hands."

The group proceeded cautiously, moving to the northeast. As they moved into the field of rocks, there wasn't any way they could protect themselves. They were surrounded by rocks, and enemy troops could be all around them. If so, they would never know it until it was too late.

It happened when they were eight hundred feet from the rendezvous area on the beach. From the left, a voice—from the side of a rock ten feet to the left—called out in English, "We're friendlies! Don't get trigger-happy!"

Another voice called out from the right, and farther to the front, "We're the ones you're supposed to meet. Stand still and we'll come to you."

The Death Merchant and the Russians stopped. All except Tystsevich and Tsipin understood English. Camellion whispered, "They're commando scouts. Don't do anything rash." Circuits of remembrance were clicking in his mind. The first voice had been very familiar. It was the voice of a man he hadn't seen in over a year and a half. *But it can't be!*

It could be and was. When the man came forward, a Heckler and Koch M-91 assault rifle in his hands, Camellion saw that he was James Victorio O'Malley, better known as the Peppermint Kid. The wiry Briton, an explosives and underwater demolitions expert, had for years been a member of Colonel Michael Quinlan's Thunderbolt Unit Omega, the most professional group of mercenaries in the world. Mad Mike and his TUO boys had fought all over Africa, Central and South America, and the Middle East.

O'Malley was dressed in a diver's black wetsuit and had a holstered SIG-Sauer P226 pistol belted around his waist. The belt also contained pouches filled with extra magazines for the assault rifle. Instead of flippers on his feet, O'Malley wore canvas tennis shoes.

"I must be in the wrong movie," Camellion said with a slight laugh, knowing that since O'Malley was there, Mad Mike Quinlan had to be close by. "How many of you came ashore, Kid? And where's Mike?"

Thirty feet ahead, the other Thunderbolt commando stepped out. He was also dressed in a wetsuit and carrying an H & K assault rifle.

"Heh heh heh." Chuckling, O'Malley looked over the group of Russians with critical eyes. For years he had fought the cockroaches of Soviet client nations and considered anything Russian slightly lower than the belly button of a beetle. Then his eyes settled on Richard Camellion. "What name are you using 'ere, Yank?"

"Arnold Scott!" Camellion laughed. "How about some answers?"

"Thirty of us came ashore, Scott. We've been here an hour. Mike's down at the beach." O'Malley motioned for Stavros Kotzias, the other merc, to move out toward the beach. Kotzias, a former officer in the Greek air force, nodded and crooked a finger at Alexey Perchany.

"I gather that you haven't detected any KGB border guard troops," Camellion said as they moved between the rocks.

"Not a single one of the bloody bastards," O'Malley replied. "But the blighters 'ave patrol boats moving up and down the coast. We 'ave another problem with Commander Wesson, the skipper of the sub. The bloody fool thinks that the damned Ivans can't detect the boat. He's either got his knickers down around his ankles or else there's something going on we don't know about, eh, Yank?"

Camellion was positive he knew the reason for Wesson's "lack" of concern. The *George Washington* was protected by the Gf mechanism, an electromagnetic cloaking device that rendered the submarine not only visually invisible but also immune to electronic detection. This did not mean that the sub could not be destroyed. Even if an enemy sub or patrol boat couldn't "see" or "hear" the *George Washington*, a missile or torpedo could make contact and blow the boat out of the water, in spite of the Gf mechanism.

In a short time Camellion, the Peppermint Kid, and the rest of the group were on the beach and snuggled down with the Thunderbolts behind rocks of various sizes. The Death Merchant, Zoya Beliyev, and Kirill Tarkovsky were on the moist sands with Michael "Mad Mike" Quinlan and Wilhelm Bruckner, who was so huge he resembled an animated bulldozer.

Close by was Andre d'Albis, the merc at the Gould PCS-2001 transceiver.

Speaking German, Camellion got down to business: Why had the Thunderbolts replaced the SEAL commandos, and why had the mercs come ashore with "Slingshot" APILAS antiarmor launchers and shoulder-fired ground-to-air Viper missiles?

"Let's not play games, Richard," Quinlan replied matter-of-factly. "We replaced the SEALs because we're expendable. We're only mercs. And I suppose that Grojean assumed that the KGB might deduce where the pickup point is. We hold off the Ivans while you get the Prize to the sub. By the way, which one is he?"

Camellion tilted his head toward Dr. Ulomov. "That pathetic-looking pig farmer over there by O'Malley and the other two Russians. They drove the tractor-trailer. What about the sub? The Kid thinks its captain has slipped his gears."

An expression of amusement dropped over Quinlan's boyish face. He was a good-looking man with expressive brown eyes and brown hair worn moderately long. At 6'1" and weighing two hundred pounds, he was an inch taller and twenty pounds heavier than Camellion. "Hell, you know how O'Malley is. He's not content unless he's worrying about something."

"Ach! Was Sie sagen!" mocked "Krautie" Bruckner with a low, guttural laugh. He then became serious. "We know that the *Unterseeboot* has some kind of device protecting it. *Ja,* that is fine for the boat. But, *donnerwetter!* It makes our work on shore more difficult."

"Yeah, the sub can't raise its radio antenna," Camellion said. "What kind of communications setup do you have?"

Michael Quinlan said, "The thirty of us came ashore in five SCUTTs. After they dropped us off, about thirty or forty yards off-shore, they returned to the sub. We're stuck here like pimples on a teenager until we get word by radio that the SCUTTs are coming back for us. Captain Wesson said he'd give you an extra half an hour past the scheduled deadline. That gives us more than half an hour yet. One of the SCUTTs should be calling any moment now. Then we can get the hell out of here."

"What's the position of the sub?" Camellion let his eyes wander to one of the Thunderbolts who was operating a Debbler listening device, which was on a tripod and whose square-frame antenna was steadily revolving. A powerful instrument, the Debbler could pick up a whisper at five hundred feet.

Quinlan glanced at Zoya Beliyev, who was staring at him. He reached into an inside pocket of the field jacket he was wearing over his scuba suit and pulled out a pint of whiskey. "The boat is about seventeen klicks to the southeast," he said, uncapping the bottle, "and submerged at a hundred fathoms. In case you're interested, that's six hundred feet, or a hundred and eighty-two meters. Naturally, she'll have to come up four to five hundred feet when we meet her with the SCUTTs. What's with the 'Snow Queen' here? I trust she doesn't understand German?" He tilted the bottle to his lips and took a long drink.

"She's only curious, Mike," Camellion said, feeling worried. "How about the dry suits and air tanks for us? I hope to God one of the SCUTTs doesn't have to bring them to land."

Quinlan went "Ahhhhhh!" from the fire of the whiskey, then capped the bottle. "Not to worry, buddy. We have plenty of suits and tanks for you and the Ruskies. They're stored down by the water's edge with our own tanks. Right now all we can do is sit tight and enjoy the scenery."

"Ten thousand comedians are out of work and you're trying to be one!" Camellion cracked. "If we don't get out of here soon, we're going to become pop up targets!"

"Scott, tell us what is happening," Kirill Tarkovsky murmured in Russian, sounding as if his feelings had been hurt. "Why are we not preparing to go to the submarine? Isn't it there?"

"The submarine is there," Camellion said patiently. "We're waiting for the word to proceed. Patrol boats going up and down the coast are holding up the show." He then explained that all of them would be traveling underwater to the *George Washington,* that they would be wearing scuba suits and riding on SCUTTs. "SCUTT is short for *S*ubmerged *C*raft for *U*nderwater *T*actical *T*ravel."

A SCUTT was nothing more than two tanks with a control column and panel, ten metal seats on top, diving planes, a rudder, two engines, and two propellers. Let water into the tanks and the craft submerged. Blow the tanks with air and the craft surfaced. Speed fully loaded: three knots.

Feeling reassured, Beliyev and Tarkovsky were moving off to

tell the other Russians what was going on when the Thunderbolt at the sound detector called out in a cold and calm voice, "Colonel, we're getting company. Maybe a dozen vehicles, coming at us straight from the southwest. Not more than three klicks away."

"Hurensohn!"—son of a bitch!" Bruckner cursed in German, then said in accented English, "Ve couldn't be in a vorse position. Ve got to get our butts to der sea!"

"Our fronts aren't bulletproof either," drawled the Death Merchant, who had gone to a crate of spare weapons and was taking out two Gonez High-Tech semiautomatic pistols, choosing .45 ACP caliber, delighted when he saw that each magazine held thirty-eight staggered rounds.

"Andre, try to raise someone on the radio," Quinlan ordered, a fierce look in his brown eyes. "I'm not going to let any damned Soviet savages steamroller us, not by a long shot." He turned and motioned to the Peppermint Kid. "Jimmie, get over here."

The Death Merchant made his way over to Zoya Beliyev, who was explaining the facts of life to Dr. Ulomov. Camellion quickly warned the scientist, "Dr. Ulomov, whatever happens, keep down between these two rocks. Zoya, you stay with him. Do you have a weapon?"

She opened her jacket and patted the butt of a Vitmorkin machine pistol stuck in her belt. "It's fully loaded."

"Are we going to die, Mr. Scott?" Ulomov asked in a weak but ordinary voice, as if dying were as common as the rising and setting of the sun.

"Sure, twenty years from now," Camellion said easily. "But not this day. Remember what I said—stay down, both of you."

"Hey, Camellion! Take a look to the east!" Quinlan called out, not bothering to use the Death Merchant's alias. At this point, it didn't matter. Camellion, Scott, or Twinkledinger! Either they would get to the *George Washington* or they would die on shore or in the water on the way to the submarine.

Feeling better because of the two Gonez H-T pistols buckled around his waist, Camellion looked toward the sea. There were three sets of red lights two and a half miles from the shore—three Soviet patrol boats, each moving very slowly, two toward the north, one toward the south. The three Turya torpedo boats carried depth charges and electronic homing torpedoes.

"Mike, how many Slingshots do you have?" Camellion asked, turning to Quinlan, who had just been told by d'Albis that he couldn't raise either the *George Washington* or one of the SCUTTs.

"Hell, this is a fruitcake operation!" d'Albis complained. "Uncle Sam thinks more of that four-hundred-million-dollar submarine than he does of us. On the other hand, why shouldn't he?"

"Richard, I know what you're thinking," Quinlan said. "We have five Slingshots. I just told O'Malley how to have the boys deploy them and the GPMGs." He stabbed a finger toward the beach. The Death Merchant saw that Thunderbolts were placing an APILAS launcher and six missiles for each tube in rocks at each end of the 150-foot-long smooth beach.

A Slingshot APILAS—*A*rmor-*P*iercing, *I*nfantry, *L*ight *A*rm *S*ystem—was bulky and ungainly looking. The main body was a fifty-two-inch one-piece launch tube into which could be thrust a 108 mm missile with a shaped HE charge. The rocket engine of the missile was very fast burning and pushed the warhead along at better than 1,200 feet per second, to give a very short time of flight to its effective range of 300 yards. The warhead was so powerful it could dig right through 700 mm of armor or six feet of reinforced concrete.

"We brought three U.S. M-sixty general-purpose machine guns ashore," Quinlan said. "Under the circumstances, it's a damn good thing we did. I'm going to center one and place the other two at each end of the southwest perimeter. We'll deploy the other three Slingshots along the line to the southwest, say thirty feet apart." He made a face. "Don't stand there and bump your gums and tell me you have a better plan!"

"I wish I could and I wish I did, but I don't," Camellion said, sniffing the night air. "We do have one thing going for us—typical Russian overkill. They're no doubt bringing up BTRs to hem in what Colonel Rudneva—he's the KGB joker looking for us—believes to be a small group armed with only light weapons. Our salvation depends on the SCUFFs arriving in time—if the patrol boats don't blow them out of the water!"

"Let's take another look at the Debbler," Quinlan suggested.

He said in a lower voice, "Without the SCUFFs getting here on time, we won't last long."

He and the Death Merchant walked the short distance to the sound detector and looked at the red needle on the small control panel. It had swung to *H,* heavy.

Quinlan reached out a hand. "Let me have the headphones, Vito."

Rinletti removed the headphones and handed them to his boss. Mad Mike put one of the phones to his left ear and listened for a moment. Then he handed the headphones to Camellion, who slipped them over his head. The sound was loud and steady.

"A mile and a half at the most," he said. He pulled off the headphones and returned them to Rinletti. "Mike, can you spare some NV goggles and a walkie-talkie? I'm not going to sit here and wait. I'm going out there to do some scouting."

"Affirmative. We can spare Cylops for you and Kotzias," Quinlan said. "He was the other man with the Peppermint Kid when they met you. He's one of the best scouts I have. He should be Indian instead of Greek."

It took only five minutes for the Death Merchant and Stavros Kotzias to slip the straps of general-purpose Cylops night-vision goggles over their heads and to adjust the instruments over their faces. Camellion also carried a MASTR Tracer II walkie-talkie in a case on his belt.

"I'll report back once we know their strength," Camellion told Quinlan. "Meanwhile, make sure none of your men fire before we get back."

The Death Merchant and the mean-looking Kotzias turned and were soon lost among the rocks.

His eyes narrowed to slits, Vito Rinletti turned and looked at Mike Quinlan, who was putting a cylinder into a CAWS *(C*lose *A*ssault *W*eapons *S*ystem) Pancor Mk-3 Jackhammer shotgun, a weapon that looked like something out of the twenty-first century. For one thing, the magazine was a detachable cylinder that held ten rounds of twelve-gauge ammo. For another, the cylinder and all the shotgun's major subassemblies were injection-molded from a new high-strength synthetic material called Rynite SST.

"Colonel, who is that bird Camellion?" Rinletti asked.

"When he's around, you get the feeling that death is grinning and waiting to tap you on the shoulder."

Rinletti was more right than he would ever know, Mad Mike thought. Seeing that Bruckner was checking on the positions of the GPMGs, Mike got to one knee, pulled out his Tracer II W-T and waited. It was not at all complicated. Before dawn they would either be on the submarine—

Or dead in the Soviet Union. . . .

I'd rather be buried in a sewer!

Chapter Fourteen

More pleased with himself than he had been in weeks, Lieutenant Colonel Boris Rudneva looked at the map spread out on the swing-down table in his ACRV-2 command vehicle. Dressed in gray-green battle fatigues, Rudneva looked over at Captain Bodgan Konstantinn and Lieutenant Andrew Berchievimiv and smiled in satisfaction.

"As you can see, our armored vehicles and troop carriers can move within forty-five meters of the target area on the beach before they are stopped by large rocks," Rudneva said, "and with our patrol boats off-shore, there isn't a single possibility that the American agents and those traitors will escape." In response to a frown crossing Berchievimiv's high forehead, he demanded with a sneer, "Well, what's wrong with you, Lieutenant? You can read a map, can't you?"

"Yes, sir, I can, Comrade Colonel." Berchievimiv, a slim young man with white-blond hair and a slight Oriental cast to his eyes, was not impressed by Rudneva's rank or reputation. He continued promptly, "I only wish to point out that we haven't any concrete information about the number of the enemy and the weapons they might have at their disposal. We have pinpointed their location by our sound detectors; however, we—"

Captain Konstantinn was blunt in his interruption of his subordinate (he was also trying to score brownie points with his boss, Colonel Rudneva). "Let's not be ridiculous, Comrade Lieutenant," he said imperiously. "There can't be more than a dozen on the beach, fifteen at the most. The largest weapons they have are assault rifles and machine pistols, or what the Americans call submachine guns. The only reason we are surrounding them with armor is because we want them to know how hopeless their situation is. We want them to put down their arms without a fight and surrender. We want every single one of them alive."

"Comrade Lieutenant, what else were you going to say?" Rudneva asked coolly.

Lieutenant Berchievimiv remained firmly cautious.

"I think it is strange that our patrol boats haven't picked up any sounds of the submarine that was supposed to rescue the enemy. Even the *Stalin,* our own submarine, has not detected any enemy below the surface except that one time. That's when—"

"Comrade Lieutenant—" Konstantinn began in a loud voice.

This time Berchievimiv refused to be cut off. "That's when the patrol boats and the *Stalin* picked up the propeller noises of very tiny craft, and they were moving away from the shore. Suddenly those sounds stopped. It was as if those underwater craft suddenly vanished. That was two hours and"—he consulted his wristwatch—"seventeen minutes ago. Comrade Colonel, I feel something is very wrong."

Rudneva folded his hands on the map and said evenly, "The only thing wrong is that you can't envision what has happened. The American submarine was frightened off by the *Stalin.* That's why the targets are still there on the beach. The submarine has left them stranded—and we have them cornered, trapped. Captain Konstantinn, order all the vehicles to move in. Tell our driver we will remain in the center rear behind the third troop carrier."

Because a GP Cyclops night-vision instrument has a 2,500X system gain, IX magnification, the Death Merchant and Stavros Kotzias could see in the dark as clearly as if it were high noon in bright sunshine. They had crept forty-five yards to the southwest and had stopped their forward recon at the edge of the larger boulders. They weren't overjoyed at what they saw. Five hundred feet ahead, spread out forty to fifty feet apart, were four BTR-40 armored cars, the light machine guns in the turrets sticking out like blue-gray arms. Fifty feet behind the armored cars were five BTR-60 troop carriers. They, too, were fifty feet apart from each other.

Watching the two lines of approaching armor from the side of a boulder the size of a pickup truck, the Death Merchant was quick to spot the ACRV command vehicle in the rear. Was Colonel Rudneva in the vehicle? Not that it made all that much difference—*That pig farmer is only doing his job.*

"All that armor. The Slingshot missiles will turn them into junk!" muttered the bearded Kotzias, who wore a large gold ring in his right ear and carried a holstered 10X .357 Desert Eagle auto pistol. Like the rest of the Thunderbolt mercs, he carried weapons of his own choosing.

"Each carrier holds eighteen troops," Camellion whispered judiciously. "That's ninety men, not counting the two drivers in each vehicle. Then we have three men in each armored car. A total of a hundred and two men. Even you Thunderbolts can't win against such odds."

"Yeah! You mean if those vodka-drinking sons of bitches ever got to us, and they won't," Kotzias retorted with a growl. "Let's get the fuck out of here. They're only a hundred and twenty yards away, if that far. Once those carriers reach these rocks, the Ivans will pile out and we'll all be in a fuckin' fix."

Camellion and Kotzias were pulling down when one of the Soviet gunners in the turret of a BTR-40 spotted them clearly through the Korvv NV goggles he was wearing. He opened fire immediately with the turret's SGMB light machine gun.

Zingggg-zingggg-zingggg-zingggg! A typhoon of steel-cored spitzer-shaped projectiles stung the front of the big rock. Others stabbed over the spots where Camellion and the Greek had been, the cloud of slugs coming only half a heartbeat after the two men had pulled back. Amid the sound of a hundred ricochets, sharp rock chips stabbed at the Death Merchant and Stavros Kotzias, some stinging their necks.

"We'd better get back fast," Kotzias suggested. He appeared puzzled when he saw Camellion pull the Tracer II walkie-talkie from its case on his belt.

"We don't have time to get back to the beach before reporting to Mike," Camellion said in a lazy and bored voice. "Those carriers have to be knocked out before they reach these rocks and start discharging their troops. If even half those Ivans reach the beach, we'll be sitting in hell before daylight."

He switched on the Tracer II and in clipped tones reported to Quinlan, finishing with "Have your boys with the antiarmor stuff open fire right now. Kotzias and I will keep very low and crawl back—and, Mike, have only your center GPMG open up on the armored cars. That will make it more difficult for them to fire at the Thunderbolts with the Slingshots. Of course, if the carriers stop and troops pile out, open up with everything you have—over."

Quinlan's voice came out of the walkie-talkie transceiver. "Yeah, I got it. You and Stavi start eating dirt. We're going to open up now—out."

"We're not going to stay and observe the hits?" Kotzias sounded angry, and the criticism in his voice was obvious.

"Being crazy-brave would only prove we're amateurs," Camellion said, shoving the walkie-talkie into its case. "There's a time to stand and fight and a time to run. Let's move it." Then as an afterthought: "A lot of those Ivans will get through. You'll get a bellyful of blood before this night is over."

They hadn't crawled ten feet on their hands and knees when the first 108 mm APILAS shot over the rocks. They neither saw nor heard it. The missile was traveling too fast, far faster than human eyes and ears could transmit images and vibrations to the brain for thought interpretation. The three border guards in a BTR armored car—the one farthest to the north—didn't see or hear it either. They didn't even feel the results of the missile's action. They died too quickly. The charge hit the foundation-mount of the turret and exploded with a terrific crash and a huge flash of bright-red fire. Within the blink of an eye, the armored car was destroyed, hundreds of its parts flying in all directions. When the smoke and flames cleared, there was only burning junk and no sign of the crew. A few severed arms and legs and a bloody head were lying on the rocks though.

Caught in a trap of Colonel Rudneva's making, the Ivans in the armored vehicles were too far from safety to retreat. Utterly astonished by the explosion, the drivers of the BTR-40s and the BTR-60 carriers began to zig and zag their vehicles, hoping they could reach the larger rocks to the northeast before more tank-busting missiles came their way. They might as well have hoped for human rights in the Soviet Union!

BERUUUUUM! BLAMMMMMM! There were two more mammoth flashes of fire and smoke and earth-quaking concussions, and numerous parts of another armored car and a

BTR-60 troop carrier took to the wind with the speed of meteors.

A well-constructed vehicle, an amphibious eight-wheeled BTR-60 is boat-shaped for good swimming and to deflect hostile fire. Power steering is on the four front wheels, and tire pressures are centrally controlled at all times. Its armor is 12.7 mm thick, which meant that it might as well have been toilet paper as far as an 108 mm APILAS missile was concerned. Nor did the troop carrier's low, sleek shape help. A Slingshot missile is heat-sensitive. Each missile can dip or turn, but it always finds the target.

BERUUUUUM! A third armored car exploded as the fourth and the last BTR-40 and the remaining four BTR-60 troop carriers began to rake the rocks ahead with hot streams of SGMB and 12.7 mm machine-gun fire.

A Slingshot missile exploded the fourth armored car just as it stopped at the line of crooked boulders, the TNT turning it into a flaming coffin for its crew of three, who were torn apart as the vehicle itself dissolved into chunks of hot metal.

A few seconds later another missile hit a second troop carrier. Again there was a terrific blast and a shower of flaming metal and dismembered bodies soaring upward, then downward to splatter on the ground and further wet the rocks with warm blood, rubble, and the leftovers from massive destruction. One of the big wheels came down, bounced, then rolled at an angle in front of Colonel Rudneva's ACRV-2 command car.

Drivers of two of the BTR carriers had not waited for any orders. They had used common sense and stopped their vehicles sixty-five feet from the large rocks, realizing that the eighteen troops inside each carrier would have a better chance for life by leaving the metal deathtraps and racing the rest of the way on foot.

The third BTR carrier had succeeded in reaching the rocks. Troops were getting out the wide rear hatch and frantically darting into openings between the rocks. However, many were cut down by 7.62 mm NATO projectiles from the Thunderbolts' three general-purpose M-60 machine guns. Now the GPMGs on each end of the area had joined the third M-60 firing down the slot from the center.

The only vehicle now fully exposed to Thunderbolts with

Slingshots was Colonel Boris Rudneva's ACRV command car. It was trapped unless its terrified driver could travel the rest of the way to the rocks—134 feet.

Colonel Rudneva, his face as white as chalk, screamed at the driver through the communications system, "God damn it! Get us out of here! Get to those rocks, you idiot!"

Stunned by the unexpected turn of events—as were Konstantinn and Berchievimiv—Rudneva realized that his career in the KGB was finished. Even if he captured the American agents, KGB Central would hold him responsible for the loss of four armored cars and two troop carriers—and how many men? He'd be lucky if he ended up as a clerk in some remote outpost!

Rudneva had worried needlessly. Not one but two 108 mm Slingshot warheads hit the command vehicle, the second only a hundredth of a moment behind the first. The explosions—they sounded as one—were so violent that jagged pieces of metal clanked down on even the troop carrier parked by the rocks, flaming chunks stabbing two border guards in the neck and back, killing them.

Not a trace was left of the command vehicle and its occupants, who had been changed into a fine spray of flesh and blood and bone now being borne by the wind on a last wild journey.

Richard Camellion and Stavros Kotzias reached the beach northeast of the rocks at about the same time that KGB border guards began pouring into the southwest side of the boulders. The two moved over to Mike Quinlan and Wilhelm Bruckner, each of whom was standing at the end of a minimonolith sticking up from the sands like an enormous flat finger. Both were facing the southwest and waiting for some sign of the Ivans.

All up and down the line, Thunderbolts were calmly waiting. They had been in similar situations many times and had always won. To a man, however, they realized that the day would have to come when they would lose. So what? No man lives forever.

"What damage did your boys do?" Camellion asked Quinlan.

"They scratched four armored cars, two of the carriers, and the command vehicle," replied Mad Mike. "There's no way of knowing how many were killed by the GP machine guns. Either way we're outnumbered. The good news came over the radio five minutes ago. The SCUTTs will be here shortly."

Stavros Kotzias cut in. "How in hell can the SCUTTs get through without the patrol boats out there detecting them and doing something about it?"

"How many men did you lose, Mike?" The Death Merchant pulled off the Cyclops night-vision instrument and shoved it into a shoulder bag. "Stavros has a good question. They must have said something to you over the radio about protection for the SCUTTs."

"Yeah, they told us over the Gould. They said not to worry about any of the patrol boats. I have to assume that the Navy boys know what they're doing."

Camellion pulled out one of the Gonez High-Tech pistols and pushed off the safety. "The Ivans will be here before the SCUTTs arrive. Mike, we're going to have to do it the hard way."

A lopsided grin twisted its way over Mike Quinlan's mouth. "We almost always have to do it the hard way. How good are the pig farmers who came in with you?"

"Ach! I never saw a Russian yet who was good for anything but fertilizer!" "Krautie" Bruckner spat contemptuously on the ground.

"Those that came in with me are different," said Camellion, annoyed at Bruckner's blind hatred of anything Russian. "They can fight, and they're more than willing, even the woman, Zoya Beliyev. She's between two rocks by the beach, she and the Prize."

"We could station some of the boys around them," offered Quinlan.

"No!" Camellion's low voice was sharp. "That would only draw attention to them. They can't be seen where they are, and if the Ivans ever get that far, we'll be dead meat and it won't make any difference. All we can—"

The sound of an enormous blast to the east made him and the others turn and look out over the shore to the sea. They were in time to see fire fading from the explosion that had destroyed one of the Soviet patrol boats.

BERUMMMMMM! Another column of fire was born, and another patrol boat was blown up by torpedos that had streaked from the *George Washington* and through the electromagnetic barrier protecting the Alpha submarine.

"I guess the Navy boys did know what they were talking about," Mike Quinlan said smugly. "The Russians have as much chance against that sub as a jungle bunny in Harlem has of learning calculus!"

"And the 'between'—between now and the time we're on the SCUFFs—will be harder than learning French," Camellion said. When he saw the faces of Bruckner and Kotzias cloud over with puzzlement, he explained that in French there are nine tenses in the indicative, two in the conditional, and four in the subjunctive. "This means dozens of special endings to memorize—if you want to speak French properly. But now's not the time to—"

He didn't have time to finish. All up and down the line, submachine guns and assault rifles, in the hands of Thunderbolts, began firing. In reply came the roaring of AKRs, AKSs, and PPS43 Soviet weapons, these being fired not only by the charging KGB border guards but also by Tarkovsky, Tsipin, Gluzman, and Tystsevich.

A tidal wave of Soviet 5.45 mm projectiles flowed over both sides of the monolith protecting the Death Merchant and the three other men, the sharp and sudden contact between FMJ spitzer slugs and granite creating a howling symphony of screaming ricochets. It wasn't that the Thunderbolt mercs were dumb enough to expose themselves as targets. The Ivans were triggering off bursts at the sides and inner edges of the rocks to make sure the enemy couldn't lean out and toss slugs at them down the crooked "avenues" between the boulders.

Fifty-four regular troops and the six drivers had gotten out of the three BTR-60 troop carriers. Fifteen had been killed by the three GP machine guns. Thirty-eight border guards charged out of the rocks onto the strip of beach. They had been told that a "foreign enemy" had invaded their land, and they didn't intend to lose. In only minutes the dark beach was filled with men, the mercs determined to kill anyone in a dark-green uniform and wearing a gray metal helmet with a red star in the front and on each side.

Tactically, the disadvantage was with the Russians, in the main, because to stay alive they had been forced to fire while racing to the target and had not had time to reload. Therefore most of the border guards had either empty weapons by the time they clashed toe to toe with the Thunderbolts, or they had to rely on sidearms, such as Vitmorkin and Stechkin machine pistols. But the real drawback for the Soviet troops was that, man for man, they were not a match for the highly experienced and battle-hardened Thunderbolts, most of whom enjoyed killing and were proud of how fast and expertly they could scratch a victim.

Two Ivans came at the Death Merchant, one trying to bear down with an AKR assault rifle, the other about to pull the trigger of a long-barreled Vitmorkin. Camellion, having pulled the second Gonez High-Tech pistol, jumped to the right to avoid the stream of 5.45 mm slugs from the assault rifle and fired both Gonez pistols.

Camellion aimed for the head, wanting instant kill-shots, his logic based on the fact that for most pistol calibers the maximum velocity of the bullet never exceeds 1,200 feet per second. At speeds between 400 and 1,200 fps, the bullet has a tendency to bore a hole through the body, creating a channel wound, with damage confined to the channel. At velocities over 1,200 fps, the bullet carries enough energy so that a more severe wound can result, but as a rule the bullet only passes through the body. It is only after the bullet has been accelerated above 2,400 fps that the high-velocity explosive wound comes into being, unless you're using special ammo—Arcane, THV, and so on. At the moment Camellion was using .45 caliber cartridges, and a .45 ACP projectile carries only enough energy to knock a man backward at a rate of about two inches per second. For this reason the Death Merchant wanted to be positive that the targets didn't have even a minimoment in which to fire—not even as they were going down.

They didn't. The .45 bullet from Camellion's left Gonez smacked the Russian with the assault rifle in the bridge of the nose. The slug zipped through the lower portion of his brain and blew out the back of his head. No human being could have died faster. The pig farmer with the Vitmorkin was hit in the neck, the chunk of .45 caliber metal from the right Gonez tearing out his throat and cutting in two the carotid artery and the vagus nerve and going out the rear of his neck. He died instantly—stone dead between two blinks of an eye.

Mad Mike Quinlan, Bruckner, and Kotzias each blew up a border guard with well-placed slugs. Yet the Russians were fast . . . very fast. In only seconds Camellion and the others found Ivans surrounding them, grabbing their arms or trying to eggshell their heads with the barrels or butts of empty weapons.

The other Thunderbolts—three had been killed in the initial Soviet charge—also found themselves steamrollered by the Ivans in hand-to-hand combat—not that the mercs were all that worried. They were experts in the various schools of karate and back-alley dirty tactics. But Semyon Gluzman and Boris Tystsevich were not. Older and not in the best of physical condition, they were killed quickly, dying with their heads caved in. Pytor Angara went down with a 9 mm Stechkin slug in the stomach, but he had taken a Russian with him, smashing his skull with an adjustable wrench.

It was different with Kirill Tarkovsky, who was strong and tough and knew all kinds of dirty tricks. When he was grabbed by the throat by a Russian bent on choking him to death, Tarkovsky clasped his hands together, gripping the knife edge of his left hand with the fingers of his right hand and tightly wrapping his left thumb around the right thumb. He then drove his hands upward between the Russian's arms, forcing the man to loosen his hold. Very fast, Tarkovsky then smashed his clasped hands down on the bridge of the man's nose, grabbed the back of the Ivan's head, and pulled it down to meet his upraised right knee. There was a low groan, teeth flew, and the man collapsed. Tarkovsky promptly stamped his right heel into the side of the man's neck. Just as promptly, Tarkovsky died! Evgeni Ekikrip had slipped up behind him, wrapped an arm around his throat, and shoved a short bayonet-trench knife into his back, just above the right kidney.

Ekikrip had only seconds to enjoy his victory. He was pulling out the bloody blade and releasing the unconscious and dying Tarkovsky when Gideon Adan, a Thunderbolt from Israel, expertly tossed an Afghan *Choora* knife with a thirteen-inch blade. The big length of steel stabbed Ekikrip between the shoulder blades, momentum burying the blade to the hilt. Blood pouring out of his mouth, Ekikrip shuddered, collapsed, and died on the dead Kirill Tarkovsky. Adan spun, pulled an icepick from a narrow sheath on his belt, and tore ten feet across the sands to help Sergei Tsipin and Vito Marsenti, a merc from Italy, who were battling three border guards only a short distance from where the Peppermint Kid was proving he was worth three Russians—pound for pound and in know-how.

O'Malley had snuffed one Ruskie with the last 9 mm hollow-point slug in his SIG-Sauer auto pistol. But two more were coming straight at him, both using empty PPS43 submachine guns as clubs. The closest Slavic silly swung his chatter box like a baseball bat while the second goon tried to jab the barrel of his music box into O'Malley's solar plexus. O'Malley ducked, arched himself back, and at the same time executed a very quick and accurate left snap kick, the tip of his foot smashing into the scrotum of the man who had tried to slam him in the solar plexus. A horrible groan of pure agony jumped from the man's mouth. His eyes bulged in disbelief and misery and he started to sink to his knees as O'Malley moved in quickly to polish off the other man. He did the job by crushing the sphenoid bone, on the left side of the Russian's temple, with the SIG-Sauer. Suddenly O'Malley found himself going down. Another Russian had come in from the right and tackled him around the waist. O'Malley and Stefan Aksentegok hit the sand, hard. Both men were only eight feet west of Zoya Beliyev and Dr. Georgi Ulomov.

All this time Beliyev and Ulomov had lain quietly between the two long, low rocks so close to the edge of the shore that the water almost lapped at their feet. Both lay on their stomachs, pretending to be dead. Zoya's forehead rested on her left forearm, her right arm under her body, her hand wrapped around the cold butt of a Vitmorkin machine pistol, her finger against the trigger. If the worst came, she and Dr. Ulomov would die in a hail of gunfire, but some of the KGB border guards would jump into eternity with them. *Do nothing!* the Death Merchant had ordered her. Now, seeing the Peppermint Kid and Aksentegok hit the sands in a tangle of arms and legs, she debated whether she should lend O'Malley a hand.

Alexey Perchany was fighting almost back to back with Andre d'Albis. He didn't know anything about karate, but he had tried boxing. He caught one Russian with a powerful right uppercut that sent the man reeling back dazed. Perchany then ducked the left-hand knife-hand chop by Rudolf Haymaski and countered by tossing a left cross at him. It was then that Perchany received another surprise of the day. Haymaski ducked and, being an expert in *Sambo,* the Russian school of karate, turned slightly to his left and executed a very rapid and high side heel kick to Perchany's left rib cage. Feeling several ribs snap, Perchany found himself letting out a reflexive howl of pain.

Meanwhile, d'Albis, fighting with a Buck Master survival knife in each hand, had slit open the stomach of one border guard and turned into bloody mush the intestines of another overconfident craphead who came at him like one-man gang busters. Then another Ivan tried to grab d'Albis by both wrists, which was the worst move Kornan Putski could have made.

"Fils de putain!" d'Albis cried, snarling. He let the Bush Master in his right hand fall to the sands, stomped on the Russian's right instep with his left foot, and—when pain and surprise forced Putski to release his wrists—promptly stabbed him high in the stomach with the Buck Master in his left hand, first pushing in the big blade, then ripping upward. With his large veins and arteries cut, as well as the celiac (solar) plexus nerves severed, Putski was dead on his feet, even if he didn't know it. d'Albis pulled out the blade and let the dead dummy drop to the sand.

Hearing Perchany's high cry of pain, d'Albis spun, scooped up the Buck Master he had let fall to the sand, and prepared to throw it at Haymaski. He was too late. Vito Rinletti had stepped up behind Haymaski, who had been stupid enough to go into battle with the chin strap of his steel helmet securely fastened.

A snarl fixed on his face, Rinletti reached over the Russian's right shoulder, grabbed the lower front rim of the helmet with his right hand, and jerked it back, automatically bringing Haymaski's head with it. At the same time he shoved his left knee into the small of the startled man's back. Any expert in karate could have broken the hold, but Haymaski didn't have the time.

There was a British paratrooper knife in Rinletti's left hand, and he used it to cut Haymaski's throat from ear to ear. Rudolf

Haymaski shuddered violently. His arms began to flop up and down. His knees folded, and he went down, the "second grinning mouth" in his neck spurting a river of red.

However, d'Albis did see the KGB border guard coming up fast behind Rinletti, his intention to smash the Italian's skull with the wooden stock of a PPS submachine gun. The Ivan was only three feet behind Rinletti and raising the empty chatter box when he stopped dead in his tracks. He had caught the big blade of d'Albis's Buck Master in the right rib cage, the tip of the sharp steel only several inches from the coronary arteries. The dying border guard fell at the same instant that Zoya Beliyev pulled the trigger of her Vitmorkin machine pistol, and Stefan Aksentegok—about to smash in O'Malley's face with the butt of a Stechkin MP—took the slug in the side of the neck, the blood spurting over his right shoulder and giving the front of the Peppermint Kid a bath of red. The bullet went all the way through Aksentegok's neck and struck another border guard, who had just broken the neck of Perry Brinnow, a Thunderbolt who made his home, between kill assignments, in Moosejaw, British Columbia. The flat-nosed 9 mm Vitmorkin bullet hit the Russian two inches below the navel and came to rest against his spine. He cried out, folded, went down, died. Simultaneously, Lieutenant Igor Gvischiev rushed in low at the Death Merchant. Gvischiev had made a lot of mistakes in his twenty-five years. This was the last mistake of his life.

Go in darkness, fool! Camellion's left foot shot out. He tripped Gvischiev and, as the damn fool fell forward, caught him in a front strangle hold. Camellion slipped his right forearm under the Russian's throat and clamped his head tightly under his right arm. At the same time Camellion clasped his left wrist with his right hand, all the while applying pressure by leaning backward and lifting on the man's throat with his right forearm.

Gvischiev, knowing he was only seconds away from oblivion, did his best to hammer away at the Death Merchant's groin and stomach—a difficult task since Camellion had lifted him up so that he was almost standing on tiptoes. All in the same motion, Camellion twisted his right arm and jumped a foot off the ground, crushing Gvischiev's trachea. The man gave a final shudder and went limp. Camellion let the corpse fall close to the body of a border guard that Bruckner had just slammed to the ground with an overshoulder toss and was polishing off by stamping his right heel into the man's face.

The Death Merchant then went after two more of the Soviet Union's "best," both of whom were rushing at him and Krautie Bruckner. Behind them came a third. It was the first man who worried Camellion. He had spotted Quinlan's Pancor Mk-3 Jackhammer shotgun, and even a piece of trash born in the Soviet Union had enough sense to know a weapon when he saw one.

Mad Mike Quinlan was having a slight problem of his own at the moment, in the form of a big Russian coming at him with an AKR assault rifle with a bayonet attached.

"You stupid son of a bitch!" Mike taunted Branko Voukelich. "I'm going to take that frog sticker away from you and use it to pin your ass to the sand!"

Enraged, Voukelich made a quick thrust at Mike's stomach, and instantly received his Big Shock of the day. Quinlan side-stepped and with lightning speed used the palm of his right hand to parry the thrust, shoving against the side of the barrel and the handle of the bayonet. At the same time he stepped to his right oblique. He was now in a position facing the bayonet, with his groin area protected by his right leg. Before the startled —and now a bit frightened—Voukelich could pull back and try for another thrust, Quinlan grabbed the upper portion of the assault rifle with his left hand and used a right sword-ridge hand to strike the inside of Voukelich's left elbow, the sharp slam causing the Russian trooper to let out a yell of pain and release his left hand from the forward underneath portion of the AKR assault rifle. Quinlan grabbed the AKR with both hands and, as he kicked Voukelich in the left kneecap with his left foot, twisted the assault rifle and its bayonet free. Just as quickly, Quinlan hooked the instep of his left foot in back of Voukelich's left ankle and jerked. Down went Voukelich, flat on his back. A quick reversal of the assault rifle by Mad Mike and an even faster downward thrust. Voukelich screamed a very short wail of agony as the blade of the bayonet cut through his colon and tickled his spine. His body jerked several times. His eyes rolled back and his mouth went slack. He was lucky. He would never suffer from cancer.

Quinlan pulled the bayonet from the corpse and turned his attention toward two Ivans fighting with Stavros Kotzias. Kotzias had locked one trooper in half a commando neckbreaker and was trying to fend off the second man with backward kicks. Quinlan was twenty feet away when the Greek's luck went sour. The pig farmer coming at him from the rear caught his right ankle with both hands and pulled.

Anton Zaisko, the Ruskie who had spotted the Jackhammer, also lost all his good fortune. Charging him, the Death Merchant leapt high and caught him around the neck with a left-legged knee strangle, squeezing with all his strength. Zaisko, his windpipe half crushed, went down, choking and gasping for breath as Camellion stormed toward the second Russian, and Bruckner—incredibly light on his feet for so huge a man—attacked the third man, who had a bayonet trench knife in each hand. Bruckner grinned evilly, called the pig farmer an "asshole" in German—*"Du bist ein Arsch!"*—and wiped him out with a left roundhouse kick to the groin.

Vladimir Shapovalov, the third KGB border guard, did not intend to lose. Snarling and grunting, he tried a roundhouse kick to the Death Merchant's chest. Camellion saw it coming, ducked, and moved in fast on the Russian with a right sword-foot kick that slammed the trooper full in the face. Camellion's blow could not have been better timed or more perfectly aimed. His foot broke Shapovalov's nose, upper jaw, and all his front teeth. Rendered helpless by pain and shock, Shapovalov was as easy to finish off as a blind dwarf with his wrists handcuffed to his ankles. Camellion let him have a dynamite kick to the solar plexus, the grand slam sending shock waves up his spinal cord to his brain, which hemorrhaged.

There were still six Russian border guards charging straight at Bruckner and Camellion, five with empty AKR assault rifles equipped with bayonets. Two of the troopers broke off and headed toward Mike Quinlan, who had just thrown the rifle and its bayonet and speared the trooper who had grabbed Kotzias's right ankle. Kotzias was now rolling over and over on the sand with the other Ivan, who had broken the Greek's commando neck-breaker hold when Kotzias had been jerked back.

The Death Merchant was now only six feet from Quinlan's Pancor Mk-3 shotgun. In only seconds, the futuristic-looking

Jackhammer was in his hands and he was pushing off the safety lever. A second more and his finger was pulling the trigger.

BLAM! BLAM! BLAM! BLAM! BLAM! BLAM! Six times the Jackhammer boomed, and each time a Russian went down to wet the sands with his blood. *BLAM!* The Jackhammer exploded again, and the Russian who had managed to free himself from Kotzias fell back, a big, bloody maw where his face had been.

Mike Quinlan looked across at Camellion, who was also surveying the area, the smoking Jackhammer still in his hands. The beach was littered with corpses, and the wind smelled of warm blood and ice-cold death.

"Look what's coming up out of the water," O'Malley yelled. "The Navy boys are here with the SCUTTs."

Six men dressed in scuba dry suits, with closed breathing systems, were coming up out of the water onto the beach, each looking like some alien from another planet, what with air tanks and hoses leading to helmets with round face masks.

"Mike, get your men organized," Camellion said. "I'm going to check on Beliyev and Ulomov. We have to be off this beach before more pig farmers arrive."

"Affirmative." Quinlan then yelled at Bruckner, "Get a body count of our people. We're going to hit the water with all possible speed."

Camellion ran across the beach and found that while Zoya was in good health, Georgi Ulomov was trembling and barely conscious.

"I'm sure he has a fever; his forehead feels hot," Zoya said anxiously. "I hope the journey to the submarine doesn't kill him!"

"It's exhaustion," said Camellion, cocking his head and listening for helicopters. "Some of our Navy people will be over here shortly. They'll suit him up and adjust the air flow and help you on with your suit."

Zoya stared at Camellion, fear in her eyes. "I've always been terrified of having my head under water," she confessed.

"It's easy," he reassured her, "and you'll be in the hands of the best divers in the world, the American Navy SEALs."

Camellion hurried back to Mike Quinlan, who was conferring with Lieutenant Robert Hoxmier, the SEAL commander, who pumped the Death Merchant's hand. "Well, Scott, I see you're one of the lucky ones." At the same time he glanced around at Thunderbolts who were putting on airtanks, helmets, and flippers.

"We lost eighteen Thunderbolts," Quinlan said, unruffled. "Of your group of pig farmers, only the woman, the scientist, and those two over there didn't buy it." He pointed out Sergei Tsipin and Alexey Perchany, both of whom were being helped into scuba suits by SEALs.

Hoxmier shifted the wad of gum to the other side of his mouth. "I've sent three of my men over to the woman and the scientist, and ordered them to stay with them until we're out of the airlock on board the boat. You two get into your own suits. As it is, we're taking a hell of a risk."

Hoxmier then told Camellion that all the materiel that remained on the beach was to be destroyed, that the less weight on the SCUTTs, the quicker they would reach the submarine. "That includes the Debbler 'ear,' your radio, and the transceiver that Quinlan brought with him. As you can see, my guys are attaching C-four charges to everything. I'll detonate the whole nine yards once we're underwater."

"The AN/URC costs seventy thousand dollars," Camellion said, "but—"

"The hell with cost," Hoxmier said firmly. "I have my orders."

"Do what you have to do," Camellion acquiesced. "How far away is the boat?"

"Only five miles to the east," said Hoxmier, "and submerged at only a hundred and twenty fathoms. Worse, there's a Soviet sub prowling around. The captain said we shouldn't worry. He didn't go into details, but you fellows know as well as I do that the *George Washington* is protected by some kind of super-duper device. Why else would her skipper take such insane chances?"

Zoya Beliyev and the SEALs with her—two of them carrying Dr. Georgi Ulomov—were the first to enter the water of the Sea of Okhotsk. The rest of the force followed. The Death Merchant and Michael Quinlan were last, Mad Mike whistling "Silent Night," the notes coming through the headphones built into Camellion's helmet.

"Christmas is over three months away," joked Camellion. "You and I could be in the next world by then."

Quinlan stopped whistling. "Old buddy, it's always Christmas—any time you can walk away from a battle like we just had."

Suddenly, unexpectedly, there was a muffled *weruuuummmmmmm* to the northeast. An area of the sea heaved and undulated.

"It was too far away to have been our boat," Quinlan said with relief.

The Death Merchant didn't answer. He almost felt sorry for the pig farmers on the Soviet sub that had just been destroyed. Then the dark water closed over his head, and he was swimming.

In submariners' light-blue coveralls, Mike Quinlan looked up as Richard Camellion entered the lounge, walked over to the narrow table, and sat down. Quinlan finished pouring the brandy into his mug of coffee. He recapped the bottle and shoved it into his pocket.

"The way you drink should be against the law," mused Camellion. Since the force had reached the sub and was safe, a space had opened up in the Death Merchant, one that was free, untrammeled, yet very private. There were still ten thousand secrets that were his alone.

"It is against the law, especially in church," Quinlan said with mock seriousness. "It's also bad for my health. I had an uncle who drank a pint of whiskey a day. He died at ninety-six. The doctors said that if he had left the booze alone, he would have lived to be ninety-seven. How's Ulomov, your 'girl friend,' and the two other Ivans?"

"Ulomov doesn't have pneumonia. He's only tired. They're pumping him full of vitamins and antibiotics. The other three are excited about going to the States. To them, it's like dying and being told you're going to the highest level of heaven!"

Quinlan took a long swallow from the mug. "I don't suppose any of the officers of this boat would tell you about the explosions we heard. And I don't mean the stuff that Hoxmier triggered on the beach."

"Surprisingly, the exec did tell me." The Death Merchant's voice took on the speed of assertion. "After all, whom can we tell? The big explosion was a Soviet sub. A nuclear job. The exec said instruments aboard this sub have already detected heavy radiation in the water."

"Moscow will have plenty of nightmares over that," Quinlan said, sounding delighted.

"The exec told me that they sent six torpedoes at the Soviet sub. She tried to turn at the last minute, but several got her. She went to the bottom in minutes, at a depth of around eighteen hundred feet. I'd like to see the Ruskies raise her nuclear reactor from that depth.

"The other five explosions we heard while on the SCUTTs were choppers. The sub missiled them out of the sky."

Quinlan's expression was one of intense satisfaction. "The nice part is that Moscow can't do anything about it, not unless Gorbachev and the rest of the scum want to tell the world how we beat hell out of them."

"And admit to the world how weak Soviet coastal defenses are in Siberia," said Camellion, who was thinking about other sands, the sands of faraway Libya. "The world at large will never hear even a faint whisper about what happened. Radiation from the sunken sub will be detected, and the world press will report the 'probability' of a Soviet 'nuclear accident' near the east coast of Siberia. That will be the end of it."

Quinlan took another swallow from the mug, then looked steadily at the Death Merchant. "It's all irrelevant. We both know that the truly big one is right around the corner. I doubt if there will be any survivors to start over again. If there are"—he chuckled—"there'll be new myths, new 'truths,' new superstitions. But man has always been a conceited ass braying about his 'glory.' "

"What difference does it make?" Camellion said casually. "A tiny speck of a planet moving around an ordinary star that's only one of trillions in the universe! Who cares if all life is destroyed on that planet—*this* planet? It's all relative."

"Yeah, the whole damned race is living in a dream with its eyes closed."

Slowly, the Death Merchant nodded—*And even the dead are part of that dream. . . .*

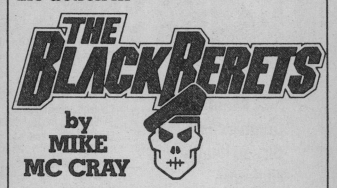

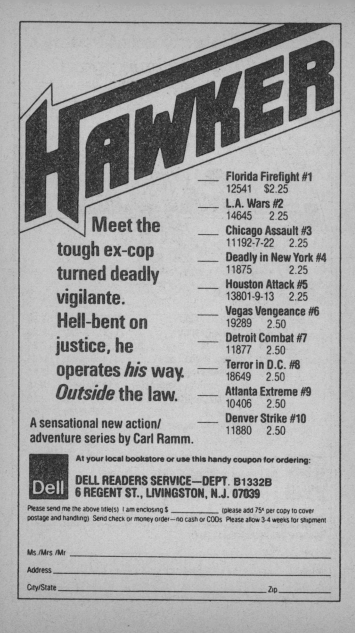